THE WHITE DEVIL OF DUBLIN

To ~~███~~

Kick back
and enjoy
this sequel to
The Tempest Murders!

P. M. Terrell

THE WHITE DEVIL OF DUBLIN
By p.m.terrell

Published by
Drake Valley Press
USA

This novel is a work of fiction. Any resemblance to actual persons, living or dead, is entirely coincidental. The characters, names (except as noted under "Special Thanks"), plots and incidents are the product of the author's imagination. References to actual events, public figures, locales or businesses are included only to give this work of fiction a sense of reality.

Copyright 2014, P.I.S.C.E.S. Books, LTD.

All rights reserved; no part of this publication may be reproduced, stored in a retrieval system, or transmitted, in any form or by any means, electronic, mechanical, photocopying, recording, or otherwise, without the prior written consent of P.I.S.C.E.S. Books, LTD.

Cover design from an original photograph by John Dorton Photography, www.johndortonphotography.com.
Original photograph copyright 2014, John Dorton Photography

ISBN 978-1-935970-22-4 (Trade Paperback)
ISBN 978-1-935970-23-1 (eBook)

Author's website: www.pmterrell.com

THE WHITE DEVIL OF DUBLIN
By p.m.terrell

The White Devil of Dublin is the sequel to *The Tempest Murders*, which is a 2013 USA Best Book Awards Finalist and 2014 International Book Awards Nominee.

What reviewers have said about p.m.terrell's books:

"…powerfully written and masterfully suspenseful, you have to hang on for the ride of your life." – Suspense Magazine

"As a reader, you are swept along on a magic carpet of writing wizardry… In my opinion, it is only a matter of time before we see p.m.terrell on the bestseller lists." – syndicated reviewer Simon Barrett

"p.m.terrell is most definitely a master wordsmith, plying her craft so well as to make us fall under her spell and never, ever want to come back out." – reviewer K.J.Partridge

"p.m.terrell is without doubt one of the best authors I have had the pleasure of reading." – Fated Paranormals

"p.m.terrell continues to amaze with how well-developed her plots and characters are… Just when you think it couldn't get any better than her last book, she surprises you and delivers a better book than the last." – Books and Bindings

1

1169, The Approach to Duiblinn

The mists swirled about the Viking ship, shrouding their approach in an ashen veil. It seemed as though the clouds themselves were reaching toward the waters, parting momentarily to reveal their advance, silent and evil, an apparition on the deadly sea.

He moved as one with the great ship, his feet spread wide and firmly planted behind the dragon's head that graced the bow. Atop a platform, he had an unencumbered view of the gray waters; though they roiled and tumbled, the waves crashing against the sides of the vessel, he remained unyielding, secure in his position. He towered above those behind him who worked the sail or labored in the rowing stations. He could feel their eyes upon him.

Though he was a young man, his hair was white and reached nearly to his waist. It was wild at the moment, swirling about his body wherever the wind took it. His eyebrows and his lashes were pale against alabaster skin that stretched over taut muscles. His shoulders were broad and his arms powerful, though he now rested them idly behind his back, his fingers entwined. His thighs were strapping and fought at the fabric that dared encase them, moving effortlessly with the sway and tug of the vessel that was more a home to him than any bed and table.

His eyes were the color of blue ice. The pupils were not black but appeared to lack any color at all. He had been told by his men that when he stood at the bow of the ship as he did now, his eyes appeared nearly completely white and otherworldly, a characteristic that unnerved his enemies.

His name was Baldr but he was known simply as Hvitr Bard, *The White Devil.*

He preferred the saffron tunic and slightly darker cloak that he currently wore, though he'd discovered years earlier that his wine-colored clothing was best in battle, as it hid blood splatters. He had never been injured himself; his arms were uncommonly long, his frame inches taller than his Norse counterparts; a giant among giants. And among the Celtic people he now approached, he was indeed a goliath. No swing of an arm, even extended with a sword, could reach his torso.

As the mists parted with the first peek of the rising sun, he spotted fishermen along the shorelines and sheep farmers on the hills. As they readied for their day, they stopped to watch the tall, sleek ship slide silently past them.

Gone were the days when necessity dictated a stealthy approach. The Ostmen had ruled Duflin—what the Gaelic people called Duiblinn, or Black Pool—for three hundred years. It was their village now, even if the Celts resented their presence; a bustling, thriving spot along the water that beckoned with good food, strong spirits, and an abundance of women to be had for the taking.

In the distance, he spotted an outcropping of buildings. He forced himself to remain perfectly still, completely rigid. His expression would remain chiseled still as stone. It was an integral part of what made him *The White Devil.*

The docks were alive with fishermen departing for a day at sea; a cacophony of voices reached his ears as they drew closer still. Women hawked pieces of bread and meat for men who would grow hungry before they would again see these shores. Men shouted to one another, inspecting the nets and tossing them onto the decks, gathering their supplies for the hard hours ahead. In the distance, bells rang, their vibrations echoing in the mists of Eire.

Young boys rushed to greet the Viking ship, eager to assist for a coin, while the Celtic men eyed them suspiciously, warily.

Only then did Hvitr Bard remove his hands from behind his back. He raised one hand, and the rowing behind him stopped. With a gesture only his men recognized, they rose as one and prepared to come ashore.

The sail unfurled behind him as they pulled alongside the docks. Under the expert hands of his men, it would be folded and readied for the next voyage, whenever that should be. At a moment's notice, they could be called to the north or the south to quell some uprising against them or to settle an old score with either the Celts or the Normans, or simply to raid another monastery or castle.

Standing near the dragonhead at the bow, he loomed above the men on shore, but when he leapt to the dock below, it was with the fluid grace and agility of a smaller, more slender man. He landed on his feet, his knees only slightly bending, before rising to his full height. The crowds parted as The White Devil stepped among them, their eyes wide, unblinking, frightened. The women clasped their hands to their chests, backing away, while the men avoided his path and averted their eyes. Many of them had seen him countless times before and yet each time it was the same: he was feared. And he was reviled.

2

North Carolina, 2012

Detective Ryan O'Clery studied a group of young men gathered in front of a corner store as he waited for the stoplight to change. Within the space of a few seconds, he observed the pants hanging so low the excess material pooled around their shoes and seemed held up only by their hands stuck into both pockets. He'd also noted the clunky jewelry around their necks and the exposed skin covered heavily in tattoos. They returned his gaze warily; most, he'd brought in for questioning at one time or another and some he'd helped to lock away for various stints. He figured if he bothered to frisk any, those deep pockets their hands seemed glued into would yield drugs and paraphernalia, along with wads of cash.

They all recognized the telltale signs of an unmarked police car and began to disburse when his watchful eye didn't waver. He knew, however, that once he pulled away, they would return quickly enough. They were up to no good, as they always were, but today he had more important things to do.

Even in the confines of the police cruiser, Ryan's height was obvious. His black hair often brushed the roofline and his hands were large as he casually held the steering wheel. His deep green eyes were observant; his black lashes shielding them so they were unreadable.

His partner yawned beside him, diverting his attention from the young men. Zuker was older than Ryan, thinner and shorter, with warm brown eyes, honeyed skin and a perpetually cheery disposition.

"Need a nap, 'ey?" Ryan chided him. His Dubliner accent was pronounced, though he'd lived in America for several years.

"I do," Zuker acknowledged. "Haven't slept for days."

"The missus keeping you up then?"

Zuker chuckled. "I wish that was it. No; it's that water tower south of town. You know the one."

The light turned green and Ryan drove through the intersection. He glanced in his rearview mirror to observe the young men congregating once more along the front of the corner store. As the distance grew between them, he returned to their conversation. The water tower was impossible to miss; it was painted red, white and blue and proclaimed to all who traveled the nearby interstate that Lumberton had been awarded the status of All-America City. "Sure, but since when are water towers loud?"

"Not loud. Bright. They're repainting it," he further explained, "and for some strange reason they keep it lit up like an airport runway all night long. We've complained; the neighbors have complained; but it does no good. They say it's for security. They've got scaffolding and paint buckets and all sorts of stuff up there."

"Seems to me," he said in his Irish lilt, "that a simple solution would be the hiring of a few decent security types."

"That's what we thought, too." He cracked his knuckles. "Anyway, they say it'll be done within the week, weather permitting."

"And blackout shades won't help to keep the light out till then?"

"We've got heavy curtains, but the light still gets through… if they're going to be finished soon, no point in changing them."

A few drops of water landed on the windshield and Ryan glanced upward at the autumn skies. Clouds were unfurling in muted shades of gray against a darkening sky. The weather had been strange of late and one never knew whether to expect days reminiscent of sweltering summers or a bone-chilling winter. The result had been storms nearly every day as the hot temperatures met cold.

"Anyway," Zuker was saying, "I waited a while for you this morning. You're usually right on time."

"Couldn't find my keys to the house."

"Oh?"

"Could have sworn I placed them on the island between the kitchen and the family room, but they weren't there."

"You finally found them, I guess?"

He shook his head. "Cait will find them, I'm sure. She was still searching when I left." At the mention of her name, his voice softened. He'd only recently returned to work after paternity leave. His assistance had been sorely needed as Cait had not only gone into labor nearly a month early but she'd given birth to two adorable twin girls they named Deirdre and Darcy.

"Well, aren't we the pair."

Ryan didn't respond as he slowed the car and turned into a neighborhood that most passersby sought to avoid. The entrance said it all: a decaying sign that once heralded the name of the subdivision was covered in graffiti and the vestiges of summer weeds stood four feet tall and would have been higher had they not been dying back.

He reduced the vehicle's speed to a crawl as they passed a mishmash of dwellings in varying degrees of disrepair. Bringing in suspects rarely led him to the nicer sections of town, he thought as he surveyed the aging clapboard houses, their sagging stoops and drooping roofs. Some homes had plastic duct-taped to their windows in an ineffective attempt to keep the scorching heat or wind-swept chill from entering unabated. Graffiti continued throughout the neighborhood, popping up on street signs or fences that appeared one gust away from lying prone.

"There it is," he said as he spotted the address for which he'd been searching.

He stopped a good half block from the home as they sized it up. It was three stories tall and most likely had a sizable attic, judging from the dormers. The roofline was sagging, and one gutter was dangling precariously away from the house. Several windows were open and even from this distance he could see that the grimy curtains dancing in the growing wind sported dramatic water stains. His eyes took in the chain link fencing that ran the length of the property, ending only when the neighboring lot picked up with plywood nailed together in a separate makeshift fence.

"I've got the arrest warrant right here," Zuker said, patting his pocket.

Ryan pulled in front of the house. "Let's go," he said curtly as he exited the vehicle. As they approached the slumped front porch, he heard Zuker's voice behind him notifying the dispatcher of their location. Before they reached the top step, he spotted movement through the window adjacent to the door. "He's going to run," he said under his breath. "I feel it in my bones."

He banged on the door. A myriad of voices began inside, followed by several toilets flushing. He half-grinned at Zuker. "They think we're here to bust them for drugs."

A woman thinner than anyone he'd ever seen before answered the door, her emaciated frame doing little to conceal the activity behind her.

"Is Johnny Gee about?" he asked.

"Naw, he ain't here," she answered, her yellowed eyes shifting.

Ryan placed one of his brawny palms against the door and effortlessly pushed it completely ajar. It was dim inside and as his eyes adjusted, he spotted activity in the hall that consisted primarily of people exiting through the back with a wary eye on the front door. Then a large man with skin the color of coal stepped into the hallway. As his eyes fell upon Ryan and Zuker, they widened. In a split second, he bolted, his massive hands hugging the banister as he cleared the bottom landing and raced upstairs.

Ryan barely registered that he'd slammed the skeletal woman against the wall as he darted past her. He saw a blur of drug-addled faces scurrying out of the way as he dashed down the hall and took the stairs two at a time. The stench of unwashed bodies, of human waste and spoiled trash assaulted his nostrils as his feet cleared the first landing. In a fraction of a second, he'd processed the hallway stretched out before him, of the faces that stared back at him, and of a high-end pair of sneakers that continued to pound the stairs above him. He rushed upward as he heard Zuker's voice behind him barking orders for the others to get out of their way.

Three men on one set of stairs, all grasping at the banister as they hurtled past, caused the aging wood to protest loudly. Ryan let go of it just as one section splintered off. His foot half-tripped along a wadded-up piece of carpet on the foul-smelling stairs but he never slowed. His eyes remained focused as he watched his suspect zip upward to the second floor and then the third.

By the time he'd reached the fourth set of stairs, his breathing filled his ears. It drowned out the voices of others who stretched their necks out of various rooms only to recoil when they saw the officers bounding toward them. He spotted a set of ankles just before they disappeared into a room at the far end of the hall. Shouting to Zuker behind him, he followed, clearing the doorway just as the suspect raised a window.

The man was huffing as he glanced back at Ryan, the sweat dripping off him onto the marred floor. Ryan threw out his arm intent on grabbing his shirt as the suspect tossed one leg out the window. He dodged Ryan's outstretched hand, straddling the windowsill for the briefest of moments before he pushed himself upward and grabbed the decaying roofline above.

By the time Ryan reached the window and stuck his head out, a volley of asphalt shingles were sliding off the dilapidated roof. He raised his forearm in front of his face to deflect the blows as rapid-fire footsteps sounded above him.

"Go, go, go!" Zuker shouted behind him.

Backing out of the window, he caught the surprised look in Zuker's eyes before he moved into the hallway. "I'll head him off!" he shouted as he raced down the stairs.

Ryan exited the back door as Zuker's legs sailed above him, barely landing on the roofline of the neighboring house. In an instant, he spotted the direction the suspect was moving, jumping and clawing his way from one dwelling to the next, winding down from four stories high to one story ranchers. Ryan rushed down the alley, clearing chain-link fences and toppling wood slats and plywood as he hurried beneath them.

The winds had picked up, bringing with them more precipitation which hit the roofs in sideways blows. He saw Zuker slip and slide across one roof and to his amazement, his partner cleared an extra-wide stretch between houses, his knees bending and flexing before becoming upright again as he lurched after their suspect.

Ryan reached the end of the street before either of the men above him. They'd progressed from older, multi-story dwellings to rooflines so low he could almost jump up and touch them. He stopped on the sidewalk, drew his weapon and shouted. The man glanced in his direction. Seeing the roofs ending and one officer waiting for him below, he seemed prepared to turn and fight his way through Zuker in the opposite direction when his foot slipped. He flailed his arms in a futile attempt to right himself but Zuker sailed through the air, catching him square in the torso.

Ryan swore as he returned his weapon to his holster, watching as the two men rolled along the wet shingles. They grappled briefly before hitting the overhang, which buckled underneath their weight. He could do nothing but watch as they plummeted downward.

They hit the ground in a combined exhale that sounded more like an air gun. He rushed forward as Zuker rolled off the big man, slamming the suspect back to the ground before he could regain his momentum. He straddled him, pinning him facedown against the pavement as he jerked his arms behind his back.

"Zuker!" he called out as he handcuffed Johnny Gee.

His partner groaned but held up his hand, half-waving in an effort to convey that he was fine. The heft of the suspect had done an admirable job of cushioning his fall.

"Make one move," Ryan shouted, his mouth against the suspect's ear, "and I swear to God—" Without finishing the sentence, he left him on the pavement and stepped toward his partner, stretching out his hand to help him up. "You okay?"

Zuker nodded. "Just winded." He looked at the man lying with his face against the pavement. "I'd say he's guilty."

~~~~~

Ryan was completing the paperwork when Zuker returned from the medical clinic. His face and arms wore an assortment of abrasions from his tumble, but considering what might have happened, Ryan thought he didn't look too bad.

"How do you feel?" he asked as Zuker sat down heavily. Their desks were arranged side by side in a large open room used by all the detectives. There was a hubbub of activity, as there always was; phones rang constantly and voices climbed over one another to be heard above the fray.

"Like I've been run over by a truck," his partner groaned.

"Johnny Gee's at the jail and I've finished the paperwork. He'll make bail within the hour, no doubt, but murder charges will stick."

Zuker nodded. He opened his desk drawer and pulled out a bottle of aspirin.

"The physician didn't give you anything for the pain?" Ryan asked.

"Hasn't kicked in yet. Drive me home, okay? I'm not feeling too good."

"Of course." He rose and reached into his pocket for the cruiser keys.

His partner remained seated. "Tell me something, O'Clery."

"And sure I will."

"I've never seen you hesitate before."

He remained standing, his hand wrapped around his keys, as he waited for his partner to continue. Instead, Zuker peered at him as if he expected him to respond. "Was that a question then?" Ryan asked at last.

"What happened?"

"I made a snap decision not to climb onto the roof, is all."

"But you've never hesitated before."

He exhaled. "And I didn't hesitate then, either, I'll have you know. What's the point you're making?"

"I want to know what happened... before it happens again."

Ryan sat back down. He studied his partner's face for a long moment. He had a cut above his brow and his eyes were bloodshot. He looked like hell. He leaned back in his chair. His wife would no doubt take excellent care of him tonight, just as Cait would do for him had the tables been turned. And he did deserve an explanation.

"I have this thing about heights," he said quietly.

"You're afraid of heights?" Zuker almost laughed.

"I didn't say that."

"You meant that."

He shrugged. "Whatever."

"Don't brush this off. You didn't pursue the suspect because you were afraid to go up on the roof?"

"I beg to differ with you. I wasn't afraid. I regrouped. And I was there, I might remind you, to apprehend the suspect. Because the way you fell, you couldn't have come to your feet fast enough to do it. And if we'd both gone onto the roof, we both would have fallen." He held his hand out to help his partner to his feet.

"I just needed to know."

"So there you have it. I've always had a respect for heights, particularly when I can look down and determine that a fall won't end pleasantly."

"Get me home," Zuker moaned.

"And there. You've proven my point, now haven't you?"

3

Ryan leaned back in the Jacuzzi with a contented sigh as he watched Cait pull her long brunette hair atop her head. She loosely secured it with a giant burled wood clip before turning toward him. The water warmed his muscles and the pulsating jets eased any remaining tension from his long day at work. He watched as Cait dipped her head a bit lower, gazing at him with eyes that laughed and teased; eyes the color of the tumultuous Irish Sea. She took her time strolling across the bathroom toward him, her long, slender fingers moving tantalizingly slow as they unfurled the belt from her thick robe. She was beside the Jacuzzi before she allowed the garment to slip from her, forming a soft heap on the tiled floor.

She knew what she did to him; she'd always known. She was the woman he'd seen in his dreams ever since he could remember. Some men fantasized of a mysterious figure, a woman indistinct except in particular places. Not him. Ryan had seen her more clearly than he saw himself in the mirror, from every hair on her head to the toes that were often adorned with Celtic rings.

When he'd first laid eyes on her in the flesh, he'd thought it was another of his dreams come to life. And when he discovered she truly did exist, he'd known then, as he knew now, that she was his eternal soul mate.

Now he remained silent as she stepped into the tub, turning her back to him as she lowered herself into the warm waters. He clasped her thighs between his hands, moving his fingers upward as she submerged her body in the gentle suds.

"Lean against me," he said, his voice deep and caressing. She sighed contentedly as she relaxed against his chest.

He reached to the wide lip of the tub and handed her a glass of wine.

"This is the perfect ending to my day," she said. Her voice was delicate and melodious; a contradiction, Ryan thought, to an inner strength.

He wrapped his arms around her and leaned his chin atop her head. "Oh, it isn't the ending quite yet," he murmured, "but I'd be thinking it's the right start."

She chuckled and after sipping the wine, she returned her glass to the tub's lip. Then she set a hand atop each of his biceps, her fingers lazily massaging them as she rested her head against his chest.

"Claire helped me out again today," she said, referring to Ryan's sister. "She knows so much about babies; she's amazing."

"Aye, and she is. But so, my dear, are you." He worked his way to her cheek and kissed it, slowly and sensuously, until she turned toward him. He lowered his hands to her inner thighs as he brushed his lips across hers. "And were the girls good for you today then?" he asked, his voice growing deeper.

"I suppose they were as good as any infant can be," she laughed. "They have such distinct personalities to be twins. Darcy is quiet and feminine and watches everything without hardly making a noise, while Dee is constantly pushing the envelope, whining as if needing attention, so vocal all the time."

He smiled. In appearance, the twins had identically shaped eyes, brows, noses and cheekbones. Their tiny bodies looked so similar that if he couldn't see their faces, he'd be hard put to know who was who. But there, the similarities stopped. Darcy had fine black hair and black brows against ivory skin, along with Ryan's emerald green eyes.

But Dee—Dee was, though he'd admit it to no one other than himself—his favorite. She had been the firstborn, and he'd delivered her himself. He remembered it as though it was yesterday; Cait had gone into labor a month early and Claire had simply happened by the house and found her. She'd attempted to drive her to the hospital but afraid she wouldn't make it, she'd driven to the police precinct instead. Ryan had been on his way to a murder investigation and was standing in the parking lot when Claire stopped the car nearly at his feet… He chuckled as he remembered. He'd climbed into the back seat with Cait and he'd delivered tiny Deirdre before they'd reached the hospital grounds.

She had nearly chestnut hair and eyes that were such a light shade of blue that he caught his breath whenever he looked at her. Cait's eyes were the color of an Irish storm; gray and cerulean, often swirling with flecks of gold when her passions were aroused. She claimed that no one in her family had blue eyes such as Dee's, and he was hard put to recall anyone on his side with blue eyes, either. She'd been born with a small red spot below the outer corner of one eye; a birthmark, the physician had called it. Ryan had worried that he'd somehow damaged her during delivery; his hands were so large, and she'd been so small… But though the doctor had assured them it would go away with time, it hadn't. As the redness faded, it looked rather like a dainty teardrop and had become, he thought, quite beguiling.

Darcy had been born directly afterward. By that time, they were parked in front of the emergency room doors but Ryan had refused to allow Cait to be moved into the hospital. With Claire's assurance that she'd look after Dee as hospital personnel whisked her inside, he'd remained with Cait to deliver his second child. Only then, with Darcy securely in the hands of nurses and Cait calmed enough to be transported, did he allow her to be moved to a gurney and brought inside. He'd left her side only long enough to check on his preemie girls—a task he did so often that hospital personnel claimed he'd worn a path in the floor.

They were monoamniotic twins; babies that shared the same placenta, versus average twins that each had their own. He was told mono babies were always identical twins, yet no one could explain why their coloring was so distinctly different. But he didn't care. They were healthy, even though they'd been born premature. And their mannerism toward one another was something to behold. They always seemed to know instinctively in which direction the other was to them, and their tiny arms were constantly jutting out, only stopping when their hands intertwined. He envisioned them in their mother's womb, their arms perpetually entwined, each one gathering solace and comfort from the other's constant presence.

His thoughts were interrupted as Cait pulled his head down to hers as she swept her lips across his, nibbling gently as her eyes sparkled.

His cell phone rang from the nightstand in the bedroom and he pressed closer to her.

She pulled back with a sly smile. "Your phone is ringing."

"Let it ring." He dipped his hands lower, racing his fingers across her inner thighs.

She giggled. "Be happy to." As their lips met once more, one of the twins began to fret, the voice growing insistent as it was broadcast over the baby monitor.

"Ugh," she said, coming to her feet.

Ryan groaned in protest.

"I'll check on the girls while you get the phone," she said, stepping onto the bath mat and reaching for her bathrobe.

"I'll be waiting right here for you, love," he answered, his eyes sweeping over her.

She entered the bedroom only to return a moment later. The persistence of the ringing phone grew louder as she held it out to him. "Answer your phone," she laughed.

She dropped the phone into the palm of his hand before turning back toward the bedroom. As he listened to her feet on the hardwood floor, he answered. "Aye, and what in blazes do you want?" His voice was brusque, but it was late and he'd be damned if the office was phoning him about a case at this hour.

"Detective O'Clery?" The voice was thin and reedy; a woman's voice he didn't recognize.

"You phoned me. Who else were you expecting?"

There was a slight hesitation. "My name is Annelise Skovgaard. Do you know who I am?"

He heard Cait's voice on the baby monitor, soft and lyrical as she soothed the girls. He leaned forward and pressed the phone closer to his ear in an attempt to concentrate. "I do. You're an historian of some acclaim. Your book on world history won a Pulitzer."

"That's right." The voice remained thin and steady; it was not filled with ego or self-importance.

"And what would you be wanting with me?" he asked.

She sighed. "I'm working on my next book. It's about the history of the Scandinavian countries."

Ryan didn't answer. Cait had begun to sing to the girls; her voice carried over the monitor in a melody that held him enraptured.

"Detective O'Clery, I've stumbled across some information about your ancestors that I think you'd find quite interesting."

"You have the wrong man," he said. "I have no ancestors from Scandinavia."

"Are you sure about that?"

"I'm as certain as the day is long. My family is from Ireland. From the beginning of time, they've always been Irish and nothing else."

"There have been quite a number of cultures that immigrated to Ireland over the centuries," she said. Her voice had grown adamant.

"My family didn't mix." His own voice was firm.

"Your ancestor was Rían Kelly, was it not?"

At the mention of his name, Ryan leaned even further into the phone. His own name was Ryan Kelly O'Clery; he'd been named for Rían Kelly, an uncle on his mother's side five generations back. It was an Irish tradition to name children after relatives whom they admired. Rían had been like a god to him, the stories of his law enforcement career morphing into mythological status. It had been the reason he'd chosen police work himself and was now a homicide detective.

There had been a time in which he'd wondered whether he was, in fact, the reincarnation of Rían Kelly. It had been the dual events of finding his uncle's journal and realizing his dreams were his uncle's memories, and a serial murder case eerily similar to one his uncle had worked, that had rocked his Catholic faith and caused him to question everything. His voice took on the quality of a hoarse whisper. "Aye."

"Have you ever heard of The White Devil?"

"The White—? No." He chuckled. "I'm quite certain I would've remembered that."

"I need to talk to you."

"I'm listening."

"I'd—I'd rather speak to you in person, if you don't mind, Detective? It's of utmost importance."

"I'm certain you have the wrong person."

"But you said—"

"It must be some other Rían Kelly you'd be talking about, if there are connections to any other country, most particularly Scandinavia."

The baby monitor had grown silent, a fact he realized as he heard Cait returning, her feet padding softly through the bedroom.

"Please, Detective. Humor me with a brief meeting. You won't be sorry."

She reached the bathroom and shed her robe.

"I'm busy at the moment," he said.

"Tomorrow, then? Please."

"Around noon?"

"Noon would be perfect." She rattled off her address. "Do you need directions?"

"No; I'm familiar with the location." In his mind's eye, he recalled a three-story, white brick home that fanned into two side wings. He was certain each wing was more than four thousand square feet. The historian was legendary in these parts and he was certain, a few others; and word was she lived in the centuries-old home completely by herself—if one didn't count the dozens of cats she purportedly took in.

"Good. Well, then," she said. "I'll see you tomorrow. Noon."

He clicked off the phone.

"Who was that?" Cait asked as she rejoined him.

He leaned past her to turn on the hot water; the bath was getting tepid. "An historian. She's about a hundred years old, I understand, and she's somehow got it into her mind that she has information on my ancestors."

"Really?" She settled in front of him. Once the water had warmed, she turned the faucet off with her foot. "As much as you're interested in your family's genealogy, you should enjoy hearing what she's got to say."

"I'm certain she has the wrong person," he said, brushing his lips against the nape of her neck. "Now, where were we?"

4

Ryan parked at the foot of the driveway; even from the street, he could see the imposing iron gate was locked. There was a pedestrian door a few feet from the gate, however, which was standing open.

"Looks as if Mrs. Skovgaard could use a lesson in security," he remarked to Zuker. "Imagine making the effort to lock the gate while leaving this one ajar."

His partner followed him through the pedestrian doorway and whistled as he got his first glimpse of the gardens. The grass was the color of bottle green, unlike most of the lawns in this area which had grown dormant with the cooler season. It was obviously a different type of grass, Ryan thought, appearing more like an upscale golf course with blades that reached tall and straight. Immaculate flower gardens were interspersed from the gate to the house, with eye-popping shades of red, pink, white and orange. Pristine hedges barely twelve inches tall separated the flowers from the grass; boxwood, he thought as he inhaled.

"I feel like I'm in Oz," Zuker said, the admiration in his voice clear. "What did you say she wanted to talk with you about?"

Ryan wound his way along the path. A tall plant swayed though there was no breeze, and he stopped to observe it. A few seconds later, a cat popped out. It was a calico and there appeared to be blood on the side of its face. He knelt, gesturing with his hands for it to come to him, but it scampered off. He spotted several more cats frolicking a few yards away.

"She claimed she had some information about my ancestors," Ryan said, rising.

"For real? Ms. Skovgaard is researching your family?"

"You know of her?"

"Who doesn't? My wife has all her books—Janie is a history professor, you know. She says she really knows her stuff. She's written a great deal about European history…"

"So I've heard."

"She has a Pulitzer, you know."

They reached the front steps. Ryan took them slowly, his eyes taking in the broad front porch, the colossal columns and the wicker furniture. Several ceiling fans rotated lazily despite the already cool air. The windows overlooking the porch were as tall as he, and old-fashioned shutters were secured with hooks to the white brick on either side of them.

One shutter had come loose, and he stopped to secure it with the ingenious metal hook.

"She used to teach at the university, you know," Zuker was saying. "Taught European history there for years… What does she have on your family?"

Ryan rang the doorbell and listened as the unique tuneful chime sounded for several seconds. "I don't know," he said. "She said she wanted to tell me in person."

"Aren't you curious?"

Something didn't feel quite right. He looked at his partner, who returned his gaze with a broad smile and friendly eyes. The cut above his brow was quickly healing. "If a noted historian said she had information about my family," he continued, "wild horses couldn't 'ave kept me away."

Ryan turned around to take in the spacious landscaping from this perspective. The front lawn alone must have been five acres, and yet it was just minutes from downtown. It was as if he'd stepped into the past. He almost expected a horse and buggy to come pulling up.

The air was still; it felt almost oppressive. He felt, he decided, as if he was standing in front of an abandoned house.

"Wonder what's taking her?" Ryan said.

"Look at the size of this place," Zuker said, waving his hand. "If she's in the back of the house, I bet it could take ten minutes to reach the front."

He turned back around and rang the doorbell once more. "I don't have a good feeling about this at'al."

"You think she's got something scandalous on your family?"

"That isn't what I'd be referring to." He raised his finger to ring the bell again but held it just an inch above it. The vision of the cat with blood on its neck loomed large in his mind's eye.

Instead of ringing the bell, he reached for the door knob. It turned easily in his hand. Before swinging it open, his other hand moved to his weapon.

"What are you doing?" Zuker's voice had dropped to a hoarse whisper.

"I don't like this."

Zuker moved his hand to his weapon as well and as the door swung wide on creaking hinges, Ryan stepped inside.

The front hall was as wide as his living room. The floors were dark, polished wood and a few feet in front of him, a staircase with a thick balustrade rose to the second floor. Ryan's eyes followed it upward; he was surprised to see not just an open second floor, but an open third floor as well. A round glass dome directly overhead allowed sunlight into the massive foyer. He turned his attention back to the first floor, his eyes sweeping the hall and the doors on either side.

"Mrs. Skovgaard?" he called out.

There was no response.

He motioned that he was going down the hall to the right, and his partner nodded, following a few footsteps behind, peering into each room on the opposite side. Ryan glanced through the first room, an ornate living area with bookcases that lined three walls, in seconds sizing it up before moving onto the next. A glance to his left caught a glimpse of a dining room with a formal table at its center; then back to the right, he stared into a study, which was also lined with bookcases. A third room appeared to be an office, with an ornate desk and a leather chair behind it; this one also was lined with bookcases.

"It's like a library in here," Zuker breathed.

Ryan nodded silently. Looking back, he spotted his partner moving into the doorway of a country-style kitchen. He was just about to check the last door on the right when something caught his eye. He hesitated briefly and then searched for a light switch. Finding it, he flipped it, transforming the room into the color of butter as antique lamps came to life.

His eyes followed the lines of the desk, the position of the leather chair set too far back from it, nearly haphazard in its angle to the rest of the room. He stepped inside, peering around the corner of the desk. A shoe lay on its side; it was a woman's old-fashioned pump, black and chunky.

He glanced behind him to find Zuker watching him. He nodded quietly, and his partner nodded in return before moving into the room with Ryan.

He continued moving silently until he was nearly behind the desk. It was then that he spotted the woman's legs. Quickly holstering his weapon, he rushed around the furniture to find her lying on her back on the plush Oriental rug.

She was thin as a rail and from the way in which she laid, he noted her spine had a curvature to it; lying on her back was clearly not a natural position for her. Her dress was elegant and simple and might have dropped to well beneath her knees, except it was bunched up just above her calves.

His eyes swept swiftly upward to encompass her arms, flailed out to each side, and her face: the eyes wide, staring straight upward as if they were still looking at something so fantastic, so engrossing, so terrifying, that she could not tear her eyes away. Her mouth was open and a trickle of blood had made a path down the corner of her lips to the floor beneath.

He did not move to check her pulse. He did not attempt to resuscitate her. It was clear that she was dead and had been for some time: she lay in a pool of blood caused by a clean, precise slit from one ear to the other.

5

Duiblinn

Baldr recognized her as soon as her face appeared in the window. Though he stood on the opposite side of the road and she was on the second floor, her image was seared into his memory. Her face was round and he imagined, cherubic; it was framed by deep brown hair that seemed always to be pulled up and back. He liked to envision what it might look like once it was freed from its constraints. He wondered also at the color of her eyes, the subtle shape of her brows, the peaks of her lips...

He stood in the shadows, lest he frighten her with his presence. She followed the same routine he remembered; she peered first to the left end of the road, as far as her eye might see, before turning to the right. Then she turned away from the window. It would take a few moments for her to don her outerwear and descend to the wide front doors of the orphanage.

Sometimes, she was accompanied briefly by a man; he'd come to learn that James O'Braoin was the headmaster and seemed only to focus on the children in his keep. Shorter than average, slight as a boy, he was almost effeminate. When they exited together, he always went to the east while she walked toward the north, alone.

She was more mysterious.

He missed her when he was away; he thought of her when he was in his native land of Norway, or when he was raiding and fighting. But it was naught but a fantasy; he knew that. One such as her could never be attracted to a man such as himself.

The drunken laughter of four men reached his ears and he stepped back into the deeper recesses of the alcove in which he stood. They wandered past, and he recognized them as Ostmen. They were larger and bulkier than the Gauls and the Celts; their hair tended to contain more red and blond strands and their clothing was that of the north. More than their appearance, their attitudes were quite different; they wandered the streets freely, unafraid and emboldened, taking what took their fancy. It was in marked contrast to the native inhabitants, who tended to avoid direct eye contact, kept to themselves and often crossed to the opposite side of the road or ducked down a side street upon seeing the Ostmen.

The men stopped walking to listen to one of them tell a story, to which they all howled in laughter, though Baldr could find no humor in it. Most likely if they were sober, they would not, either, he reasoned.

The doors across the road opened, drawing his attention back to the reason he was there.

She was tall, most particularly for a Celt. He supposed if they stood side by side, the top of her head might approach his chest. Though she was dressed in a heavy cloak that hid her figure, he knew she was slender. The first time he'd ever laid eyes on her was on a warm summer day when the breeze had wandered off the sea to caress her. As she'd struggled to keep her gown from clinging to her, he'd been treated to the sight of a small waist and hips, above which her breasts had tantalized him so badly that he'd sought release in the arms of a whore afterward, whom he'd fantasized was her.

James followed her out of the orphanage, nodding cordially but formally as he departed for the east, while she turned to the north. She walked with her head erect and proud. As others passed her in the opposite direction, she did not avoid their eyes but looked directly at them, sometimes nodding her head in a slight and unspoken greeting. Her arms were folded neatly in front of her, perhaps to keep out the frigid winds that whirled unchecked through the streets.

He waited until she was a short distance ahead of him before he began to follow from the opposite side of the road.

The four men crossed the road, their drunkenness becoming more apparent as their voices grew louder and more belligerent. They passed her, turning to walk backwards as they spoke to her, but she neither slowed nor hurried her step and as best as he could determine, she did not respond.

Baldr peered in each direction but other than the initial few who passed a moment before, there were no others out on this late afternoon. A glance toward the skies revealed darkness descending. Black and gray mottled clouds tumbled, heralding a stormy night ahead.

The men retreated into a stable, leaving only Baldr and the woman. She continued at the same pace, never turning to look behind her. She never did, he realized.

She was nearly past the stable doors when two of the men appeared. They worked like jackals, one moving swiftly to one side to grab her above both elbows, while the other covered her mouth with one hand while the other hand clutched her hair, pulling her into the stables. The door swung shut behind them, her cries muffled.

Baldr crossed the road in great strides. He did not think; he did not reason. Four or twenty made no difference to him. He operated on an instinct born of fighting.

He threw open the door to the stables, simultaneously drawing his sword. The clang of the metal as it left its sheath was unmistakable, and even in their drunken melee, the men froze at the sound.

In the fraction of an instant, he took in the scene before him: she lay unceremoniously atop a heap of hay, her cloak askew, her skirts pulled above her knees. One man straddled her, his hands hidden from Baldr but their location leaving very little doubt as to his intention. Another held her wrists above her head. A trickle of blood swept down her cheek. Her cries stopped as she laid eyes on him, despite her dangerous predicament.

"Leave her be," Baldr ordered. His words were even and measured but in the ensuing silence, they sounded like thunder.

From their widened eyes, he knew he filled the stable door with his formidable shoulders and wide stance. The wind caught his hair, causing it to billow about him. A lantern hung not far from him and he knew his eyes had caught the light, causing them to appear like two almond-shaped beacons, glowing white and steady. He did not blink and he did not move.

The men did not turn to their own swords. One whispered *"Hvitr Bard"* under his breath in the same tone he might have used if the devil himself stood before him. Three backed away.

Though her wrists were now unencumbered, the woman remained perfectly still. She did not look at him in fear or revulsion as others did. She simply watched.

The man atop of her came to his feet.

Baldr stepped further into the stables, allowing a path for the men to escape. Nervously, they shifted toward the open door, glancing back as he moved closer to the man whose pant front dipped below his hips.

The English fought with a sword in one hand, sparring, dipping and clashing. Not the Ostmen; Baldr held his sword with both hands as was their custom. With one fell swoop, he split the man open from his chest to his lower abdomen. It happened so quickly that the man simply stared at him, his eyes wide. Then he fell to his knees before crumpling forward in the hay.

Baldr whipped around to face the others but they were stumbling over one another to get through the door first.

He waited until they had retreated before turning to the woman.

"Are ye injured?" he asked, offering her a hand.

She placed her hand in his without hesitation, allowing him to pull her gently to her feet. His palm dwarfed hers and she rose with barely the weight of a feather. She shook her head. "Thank ye."

Her voice was silky; though slightly unsteady, she did not border on hysteria the way he imagined other women might—the way other women had with him on other days, other times, other locales.

He realized her cloak was ripped, as was her bodice. One breast lay exposed to him, and without taking his eyes off hers, he pulled her cloak about her for modesty. She seemed to come to her senses then, grasping her clothing in her hands and pulling it closer to her neck to cover her cleavage.

"Ye are not afeared," he said.

"Nay. I do not fear ye."

The simple statement rendered him speechless. He realized he still held his sword and he wiped the blade across the fallen man's clothing, first on one side and then on the other. He sheathed it before looking at her again.

"What do they call ye?" he asked.

"Maeve."

"Maeve," he repeated. Then, "I am—"

"I know who y' are," she interjected. "Ye are the one they call Hvitr Bard, *The White Devil*."

He cocked his head. "And yet ye do not fear me."

She smiled shyly, revealing perfect, small white teeth. Her lips were deep pink and slightly swollen. He found himself staring at them as she said, "Why should I fear ye? Y' have had ample opportunities to assault me; yet y' do not."

He felt the color rising in his cheeks and he tore his eyes from her mouth to look into her eyes. They were green, as green as the fields and the valleys that made this island so breathtakingly beautiful. He felt his breath catch in his throat.

"Ye do not think I have seen y' watchin' me?" she asked quietly, peering upward to look into his eyes.

He narrowed his eyes in an attempt to shield the light color with his lashes as he averted his gaze.

She placed an open palm on his shoulder. The slight touch was charged, as though a bolt of lightning had split straight through him. "Ye need not turn away from me," she said.

He stepped back from her, his heart pounding.

"Is the warrior afraid of me now?" She continued smiling, her chin tilted slightly down but her eyes dancing as she looked at him. One brow rose slightly as if she waited for an answer.

"It gets late," he said. His voice sounded rough and strained. "Ye had best hurry home."

Her smile faded and she peered downward, taking in her appearance. Her clothing was covered in grime and she picked hay from the fibers, tossing them at her feet. She placed one hand inside her cloak, and though he knew he should look away as she attempted to adjust herself, he could not bear to do so. He wanted to remember this moment for as long as he lived; he wanted the color of those emerald eyes to sear into his memory. He knew when he bedded down this night, he would close his eyes and see those cherry lips and those flushed cheeks in his mind's eye. And no matter how long it took for morning to arrive, it would come too quickly.

"I cannot go home," she stated. For the first time, her voice shook.

She must be otherworldly, he thought. She has rendered me speechless not once but twice.

When she looked at him again, her eyes filled with tears.

"Ye are unharmed," he said.

"Aye." She motioned toward her clothing. "But if I cross the threshold of my father's home appearin' thus…"

"He cannot blame ye for what happened here."

"No. He will not." She took a deep breath. "But my brothers will want to exact revenge."

He gestured toward the man who bled out at their feet. "There is yer revenge."

"He is but one. They will seek the others."

Her words began to sink in, their meaning both clear and ominous.

"Nothin' but trouble can come o' this."

He knew she spoke the truth. The Celts were a conquered people. The Ostmen ruled. And though the men had clearly wronged her, they were Ostmen. Any who dared to harm them—save another Ostmen such as himself—would be tortured or put to death.

His eyes roamed over her hair, which threatened to escape the confines of the elaborate bun. Without thinking, he removed several pieces of straw from the brown tresses, smoothing it down.

"I have a room not far from here," he heard himself saying. "Ye can arrange y'self in private; clean the debris from yer clothing."

She did not respond, and he felt his face grow hot. What was he thinking? "M' apologies," he stammered, "I did not presume to—"

"Thank ye," she said. "I accept yer offer."

~~~~~

He sat in a simple chair at the end of the hallway. On one side, a narrow staircase wound its way to the back of the building. At the opposite end of the hall, a wider staircase descended to a dining hall, where the sounds of voices, laughter and music wafted upward.

Though he sat alone, his senses were razor-sharp, his thoughts wandering to his room on the other side of the hall. She had been inside for only a few minutes and yet he knew when she left he would be able to inhale her scent in his room for the remainder of the night. He would sit on the edge of his bed and envision her movements, wondering if she used his comb, knowing she'd made use of the bowl of water he'd fetched for her… He would hold the coarse linens to his nose, knowing she'd dried her skin on them. He would look for imprints in the dusty floor and know that she'd tread in his room.

The door opened, interrupting his thoughts. He rose instinctively.

She smiled. "What is yer given name?"

"Baldr."

"Baldr." The manner in which she repeated it was silky-smooth, the 'r' pronounced more heavily, in the Celtic way, and he realized she made his simple name melodious.

"Well, Baldr, thank ye for rescuin' me."

No man and no woman had ever before rendered him dumbstruck as she did.

"I must be gettin' home now."

"I shall walk ye."

"Nay; I—"

"Do not argue w' me, woman." His tongue found at last, he continued, "The skies are dark and an ill wind blows. I shall walk behind ye if ye wish, but I shall see to it that ye reach yer father's home in safety."

She reached for his hand and before he could determine her motive or movements, she held one strapping hand inside both of hers. A bolt of lightning seemed to sizzle from her palms into his, an effervescence rising up his arm into his chest. "I would be quite honored for y' to accompany me."

6

North Carolina

Ryan knelt in front of the corpse. Though the crime scene techs had already taken pictures from every angle and he knew those pictures would grace his desk until the case was solved, he felt obligated to memorize every aspect of her condition.

Annelise Skovgaard's hair was silver. It was cut short in what used to be referred to as a pixie; it might have appeared boyish had it not been for the feminine features of the woman. He'd found her pocketbook on the kitchen counter and her driver's license inside the wallet. She was ninety-two years old.

Her driver's license had her eyes listed as brown but they had lightened, most likely due to age, he thought. They were outlined in blue and very large. She'd seen her attacker; there was no doubt about it.

Yet there were no signs of a struggle. He slipped on a crime scene latex glove and lifted one hand to study the immaculately polished nails. They were painted blood red. He turned her hand over to peer underneath them. There was no skin, no blood; no tears in the nails that would provide evidence that she had clawed at the attacker. He placed the hand on the floor and inspected the other hand and found the same.

He gingerly lifted her skirt. She was wearing hosiery which did not appear to have been pulled down or otherwise tampered with. He could see the telltale lines of her panties underneath. Dropping her skirt, he took in her dress; it had risen higher than intended, but he supposed it was due to her fall.

He studied the chair and its haphazard placement in the room. She'd been sitting at her desk, he surmised, when she was startled by the intruder. She'd risen quickly, and she'd stumbled. At that point, she'd lost one of her shoes.

The question, he wondered, was whether she had been pushed to the floor or had fallen independent of the intruder.

After that, he knew what had played out. As she lay on the floor, unable to rise, the killer had cleanly and neatly slit her throat from one ear to the other. From the look in her eyes, she had seen it about to happen. She might have stared into the eyes of the killer as she'd bled out. And she had been completely unable to save herself.

"I've checked her purse," Zuker said, bringing Ryan back to the present. "She had more than a thousand dollars in it."

"So the motive wasn't robbery." He lifted one hand again. "How much do you think this ring is worth?"

He whistled. "What is that, a two carat diamond?"

"Quite possibly. I'd surmise it's worth at least ten thousand." He fingered the bracelet at her wrist; it alternated between emeralds and diamonds. "This doesn't appear to be costume jewelry." As he dropped the hand once more, his eyes traveled back to her throat. Just beneath it were multiple strands of pearls, now turned red with the woman's own blood.

"I have several officers checking for points of entry," Zuker offered. "The house is too large for one person to go through. They're bringing in a dog in case the killer is still here."

"I'd imagine he left through the pedestrian gate," Ryan said. "But it's best that we're certain the house is clear." He rose to his feet and motioned to an officer who stood nearby. "This body can be transported whenever they're ready. Tell them—" he stopped and looked back at the body "—tell the medical examiner that I want to know if there are signs that she'd been Tasered."

"You don't—" Zuker's mouth dropped open.

"I believe it's a copycat crime," Ryan said. "You remember the serial murder case we worked last year?"

"How could I forget it? There were several women killed in the span of a few days. The killer then went after Cait. But you killed him; on the Outer Banks as Hurricane Irene came ashore."

"Each of those women fit a particular profile," Ryan said, moving behind the desk. "They were all in their twenties. They all had long, brown hair. They had a specific body type." He looked at the leather chair for a moment. "This woman—Mrs. Skovgaard—obviously does not fit that profile."

"But you killed that man."

"Diallo Delport. I watched as he was swept out to sea in the hurricane."

"They never found his body."

"He's dead. I'm certain of it."

"Then why—?"

"The media reported the cause of death of each of the women. You remember; it solved cases in the Atlanta area as well. It was reported that each of the women had been Tasered. It also reported the cause of death." He watched as two men hoisted the body into a body bag and zipped it. "The throats were slit from ear to ear, just as Mrs. Skovgaard's was."

"So you think we're dealing with a copycat." Zuker's voice was flat.

"Aye. I do." He turned his attention to the desk. "She knew I was coming. And some time earlier, she sat at this desk." He waved his hand over it. "What do you see here that she could have been working on?"

Zuker walked around the desk, stopping at each angle to study it. "Nothing."

"Precisely. There's no open checkbook or bank statement, as if she was balancing her accounts. There are no pads of paper as if she was working on her next book; there are no notes."

"If she knew you were coming, where is the information she wanted to show you?"

Ryan opened a desk drawer and then another. He shook his head. "Indeed."

"Could she have been killed for what she knew?"

He looked up, startled. "I can't see how she could have been. Whatever she had, it had to have been historical, certainly nothing current. There would be no need to murder someone for something that happened years before, is there? All the parties would be dead and gone, long buried."

"I suppose you're right." Zuker glanced around the room. "I'm going back through her purse and her cell phone. We'll have to notify next-of-kin."

"Do you know much about her private life?"

"No, but Janie might. She read all her books… Come to think of it, Ms. Skovgaard had been married at one time. Seems her husband died maybe fifteen or twenty years ago. They had no children."

Ryan continued going through the desk drawers. "Did she have a computer?" he asked suddenly.

"I don't know. Why?"

He pointed at the desk. "It's nearly empty. There are no note pads. Perhaps she'd been working on a computer here?"

"And the killer took it?"

"Just a thought."

"The question is, 'Why?' then."

"Precisely. Why would someone enter this home, startle the owner, slit her throat and leave her to bleed out… yet not take her jewelry, her money, or ransack her home?"

"Maybe he was interrupted."

"Maybe we interrupted him," Ryan said. The body was being transported down the hallway and now he stared at the pool of blood on the floor. "No," he corrected himself. "The blood is too old. Some of it's already dried."

His cell phone beeped and he glanced at the screen. "Text message from the Chief," he said. "He wants to see me when I'm finished here."

"I don't doubt that he does," Zuker said as he returned to the kitchen. "I'll find the next-of-kin," he added over his shoulder.

Ryan sat back in the leather chair. The woman's shoe still lay on the floor a few feet away. The desk was nearly empty, save for a cordless phone, a pencil cup filled with pens, pencils—and a pair of scissors. He carefully extracted the scissors by slipping a pencil through the handle and lifting it up. There was no blood on it. He returned it, but called to a technician to process it. He didn't think it was the murder weapon, but one couldn't be too careful. It could have been wiped clean.

With a heavy sigh, he rose from the desk. He had other rooms to examine, and the Chief was waiting on him.

7

Duiblinn

The days had turned to weeks and the weeks to months. Each afternoon that he was in Duiblinn, Baldr waited for Maeve to finish her workday at the orphanage, walking her nearly all the way home. They always stopped as they rounded the curve in the road, beyond which her father's house could be seen. There, he would leave her. It would not do for an Ostman to be seen by her brothers and father; and most particularly, not *this* Ostman.

Sometimes, he would retreat to the small rise between her father's home and Duiblinn proper, where he would watch her as she walked across the open fields. Sometimes the breeze would catch her hair, and though he was too distant to see the strands themselves, he imagined them breaking free to swirl about her face.

She never looked back, and yet in his heart he knew she was aware that he was there, watching and waiting.

Sometimes the door would open to the cottage and she would disappear inside to the warmth and glow of the fireplace and he would remain on the hill, his cloak pulled about his hair to shield the stark white color from the penetrating moon rays, lest he be seen. He would stay there until his hands grew cool, the warmth from her skin dissipating into the night. Then he would wander the streets of Duiblinn, his thoughts remaining with her, until he found himself back in his room and asleep, with her voice and her smile pervading his dreams.

He learned that she was a studied woman who taught the most promising children in the orphanage how to read and write. Her eyes danced when she spoke of her charges, and they grew dark when she relayed instances of cruelty perpetrated against them. Her voice always pranced and shifted like musical notes, at various times growing excited, serene, animated and placid.

He did not have to speak. He was content to listen to her, to feel her smooth skin against the palm of his hand. The walks home went by too quickly; and then he was left alone to relive each moment until the morrow came.

~~~~~

She wore a broader smile than usual. Just a few yards from the orphanage, she pulled him into an alcove, her eyes glinting in merriment.

"M' father has gone away on business," she said.

"Oh?"

"And he's taken m' brothers with him."

He gazed into eyes that appeared to grow greener and wider with each passing moment.

"Do y' know what this means?" she asked.

"Yer mother—"

"She is tendin' to h'r sister, who is ill. There is no one at home, Baldr, no one but me."

He leaned back on his heels. A distant hint of logic pleaded with him not to vary their routine, but as his heartbeat gained in momentum he knew that his brain would be no competition for his heart and his soul. "Will ye sup with me this eve?" he asked.

"Aye," she answered instantly. "And I thought I would have to beg y' for the invitation."

He took her hand and they continued walking in silence. Then he stopped abruptly and turned to her. "We cannot be seen in the public dining hall."

"And why not?"

His hand went to his chest. "I am an Ostman, and ye—I shall not harm yer honor." He began walking again. "And I am—different."

"Aye," she said, taking his hand in hers again. "Y' *are* different. Y' are a gentleman in a world that has gone mad."

"Ye were in my room once, do ye remember?"

"I shall ne'er forget."

"I did not harm ye then. Will ye trust me to sup with me in my room?"

She laughed so heartily that he stopped walking to watch her. Her laughter sounded like a chorus of angels singing. "Aye," she said when she stopped to catch her breath. "But do y' trust *me?*"

~~~~~

He knocked lightly on the door before cautiously opening it. He found her just as he'd left her, seated next to a square table in the center of the room. He closed the door behind him before depositing bundles of meat, cheese and bread in front of her.

"Did y' have any troubles procurin' all o' this?" she asked, eying him as he retrieved a flask of wine.

"Nay," he answered. "I simply informed them I would be dining in my room this eve."

"And they didn't question ye? Or the amount o' food y' needed?"

He poured some wine in a bejeweled cup, a souvenir from a monastery he'd raided a few weeks back. They were easy targets, the monasteries were, but of late they were yielding less. Between the Normans' and the Ostmen's relentless raids, most of their cache was already spread out over all of Eire and beyond.

He placed the cup in front of her and said, "No one dares to question me. And this is the amount of food I eat at every meal." He sat in the chair beside hers.

He had just begun to unwrap one of the bundles when she stood abruptly. Wide-eyed, he watched as she stepped toward him. Adjusting her skirts, she straddled him on the chair.

"Ye mustn't—" he began. Self-conscious, he averted his gaze downward, only to find himself staring at the folds of material now deposited in his lap.

She placed a slender finger under his chin and lifted his face to hers. "Why do ye look away from me?"

"My eyes," he said, looking downward once more.

"I love yer eyes."

Startled, he looked back at her. He expected to find her laughing or some sort of telltale sign of her teasing him, but though she smiled, her eyes remained serious. "Yer eyes are the color of a beautiful winter sky… They are the lightest blue I have e'er beheld. And sometimes, it is as if they become invisible, just as wavin' yer hand through the air shows the skies not to be blue at all but utterly clear."

"And that does not frighten ye?"

"O' course not. Y' do not frighten me." She lifted one of his hands to hers and compared the palms against one another. Hers was so tiny, it might have been a child's hand placed within his. But while her skin was rosy and vibrant, his was as white as marble. She studied his skin for a moment before turning her attention to his face.

His face was soft as a baby's skin. While many of his men had long, braided beards, he had never been able to grow hair on his face. She placed a hand on each cheek, her fingers caressing him, pausing slightly over his dimples before they moved downward to his jawline.

"Maeve," he whispered.

When she looked in his eyes, she appeared utterly serene and amazingly beautiful. Her brows were dark and arched, setting off the color of her eyes. He placed his hand beneath her chin and allowed his thumb to gently brush her lips.

"Maeve," he said again, enjoying the sound of her name on his tongue, "I have loved ye since the first day mine eyes laid upon ye. But I did not dare hope—I thought always to have ye in my dreams only."

She leaned her cheek into his hand and closed her eyes with a gentle sigh. When she opened them a moment later, she placed her hands on his shoulders. "And I love ye," she whispered, "Baldr, Hvitr Bard. Y' have always had mine heart."

"But how could it be? I am—different."

"We do not choose the one we love. The love chooses us."

She leaned toward him and he brushed his lips across hers in a slow dance, feeling his way from one mesmerizing corner to the other. She parted her lips slightly; he began to move away when she pulled him back to her. She sucked softly on his bottom lip and he found himself wrapping his arms around her, pulling her closer to him, and opening her mouth more fully as he tasted her.

She felt better than anything he might have dreamed. She tasted sweeter than the juiciest fruit and smelled more pleasingly fragrant than the finest bouquet. She was intoxicating, this waif on his lap, utterly and completely intoxicating. Her sighs were like velvet, smooth and insistent.

When she pulled back, he heard himself moan and he sought to bring her back to him only to find both her palms against his chest. Before he could speak, she tugged at his tunic. "Remove it," she said. No order could be spoken so demurely or so softly; and no order could ever invoke in him more allegiance.

Once the tunic was pulled over his head and discarded on the floor beside them, she leaned back to gaze upon him. He steeled himself for her revulsion, but with an easy smile, she raced her fingers along his muscled chest before moving to his biceps. Unlike others who sported massive amounts of chest hair, his skin remained perfectly smooth and completely hairless. His arms dwarfed her; he hailed from a land to the north that was known for their large-boned inhabitants and even then, he was taller and huskier than most. He had not realized just how large he was until he watched her outstretched palm against the inside of his arm and realized from her thumb to her smallest finger, she could not reach halfway around his bicep.

"Ye have no scars," she said as if mesmerized.

"That is true."

"And yet y' are a warrior."

"Aye."

"How have y' managed to avoid injury?"

"The gods have been with me," he said. As she continued to feel his biceps and then his muscular triceps, he added, "I have been blessed with long arms. In battle, it has been difficult for one to get close enough to do me harm."

In reply, she kissed each bicep in turn, her lips traveling along the outlines of his muscles, slowly and sensuously.

He knew exactly when he moved to her clothing; he would relive this moment countless times in his dreams and memories. He would remember her soft smile as he slowly and meticulously loosened the ties, slipping her blouse from her shoulders and eventually from her breasts. He would reminisce to his dying day the touch of her fingers strumming through his long, white hair and the sensation of hers as he freed the deep brown tresses from its bun, allowing the strands to surround them like silk threads.

The memory would forever remain etched in his consciousness of rising to his feet and feeling her legs wrap around his waist, of carrying her to his bed and laying her down as softly and gently as he knew how. Later, he would close his eyes and see her emerald eyes the way they'd been at that moment; the pupils large, her cheeks flushed, as he slipped out of his breeches. And he would never forget how her hands trembled as she helped him with her skirts until they were left, skin against skin, lips exploring one another, hearts beating as one.

He pulled slightly away, searching her eyes for any indication that she had second thoughts. At any sign of hesitation, he would go no further.

But as their eyes met, hers appeared almost almond shaped as she smiled. "Y' are so beautiful," she whispered.

At that moment, his heart filled with a joy that he'd never known before and in his wildest dreams, he never thought he'd ever experience. He took her securely in his arms, holding her as tightly as he dared, wanting her to remain so close that he would not be able to tell where he ended and she began.

8

North Carolina

The police station hummed with activity. There was a constant stream of people entering amid an oppressively tense atmosphere. Ryan glanced up as a woman's voice grew increasingly loud. It wasn't as if people visited the police on their best day, he thought. He always seemed to encounter people on the worst days of their lives—an assault, a burglary, a robbery… a murder.

He turned back to the cell phone he held in his hand. He connected it to his computer and logged onto the software he needed. Then he downloaded the contents of Annelise Skovgaard's phone onto his computer. Once that was done, he ran an analysis of her call records.

She telephoned a specific number at least once a day, he noted, and sometimes twice. The same number was responsible for calls to her as well, with slight variations; the last one or two digits seemed to vary. So she was in constant communication with a company, he thought, and a large company at that.

He switched to the Internet and ran a reverse lookup of the phone number. Ah ha. Her publisher.

Zuker placed a cup of coffee on Ryan's desk as he dialed the number. "Thanks," he nodded. Then, "Aye. This is Detective Ryan O'Clery with the Lumberton, North Carolina Police Department. Would you happen to know which editor works with Annelise Skovgaard, the author?"

"Hold, please." The voice was curt, which made him wonder if the operator had heard anything he'd said.

A moment later, another woman's voice came on the line. "Jacqueline Janssen. What can I do for you?"

He introduced himself again. "I'm searching for Annelise Skovgaard's editor. Would you happen to know who that might be?"

"I am her editor." The voice was tinged with something he could only describe as irritation, as though he'd interrupted her busy day.

"And what did you say your name was?"

She repeated it with more than a little annoyance.

"Your last name is spelled—?"

"Look, Mister—"

"Detective. Detective Ryan O'Clery."

"Look, *Detective*, I'm a very busy lady. What do you want?"

"You have a detective telephoning you from the police department where one o' your most noted authors happens to live. And you're too busy to speak with me? Aren't you just a bit curious why the police department is phoning you on official business?"

There was a brief silence followed by a sigh. "I'm sorry, Detective—"

"O'Clery. Ryan O'Clery."

"I assumed you had written a book and wanted it published. You haven't, have you?"

"What would that have to do with anything?"

"It's just—well, we get a lot of unsolicited calls."

"Sure, and you can rest assured that I haven't written a book and have no intention of doing so. I'm phoning you because I have some questions for you about Annelise Skovgaard."

"I'm sorry; you'll have to speak with her if you have any questions. I can give you her number…" Her voice faded off and he thought he heard papers shuffling.

"There's no need to look up her number. I'm holding her mobile in my hand. It's how I got your number."

"Oh?"

"Mrs. Janssen, you say?"

"Miss Janssen."

"Miss Janssen, when was the last time you spoke with Mrs. Skovgaard?" He eyed the call list as he waited for her answer.

"This morning."

"And what time would that have been, do you suppose?"

"I don't know… I'd just come in to work. She's always the first author I touch bases with. I suppose… I suppose around nine o'clock."

Nine-oh-five, he thought, eying the call list. "And did she sound okay to you then?"

"Yes. Why? Did she—is she okay?" Her voice elevated a few octaves.

"Did she seem concerned about anything?"

"No. I don't think so. She was deep into her research on her next book. Look—"

"Had she found anything of any particular importance? Something that might have worried her?" He glanced up to find Zuker watching him curiously.

"What is this about, Detective?" Without waiting for an answer, she continued, "I'd like to talk to Mrs. Skovgaard before our conversation goes any further."

"Well, I'd like to oblige, Miss Janssen. Truly I would. But I'm afraid that's impossible."

"Then you'll have to talk to our corporate attorneys—"

"You see, Mrs. Skovgaard was found murdered today."

There was a stunned silence on the other end of the line.

"Miss Janssen?"

"I just talked to her this morning." The editor's voice had become hushed.

"So, would you happen to know her next of kin?"

"Her—what? No. Her husband died years ago. She has no children."

"Well, you see, I'm trying to notify her next of kin of her death. And I've got very little to go on."

After a brief silence, she said, "In our contract with each author, we ask for a point of contact in the—rare—event that the author can't be reached. I'll have to check."

"Can you do that for me? I'll be happy to hold."

The phone clicked so suddenly that he wasn't sure whether she'd placed him on hold or hung up entirely. But after a couple of minutes, she returned. "Detective?"

"I'm still here."

"She has a nephew in Norway. His name is Kaj Skovgaard."

"And would you have contact information for him?"

She read off the phone number, address and email. Then, "How do you know she was murdered? I mean, could it have been a heart attack—she was in her nineties…"

"May I have your mobile number as well, Miss Janssen? In case I need to speak with you further."

"Yes. Of course." Her voice was subdued as she provided it. "I'll have to issue some sort of a press release…"

"Would you mind waiting on that? Perhaps twenty-four hours. By then, I'll have more information for you—for the press, you know."

"Yes. I suppose."

"Thank you. You've been quite helpful."

There was no response and after a moment, he hung up.

"Twenty-four hours, 'eh?" Zuker said.

"I don't want word to get out just yet on the cause of death."

"Oh?" The voice came from several feet away. Ryan turned to find Chief Johnston watching him. "And why is that?"

Ryan rose. "May we speak with you now?"

~~~~~

"You're saying her throat was slit?" Chief Johnston leaned against his desk and crossed his arms. The room was dark though the blinds were open, a reminder of the volatility of the season.

Ryan motioned with one finger from one ear to the other.

"Who found her?" he asked. "Was there a witness?"

"As far as we know, there are no witnesses." He glanced at Zuker, who remained silent beside him. "Mrs. Skovgaard telephoned me last evening. She said she was working on a new book, and she'd discovered some information that she thought might interest me."

"She was a Pulitzer Prize winning author, you know."

"Aye." He cleared his throat. "So I've been told."

"And a noted historian."

"Aye."

"Why do I have the impression her murder has something to do with you?"

Ryan peered at Zuker out of the corner of his eye. "We're considering the possibility. You see, since her throat had been slit—"

"Just like the serial murder case you worked last year."

"Aye, but—"

"You said the killer died."

Ryan hesitated. Chief Johnston's head was slightly lowered, but his eyes peered upward. His gaze didn't waver from Ryan's face as he waited for his reply. "I saw him swept out to sea," he said quietly.

"In your statement last year, you were certain he was dead."

"He could not have survived. Not under those circumstances. As you'll recall, Hurricane Irene was coming ashore. The winds were—well, beyond strong, to be frank. They were hellacious. The waves were crashing over the tops of houses three stories tall. He couldn't have survived."

"Are you willing to bet your career on that?"

"I believe this to be a copycat crime," he said. He was certain his evasive answer was not lost on the chief. He was intelligent and quick-minded.

He looked at Zuker. "Are you in agreement?"

"It's the same modus operandi. O'Clery asked for the medical examiner to check for Taser marks."

"I don't have a good feeling about this," the chief said.

"I didn't like seeing the sight myself," Ryan said. "I thought I was all and done with women whose throats were slit."

"And this victim's profile?"

"It does not fit the profile of any of the other victims. Not at'all."

Chief Johnston peered at Ryan for a long moment. He cupped his chin in his hand and thoughtfully rubbed one finger along his jaw line. "So, where do you go from here?"

"I've spoken with Mrs. Skovgaard's publisher, Jacqueline Janssen. She's provided me with the contact information for the next-of-kin. I'll be contacting him—a nephew in Norway—and I'll also be following up with the publisher on what the author was working on at the time of her death."

"You said you were there because she'd contacted you?"

"That's right."

"She'd come across something she thought you'd be interested in? Personally or professionally?"

"Personally." He looked into the chief's eyes without blinking.

"Elaborate."

"I wish I had more to tell you. She said she'd come across something about my family's history. But, to be quite honest, I think she had me confused with someone else."

"Why is that?"

"She said it had something to do with Norway. And my family is from Ireland, not Norway. We have no relations in Norway—or any other Scandinavian country. Well, my sister married a Norseman, but his family has been in America for centuries... I honestly don't believe her murder had anything to do with history. How could it?"

"Are you trying to convince me or yourself?"

"I've just begun my investigation. I'm not closing any doors yet."

"And if this gets personal?"

"It won't."

Chief Johnston studied Ryan for a moment before turning to Zuker. "Zuker's in charge of the case."

"Why?"

"Did you just ask me *why*?"

"I've years of experience. And—no insult intended, Zuk—but he just made detective rank a month or so ago. This is an unusual case—"

"A case that bears too much of a resemblance to the one that almost had your wife killed."

Ryan stopped, stunned.

"You'll help your partner, of course," the chief continued. "Use your expertise. But keep a level head."

"Aye." Ryan rose from his chair.

"You hear me, O'Clery?" Chief Johnston asked. His tone took on a demanding quality. *"Keep a level head."*

9

Ryan opened the front door to the sound of laughter and voices. He stepped into the foyer and silently closed the door behind him before heading down the hall.

He stopped at the doorway of the living room, his eyes moving over the scene that unfolded in front of him. His house was small; it had been the perfect size for him when he had been a bachelor, but now that he was married with two infants, it felt like they were busting out at the seams. Still, he had to admit, Cait had made his bachelor pad a true home. The leather couch sported beautifully designed throws that matched each season, and decorative pillows adorned the chairs. The fireplace mantle sported a variety of china figurines; she particularly loved collecting angels. There were cherubs holding birds in their hands, seraphs smelling flowers, angels in prayer… She even had them adorning the corners of every door leading out of the house; they protected them from harm, she said. Whether they did or not, he didn't care. As long as it made her happy, he'd accept the winged figures over every inch of the house. At least they weren't gargoyles.

His eyes took in Cait and Claire in the kitchen, which was separated from the living room and dining area by a wide island containing a sink. Their backs were to him as they labored over the stove together. They were laughing like high school girls, he thought. It did his heart good; his first wife had not been accepting of his close relationship with his sister Claire. Cait was. That went a long way in his book.

Claire stood several inches taller than Cait. She was neither buxom nor slender but somewhere in between. Her hair was shoulder length and its natural color was such a deep red that it almost appeared to be burgundy. It was straight and thick and often tucked behind her ears. Her skin was ivory as much of the Irish skin was; she had her sleeves rolled up to the elbows and though he couldn't see them from this distance, he knew they were sprinkled with freckles. When she spoke, it was in the melodious cadence that was uniquely Irish; a tone and descant that reminded him of home.

In contrast, Cait was more petite and slender. Her long brunette hair was haphazardly pulled up with clips that fell short of containing it. Her voice was soft and feminine; a voice that often unnerved him with its quiet strength.

His eyes moved from the two women to Claire's twins, Emma and Erin, who were setting the table. They were now six years old but they acted as if they were twenty; especially after his own girls had been born, they seemed to have matured even further.

They both sported red heads, though they varied in shade; a combination, Ryan thought, of the Irish blood and their father's Norse ancestry. They were both speaking to each other non-stop. They didn't seem to be listening to what the other said; yet in their next breaths, they answered the other's questions or commented on what they'd just heard. It was the craziest thing he'd ever witnessed. He wondered if his two girls would do the same.

His eyes wandered to the playpen, where Darcy and Dee lay sleeping peacefully, despite the clamor around them. They lay side by side with the fingers of both hands intertwined with the other's, as if they were concerned that their twin would disappear while they slept. When he'd returned to work, he'd missed them more than he had expected. While at home, he'd missed the camaraderie of the men and the challenges of his cases. Now that he was back at work, he found he missed holding his children and marveling at every noise they made, every expression they offered, every inkling of growth they exhibited.

A movement on the other side of the playpen caught his eye, and he recognized his brother-in-law, Tommy. He was a large man; not as tall or robust as Ryan, but he towered over most and exhibited the physical fitness of most military men. He had bright red hair, a freckled face and an easy smile. "Tommy," he said in greeting.

His brother-in-law's response was lost as Emma's and Erin's voices drowned him out.

"Uncle Re! Uncle Re!" They both rushed toward him as if they hadn't just seen him the day before. Each grabbed one of Ryan's massive thighs, wrapping their arms around him as though he was a lifeline.

He laughed and swooped each into his arms. "I need a kiss from my favorite ladies," he said. Each pecked him on the cheek and he returned the favor. "Oh, I'd say you both have gained a few pounds since I last saw you!"

"That's impossible," Emma said matter-of-factly. "We saw you only yesterday."

"It's about time," Claire said, her Irish lilt taking on a cadence as no-nonsense as his mother's. But she smiled as she wiped her hands on her apron and came to his side. "Don't you know, we've been holding supper warm for you, Re."

"Apologies for keeping you waiting," he said. "I lost track of time."

Erin lifted his wrist. "And just what do you think your watch is for, Uncle Re? Use it, why don't you."

He laughed. "Aye, and you're a force to be reckoned with. And I thank you for the reminder." He reluctantly set the girls on the floor. They returned to folding the napkins at each place setting and talking to each other non-stop.

"We made lamb stew," Cait said, setting a casserole dish on the table before turning to him. She kissed him lightly, but her lips lingered on his. As he looked into her eyes, they crinkled as if thinking of a private joke.

"Oh, what a wench," he breathed so only she could hear.

"Have a seat," she said, winking. "Tommy, you too."

"And how are things at Fort Bragg?" Ryan asked as they took their seats.

"Wait until after the prayer please," Emma said. She spread her arms to either side. As the others settled into their seats, they joined hands. Without hesitation, Emma said a prayer as fervently and professionally as a nun.

"Budget cutbacks," Tommy said as he passed the rolls around the table. "Seems like I'm always trying to do more with less."

Ryan picked out a roll and did a double-take. "What is this?" he asked, holding it up.

"It's a rabbit, Uncle Re," Erin said. "Can't you tell by the long ears?"

"Is that what that is?" he laughed as he bit into a long piece of dough.

"Why were you so late?" Cait asked.

"I was working a homicide."

"Is that so?" Claire prepared to pass a bowl of fruit compote. It had jelled in a pan shaped like a fairy but now looked more like an indescribable mass. "You haven't had a murder in quite a while, have you now?"

"Not one like this. That's for certain."

"Can you talk about it?" Claire asked.

"Funny thing," Ryan said, buttering his roll. "Her throat was slit from ear to ear."

The table grew completely silent. He looked up to find all eyes on him. Claire was holding the dish as if to pass it, but she held it suspended in mid-air. Cait had her fork half-raised to her lips, where it also remained as if frozen. Tommy's eyes were wide, his hands still.

"You need to rethink 'funny', Uncle Re," Erin chided.

"Her throat was slit?" Cait's voice was hushed.

Ryan gently placed his hand on hers and lowered the fork before the food dropped from it. "Don't you be worried now, darlin'. It is nothing like the Delport case."

"What's different about it?" Cait asked, not taking her eyes from his.

"First off and let us not forget, Delport is dead. Besides, the profile is all wrong. She's not young; she doesn't have long, brown hair…" His eyes instinctively moved to Cait's hair. One thick tress had escaped the hair clip and tumbled over her shoulder, curling as it cascaded over her breast.

"Who was she?" Tommy asked.

"Annelise Skovgaard."

There was a collective gasp among the adults.

"Annelise Skovgaard?" Claire breathed. "The world famous historian?"

"The one who called you last night?" Cait asked.

Ryan took a hefty bite of the lamb. "This is positively delicious," he said. Looking up and realizing all eyes were on him, he continued, "Aye. The one who phoned me last evening."

"Annelise Skovgaard, the famous historian, telephoned you, Re?" Claire leaned forward.

"She said she had information on our ancestry," he said in a dismissive tone. "But I'm certain she was mistaken."

"She's a Pulitzer Prize winning author," Claire said. "I don't suppose they'd be making mistakes."

He tore off a piece of his roll. "Sure, and this one did."

"How can you be certain?" Tommy asked.

"She said she was researching Norway's history," he said. "And we have no ancestors from Norway."

"You told her that?"

"Aye. I did. But the lady was insistent."

"How can you be so sure she was wrong?" Tommy pressed.

"The Irish weren't exactly enamored of Vikings," Ryan said. "No disrespect intended, Tommy."

"None taken… While my ancestors were from Scandinavia, I have no idea if they were Vikings, or if they'd ever been to Ireland."

"Well, and there you have it. You aren't familiar with all there is to know about your ancestors. But my family made certain that we were."

"Re is the keeper of the family history now," Claire said. "When Auntie died, he inherited all the paperwork and journals dating back hundreds of years."

"A thousand or more," Ryan corrected. "I've been in the process of cataloguing it all, scanning it in, and computerizing it. I've converted the spare bedroom to a study for that express purpose."

"But," Cait said, "you said this historian, this Pulitzer Prize winning author, was found dead, her throat slit?"

Ryan glanced at Cait's plate. "You haven't touched your food at'al, love."

"Do you have a suspect?"

"Not yet."

"Who found her?"

"I did."

Everyone gasped again.

"You did, Re?"

"She was very insistent about the information she had, so I arranged to meet her at her house today for a chat. When I arrived, I found her quite expired." He looked at Emma and Erin. "Anyway, I suppose it's not what you'd call polite dinner conversation. You two are certainly quiet."

"It's when we're quiet that we're taking everything in, Uncle Re," Erin said in a haunting tone.

"Roll, anyone?" Emma offered, holding up the bread basket.

~~~~~

Ryan leaned back in the recliner and pulled Darcy and Dee closer to his chest. Just beyond him on the coffee table sat two half-empty bottles of formula.

Though she'd indicated she was full, now that the bottles were no longer within reach Dee tried to suck her entire hand. Ryan grappled around the seat cushion until he found her pacifier and popped it into her mouth.

He didn't know how she knew, but his daughter certainly did know which pacifier was exclusively hers. The nipple was uniquely shaped, rather flat and wide, and the ring was hot pink. The shield was a translucent purple with several ventilation holes. And Lord forbid if they couldn't find it when she wanted it; no other pacifier would do.

Now that their bellies were full and their lids were heavy, they settled against him contentedly. As he waited for Cait to take her evening shower, he kissed the top of each of their heads in turn. His sister and her family had left a half hour earlier. The truth was that he loved these moments with them. It didn't matter to him whether they were screaming or crying or eating or burping, he cherished every minute. He'd seen how quickly Claire's girls grew and he knew his would do the same. In the blink of an eye, he'd be threatening some hormone-crazed boy within an inch of his life, and in another blink, he'd be walking each down the aisle.

He loved them equally, he was sure; but he was always drawn to Dee and her distinctive birthmark. He brushed it now with his thumb and she cooed and sleepily gave him a toothless grin. When she opened her eyes just a bit, the blue color was startling; they seemed to be the eyes of a mature adult. They appeared wise, intelligent and knowing.

Cait stepped into the room. Her hair was still damp and the honeysuckle scent of her shampoo almost seemed to precede her. "Are they sleeping?"

"They're drifting off." He nodded toward the bottles. "They've each had their fill."

"Thank you, Ryan," she said, perching on the corner of the coffee table. "You have no idea how much this helps me."

"I love doing it," he said quietly.

"Darcy is the spitting image of you."

"I hope not," he laughed. "My mug is much too ugly to be a little girl."

"That is not true." Cait pulled the towel from him. "You are the most handsome man I've ever known."

"Ah, the love of my life you are indeed."

She rose, gathered the bottles and carried them to the kitchen. She tossed the towel into the laundry room hamper and quietly cleaned the last of the dishes. When she turned back to Ryan, he was watching her intently.

"By the way," she said, "I found your keys."

"Where were they?"

"On the island."

"I thought we looked there."

"I did, too, but apparently we overlooked them."

He cocked his head. "I must be losing it."

She laughed. "Then we both are." As she moved toward him, she reached out her arms for the closest girl. "I'll take Darcy."

The little girl whimpered as Cait attempted to gather her and he chuckled. "It's no bother, love." He stood and both girls snuggled against his broad chest, reaching instinctively for one another. "Just make certain their crib is ready, and I'll put them down."

~~~~~

A few minutes later, the girls were asleep in their crib and Ryan was finished with his shower. As he entered the bedroom, he found Cait lying in bed, staring at the ceiling.

"A penny for your thoughts," he said.

She didn't answer immediately. He leaned across the bed to kiss her, and she wrapped her arms around his neck. Her eyes were stormy, the gold flecks sparkling against the blue-gray color. Her dark brows were knit. "I'm frightened, Ryan."

He pulled back so he could study her face more clearly. "Of what?"

"Of the man who killed that woman today."

"You have nothing to be frightened about, I assure you."

"How many killers slit someone's throat?" she pressed.

"It's quite personal," he admitted. "It's one thing to shoot someone, which can be done at a distance. It's quite another to look into someone's eyes and…"

"I saw Diallo Delport kill my cameraman," she said.

He nodded. She'd been duty-bound to recite the details when she was interviewed by the police. He'd been present but he hadn't been the one to question her; that had been the responsibility of the Outer Banks police. She'd been a reporter then, working for an Atlanta television station, and she'd been covering the hurricane's devastation along the North Carolina coastline. After she'd given her statement, he'd held her so tightly that he didn't believe she could ever be pried from his hands while she cried and recounted the horror with raw emotion. The scene had been repeated until she seemed to have cried out all the distress of that fateful night.

"Do you have a suspect?"

"Not yet. But don't worry, Cait. It's probably a copycat crime and I'm certain I'll have the killer in short order." He eased under the comforter and pulled her to him. She smelled of honeysuckle and lilies. "There is absolutely nothing for you to be concerned with. I promise you that."

She snuggled against him, sliding one smooth leg over both of his as she pressed her face against his shoulder. "I trust you, Ryan. I know you'll get him."

"Do you miss your job as a reporter?"

"Sometimes," she said sleepily. "Sometimes I wish I had more adults to talk to."

He wove his fingers through her silky strands and inhaled her scent more deeply. As she settled against him, her breathing grew measured and steady and he knew she was drifting off to sleep. But he remained awake, his eyes on the same ceiling she'd stared at moments earlier. He fought a lump in the pit of his stomach and an uneasy catch in his throat that made his breathing irregular. He could sense when something was wrong, and there was something very wrong about this case.

10

Duiblinn

The land was filled with discord. Five years earlier, the High King of Eire, Rory O'Connor, had exiled Diarmait MacMurrough. Now MacMurrough was returning with an advance force of Norman warriors. In Baldr's opinion, the Vikings had transformed Duiblinn Village to a thriving city, and now he and Maeve could only watch from the sidelines as political rivals clashed and struggled for control of all of Eire. He would have gladly fought to maintain control of Duiblinn along with his Norse allies but their hands were tied by politics, other than skirmishes that erupted and were over as quickly as they'd begun.

The Normans were particularly fierce. Word traveled from western Eire that Celts were hung from castle walls as they were overtaken, and they cared not whether they were men, women or children. When the Ostmen clashed with the Normans, it became particularly bloody. Often the stench of dead bodies would travel on the winds for miles.

Those who remained loyal to the Norse gods, including Baldr, found themselves increasingly on the outskirts of society. Pope

Alexander III was strengthening the Catholic Church's reach into Aquitaine, Normandy, England and Scotland and now had set his sights on Eire itself, which he considered a barbarous nation without civilized rules or customs.

There was an undercurrent of change that rippled like a giant whale about to burst through the surface of a tumultuous ocean; those who adhered to the old ways were considered indecent, no better than livestock. Yet they were also deemed to be an imminent and growing danger in much the same way as a pack of filthy, rabid dogs. As the unrest grew and festered, Baldr saw many of his friends and fellow warriors take to the seas to return to the land of their birth or to find new, uncharted realms that might prove more hospitable. Reinforcements from the north were not forthcoming as their distant leaders no longer felt that Eire was worth fighting the Normans for control. As hard as their ancestors had fought for domination of this beautiful and mystical land, it seemed they were now ready to give it up without much of a struggle.

But the Vikings had become, in Baldr's opinion, more Irish than the Irish themselves. Though he himself had been born to the north, it was common knowledge that the Ostmen had lived in settlements all over Eire for two centuries or more. Yet with the persecutions that became more rampant and bold, it seemed the only path to remaining in the country was to renounce their pagan gods and fall in line with the Catholic Church. Many did, marrying their Celtic loves in the church condoned by the Pope, following the ways of this new religion and pledging allegiance to the Pope himself, though he lived in a land so far removed from Eire that none he knew would ever see him.

Norman, Welsh and Flemish warriors had landed in Eire in 1169 and now as the summer solstice beckoned in 1171, friction was rising to a fever pitch. It was not enough, it appeared, for the Normans to oust the Ostmen from the island; now King Henry II threatened to invade the country himself. With a proclamation from the Pope, who considered himself and the church above any king, Henry II was free to conquer Eire and proclaim it part of England.

Duiblinn was separated from England by the Irish Sea, and many a time did Baldr stand along the fishermen docks and stare eastward as though he could see the King of England himself rise from the mists. There were skirmishes between the Ostmen and the Normans; between the Normans and the Celts; and between the Celts and the Ostmen. There were allegiances on all sides and passions grew heated to the point of boiling.

But when he was alone with Maeve, the rest of the world seemed completely shut out. Politics, religions, gods and fiefdoms no longer mattered. Oh, to be sure he noticed the growing suspicions from the proprietors of the boarding house in which he stayed; he could feel their shortened tempers, could see them biting their tongues, but he thought he could remain beyond their reach. He kept most of his fighting to the north, the south or the west of Duiblinn. When he was in the city proper, he had eyes only for Maeve. He did not cower from any man; he did not avert his gaze; but neither did he seek to fight. He sought only the company and solace of the woman he loved.

She had four brothers: Daegan, Stiabhan, Keegan and Royan. He had only seen them from afar and only knew who they were because Maeve or one of his comrades had pointed them out to him. All were raven-haired. Three were larger than most Celts, while one, Keegan, was slighter and appeared to be no more than a boy.

Maeve and Baldr kept their relationship private and discreet, either meeting at his room by the back steps, or to the south of Duiblinn, where they would ride his black steed. He liked the way she fit in front of him as they rode, the manner in which her back relaxed against his chest, the means by which he could lift her atop the horse with just one hand as if she weighed no more than a feather… They often rested at stone bridges and watched the fish swim by beneath them, or in fields of lavender where they lay for hours observing the clouds. And on those rare occasions when her family was away, they would steal the night, relaxing under the stars and the moon, feeling each other's bodies until he sensed that he belonged more to her than to himself.

And on this high summer day, they spread a cloth next to a gentle creek, opened a flask of wine and a package of cheese and whiled away the late afternoon.

"Talk to me about yer homeland," Maeve pleaded.

Baldr lay back against the wool and watched the clouds sail across a beautiful blue sky. "It is much like Eire," he said. "The summers are shorter but everything turns very green and the flowers are vibrant."

"And the winters?"

"Ah, the winters, they go on forever it seems. The days are short and the nights are long."

"And is it cold there?"

"For ye, aye, I suppose it would be indeed. For those born there, we are accustomed to it and it does not bother us."

"The winters, are they dreary?"

"Eire's winters are much more dreary, I believe." He snatched a blade of grass and chewed on it as he reflected. "Inland, we have so much snow… It is very white, most pristine, and the very nature of it reflects what little bit of sun we receive in the winter, so it appears as if we have much more."

"And what do ye do in the winter months? Can ye sail as ye do now?"

"Sometimes." He winked at her. "But if ye were there w' me, ah," he sighed, "we would spend those long winter nights in one another's arms, keeping each other warm, and wishing the winter would ne'er end."

"Oh, would we now?" She kissed his fingers mischievously.

"Come with me," he said suddenly. "There is unrest here in Eire. Nothing good will come o' it; I am convinced o' that. We could be happy to the north, among my people."

She grew serious. She studied his fingers before wrapping both her hands around his larger one. "I would be leavin' m' family; m' brothers and m' parents… all I have e'er known."

"Ye would. But it need not be forever; we would visit them on occasion."

"I do not believe they would understand m' leavin'."

He sat up and pulled her to him. "I want to make ye m' wife," he said with a tone of urgency. "I want to live w' ye as man and wife. I would fashion ye a beautiful home to the north. Ye would not want for anything."

"I know that ye would." Her voice was low.

"So why the hesitation? Do ye not love me as I love ye?"

"Of course I love ye. I love ye more than Life itself. It is just…"

He waited for her to continue.

"M' father," she said at last, picking at a non-existent piece of lint on her dress, "and m' brothers… They think o' the Ostmen as enemies."

"I know. And yet, ye are here with me now."

"Aye. I risk their wrath to be w' ye. And yet, when I am w' them, I hear the hatred in their voices. They plot against the Ostmen, Baldr. They plot against the Normans as well. They wish for Eire to be completely Irish, as it was long a'fore any o' us were born."

"That may never happen," he said softly. "Sometimes the world continues to evolve. Sometimes there is no going back. Sometimes what we remember—or what our fathers or our fathers' fathers remember—is no more, and will ne'er be again."

"I know that." She sighed. "But I am their only daughter; m' brothers' only sister."

"Then shall I convert to yer ways, yer religion?"

"Would ye do that for me?" Her brows knit in worry.

"I would do anything for ye."

"You would renounce yer gods?" she pressed.

He looked toward the distance for a long moment before turning back to her. "I cannot lie to ye, Maeve. I will ne'er completely renounce m' gods for fear o' their retribution ag'in me. I would rather suffer yer families' hatred than the wrath of m' gods."

"Then—"

"But I can join yer faith, can I not? Is there not space for both my gods and yers?"

She smiled. "I do not believe it is that simple."

He wanted to ask then what would become of them. He wanted to know if this day and all the days in which they snatched a little time with one another, would be all that there could ever be. He wanted to know if his life was destined to be lived in a room in a boarding house; if he would forever stop just shy of walking her home lest her family spot them together. But he could not. If this was all there could be, he would have to be content with that. She was worth the long days of waiting, the slow nights of yearning, for those times when he could hold her, however briefly.

And, he reminded himself, Life was good in the cocoon they'd fashioned for themselves. It was not perfect; he was still Hvitr Bard, The White Devil, a man to whom no respectable family would relinquish their daughter. He was still a heathen, loyal to the Norse gods; they had kept him safe, without so much as a nick in all the skirmishes he'd fought, and he did not, after all, wish to incur their wrath by shifting his allegiance to a pope.

She was right for him, even if her family was unaware of their relationship. And though he much preferred to establish a home with her as his wife, he would take whatever morsels she was prepared to give him.

11

North Carolina

Ryan stood at the door to Mrs. Skovgaard's office. He had been through every room in the house. It was insanely large, he thought; perhaps twenty of his house would fit into one of hers. He stopped counting the number of bedrooms and baths and wondered at the absurdity of one woman barely five feet tall roaming about a mansion like this all by herself. Judging from the amount of dust on most of her belongings, she did not have a housekeeper, and it appeared as if she lived primarily in the main wing of the house where he now stood, as well as a bedroom and bath at the top of the stairs.

The Humane Society had come and gone, taking with them more than four dozen cats. It was a no-kill shelter and they'd find loving new homes, even if their futures would be spent without a clowder of felines.

The heavy layer of dust that pervaded the house made it easier to spot if anything was missing. Television sets, stereos and speakers were all in place, and judging from their overly chunky dimensions, they appeared not to have been moved for at least thirty years. He found a gun cabinet in the wing to the right; studying the weapons, Mr. Skovgaard must have been a hunter. There were no pistols but many rifles, some of which appeared to be collectors' items.

Mrs. Skovgaard had accumulated a sizable cache of jewelry. Her most valuable pieces such as diamond necklaces, gem-studded bracelets and diamond rings, were in her underwear drawer—where, Ryan noted, most professionals knew to look first. She had a variety of jewelry boxes, ranging from burled ones that rested atop her dresser to towers in her dressing room which were significant pieces of furniture.

Nothing appeared to be missing.

Nothing, that is, except a laptop computer.

He could see a layer of dust on her desk from his position at the door. But in the center of the desk, there was a pristine area perhaps eleven inches long by fifteen inches wide. The imprint had to have been a laptop, he reasoned.

So Mrs. Skovgaard, at the ripe old age of ninety-two, wrote her books or compiled her research on a laptop computer. And whatever she was working on, the killer thought it was more important than the jewelry, the electronics, the weapons and the money that was there for the taking.

No room had been ransacked; not even this one. The killer knew what he wanted. But why not just break in and steal it? He thought. Why kill a defenseless old lady?

He walked to the corner of the desk, where he could see the stain where Mrs. Skovgaard had lain. Why slit her throat? Why not just walk in with a gun and shoot her from across the room?

Knives were personal, he thought. It took a certain type of person to look someone in the eye while they pressed a knife against their flesh and ripped them open. It took strong emotions: hatred or rage. Who hated her? Who was so angry with her that they wanted her dead?

He heard the sound of a door closing, and he quickly drew his weapon. He pressed himself against the wall and listened. The house was silent—quiet as a tomb. He moved across the room, staying as close to the wall as possible, while he tried to peer through the door into the hall.

As he reached the edge of a bookcase, he spotted a mirror in the dining room across the hall. He kept his eyes on that mirror until he saw a leg come into view: a woman's shapely calf, stiletto heels, a skirt that seemed too short for comfort… She stepped further down the hall, her steps cautious, and his eyes swept over her fitted clothing, the black belt, a sleeveless top and toned arms. She had shoulder-length blond hair, perfectly straight and all one length.

"Police," he said. He hadn't meant to yell it, but in the stillness of the house, his voice sounded deep and strong. The figure froze. "Stay right where you are," he said. "Don't make a move."

He kept his weapon drawn as he made his way into the hallway. The woman stood with her hands raised. In one hand was a thin leather pocketbook; bracelets dangled from both wrists. Her eyes were dark blue, nearly violet. She had high cheekbones, a smooth tan, and rosy lips.

"I—worked with Mrs. Skovgaard," she said as Ryan approached. "Are you Detective O'Clery?"

"Did you not see the crime scene tape across the doors?"

"I did." She ran her tongue across her lip as if she was parched. "But the door was ajar, and I thought—"

He holstered his weapon. "You were taking quite a chance. There might have been someone here who might have done you harm."

"May I put my hands down?"

"Aye. Slowly. Do you have identification?"

"In my bag."

"Get it. Slowly."

"I have a gun in my bag."

He raised a brow.

"I have a permit."

"Do not pull the gun out of your bag. Only your identification."

He watched as she opened her pocketbook. Her fingers were slender and her nails were long and immaculately polished in deep pink. He thought of Cait's nails; since the birth of the girls, they were kept short and unpolished. This woman, in contrast, did not do dishes.

She offered him her wallet, opened to her identification. He took it and with one eye on her, he examined the driver's license. It was a New York license. She was twenty-seven years old.

"So you're Jacqueline Janssen." He handed her back the wallet.

"And you're Detective O'Clery?"

"I am. What are you doing here?"

"I worked closely with Mrs. Skovgaard. We communicated every day." He didn't respond but continued looking at her. After a moment, she obliged with more information. "I am quite distraught, as you can imagine. I thought if I came here, there was something I could do…"

He motioned toward the living room. "Now that you're here, there are some questions I'd like to ask of you." He led her into the living room, away from the room where the historian had been murdered. They sat on dusty chairs set on either side of a substantial granite fireplace.

"Do you know of anyone who disliked Mrs. Skovgaard?"

"Personally? No." She averted her eyes and appeared to be thinking through her answer. "Professionally? There will always be people who are envious of a popular author, a famous historian, a Pulitzer winner."

"And who might they be?"

"No one who would murder her," she said. Her chin trembled slightly. "There are people who would like to discredit her. But not kill her."

"I'd like the names of those people anyway."

"Sure."

"I'll take you down to the police department, where you can write out a list."

"Her office is right down the hall. I'm sure there's paper and pens there."

"Were any of the people," he continued, ignoring her statement, "angry with her? Beyond envy?"

She shook her head. "I don't know of anyone I'd call angry."

"Emotional?"

"Emotional?" she repeated.

"Mrs. Janssen—"

"Jackie. And it's *Miss*."

"Jackie." The color rose in her cheeks as he said her name. "Mrs. Skovgaard was killed up close. It was personal."

"How do you know it wasn't a robbery?" She waved her hand. "You see her home."

"Nothing is missing." He considered telling her about the laptop, but thought better of it. "This was personal. Do you happen to know what she was working on at the time?"

"She was doing research for her next book."

"And what was that book about?"

She hesitated. "Mrs. Skovgaard's success came because she took periods of history that we think we already know… and she dug deeper. She put a face on history."

"And whose face was she working on?"

She sighed. "I—I don't understand."

"Could she have been working on a particular person, someone whose family would become irate? Perhaps something that could sully someone's reputation, and the descendants might have objected?"

"I don't know." Her eyes met his. "I honestly don't know."

"What period of history was she researching?"

"The twelfth century—with a focus on Norway, Denmark and Sweden."

"Is there something that happened in the twelfth century that could be considered scandalous?"

"Detective," she said, her voice gaining traction, "even if she discovered something shocking; that was nearly a thousand years ago. Do you really think that a descendant would kill her over something she uncovered from that long ago?" Her brows knit as the last words came out rapidly and impatiently.

The front door opened and he recognized Zuker's voice as he called his name.

"In here," he shouted.

Zuker was mid-sentence as he stepped through the door. He abruptly stopped speaking. "I didn't know—"

"Detective Zuker, meet Jacqueline Janssen, Mrs. Skovgaard's editor."

He nodded in greeting.

"Mrs. Janssen—*Miss* Janssen—was just about to accompany us to the police department. I'd like for her to write out a list of people who might have been—*envious*—of Mrs. Skovgaard's success."

They rose and as they made their way through the living room, Ryan's eyes fell upon a book in the center of the coffee table. Curious, he stopped to pick it up. It was titled *Before Columbus: The Contributions of Vikings to the Development of the Americas*. It was authored by Annelise Skovgaard.

"What is this?" he murmured.

"That's the book Mrs. Skovgaard won the Pulitzer for," Jackie said.

"May I take this with me?"

She shrugged. "I don't know who would stop you." She started toward the front foyer. "I don't know why it was out. Mrs. Skovgaard was quite sick of hearing about it. It trumped all her other books; some of them she thought were better."

Ryan tucked the book under his arm as he followed her. He had a strange sensation, as if the book was actually vibrating. He stopped and adjusted it but the phenomenon continued. It was perfectly ridiculous, he thought. Everyone knew books were simply objects of paper and ink; it was impossible for them to vibrate.

Still, as he locked the door behind them and they left the empty mansion behind, he had the distinct impression that this book contained a clue.

~~~~~

"I'm afraid I've wasted your time, Detective," Jackie said as she stood before Ryan's desk.

He stopped reading his email and eyed the paper she held in her hands. "I venture to say you haven't. The slightest bit of information could lead us in the right direction, like pieces of a puzzle."

"Well, this is literally one piece of the puzzle, and I don't know if it fits." She slid the paper across his desk.

The name read Albert Petrironcalli.

Ryan glanced up at the woman, who raised one eyebrow in return.

"Albert Petrironcalli," Ryan read aloud.

"That's right. As I went through all the people I knew disliked Mrs. Skovgaard, there was really only one who stood out as vicious. Petri—his nickname—hated her; absolutely despised her." She smiled wryly as if she had handed him something important.

"I am not familiar with this name," Ryan said.

"Of course not. That's the point."

"Pardon?"

"Petri wrote a book about Vikings in America. It covered the same era as Mrs. Skovgaard's Pulitzer Prize winning book. Mrs. Skovgaard's ended up on her agent's desk shortly before Petri finished his. Her agent shopped it around, which meant every publisher worth its salt got a copy of the manuscript. They were all bidding on it. When Petri finished his shortly after and the queries went out to the publishers, they all turned it down without even a glimpse. She'd beaten him to the punch."

"And there wasn't room on the bookshelves for more than one book about Vikings?"

She laughed. "It was the same thing as Mrs. Skovgaard's, just rehashed. It had nothing new in it; no compelling reason for a publisher to want it."

Ryan nodded. "I see."

"And Petri lives not far from here."

"Are you serious?"

"Maybe three miles from Mrs. Skovgaard's house."

"The town has two noted historians in it?"

"No. The town has one noted historian and one wannabe."

Ryan looked at the paper with renewed interest. "Thank you."

"Whatever I can do to help catch her killer."

Ryan stood. "Will you be remaining in town?" She smiled provocatively, and Ryan glanced at Zuker as he cleared his throat. "In the event I need to interview you further," he added.

"Are you telling me not to leave town?"

"I'm asking you to notify me if you do."

She nodded. "Agreed."

"I'll walk you out." He motioned toward the door. As he followed her through the busy station, he said, "Jackie, don't go to Mrs. Skovgaard's home again. It's a crime scene and I haven't cleared it yet."

"So if I find the door open again, I'm not to go through it?" She smiled slyly.

He handed her his card. "Call me instead. My mobile is listed there as well as the police department number."

"Thank you, Detective." She placed the card inside her pocketbook before snapping it shut. "I'll see you around."

He watched as she strolled across the parking lot to her rental car. She seemed to sachet with just a bit more enthusiasm than he would have expected from an editor who'd just lost one of her most famous authors. After a moment, he turned around to find Zuker watching him from across the room.

"So what's on your mind then?" he asked, returning to his desk.

"Oh… just that the woman clearly is interested in you."

Ryan didn't respond. There was nothing he could say that would make his statement more palatable. He pulled out his chair and resumed checking his email. "Got an email from the medical examiner," he said.

"Already?" Zuker walked behind Ryan's desk to read over his shoulder.

He opened the email and scanned it quickly, then went back through to make sure he understood it correctly.

"Well, there you have it," Zuker said.

"Exactly as I suspected," Ryan agreed. "She was Tasered."

"A defensive wound," his partner said. He held his arm in front of his face; his forearm was in front of his eyes with the palm outward. "The Taser mark was on the inside of the forearm, it says. I suspect she was seated at her desk, probably working on her laptop, and she looked up to find the intruder in the room."

"Aye," Ryan agreed. "She stood; she probably knocked the chair out from under her, which would account for its haphazard placement behind the desk."

"She started to move around the other side of the desk—probably trying to get to the door."

"And she saw the Taser. As he plunged it toward her, she threw up her arm to deflect it. But one zap…"

"And down she went."

They both became silent. Ryan knew what happened after that. She lay on her back—if she didn't fall that way, he rolled her over—and as she stared at him, unable to move to protect herself, he sliced her throat from ear to ear. She bled out, perhaps still staring at her assailant. He wondered if he had remained there to watch her die.

Zuker pulled his chair across to Ryan's desk. "O'Clery, I've got to ask you something."

Ryan chose to print the email. As the printer whirred behind him, he said, "They're going to do a full autopsy. Though we both know the cause of death."

"Yes. We do."

He wheeled his chair around to get the email out of the printer. When he turned back around, he found Zuker watching him intently. "You said you have a question for me?"

Zuker cleared his throat. "Look, O'Clery, I want you to understand that I'm just doing my job."

"Aye. And I'd be doing the same."

"How do you suppose the intruder got in her house?"

"You inspected the house, same as I. There was no sign of forced entry."

"Exactly."

"Which means she left the door unlocked."

"And why would she have done that?"

"What are you getting at?" Ryan asked.

"She left the door unlocked—and the pedestrian gate open—because she was expecting *you*."

He nodded but didn't respond.

"She phoned you the day before and said she had information about your family."

"I'm quite certain she was mistaken."

"But what if she wasn't? What if she had something on your family that marred its impeccable reputation?"

"What are inferring, man?"

Zuker glanced through the office. Though the room was full, no one was paying the slightest bit of attention to them. "Everyone knows you come from a long line of law enforcement officers."

"Aye."

"It's in your blood, the law is."

"I'd say so."

"So, what if Mrs. Skovgaard found something about the O'Clery family that was—criminal."

"Excuse me now?"

"There was only one thing missing, at least that we're aware of."

"Her laptop."

"Now, why would someone Taser her and slit her throat, knowing she would die, to steal her computer?"

"What are you saying?" Ryan could feel the color rising to his cheeks.

"The intruder Tasered her. She lay helpless on the floor. He could calmly unplug the laptop, tuck it under his arm and walk out—which is apparently what he did, anyway. Why go through the extra step of killing her?"

Ryan steepled his hands. "Obviously, the intruder wasn't stealing just a piece of technology."

"Of course not. You and I both suspected that from the very beginning. What he was stealing was the data *on* the computer—the information about your family."

"Now, that's where I beg to differ with you, Zuker. The information *allegedly* to do with my family might have been on the computer, but I doubt seriously if anyone would kill her over that. Why would they?"

"Precisely. Why would they? Who would have a motive to do something like that?"

His mouth went dry. "Are you saying that I'm a suspect?" His voice was louder than he'd intended and the room grew quiet. He could feel all eyes on him.

"Ryan, where were you earlier in the day?"

He pushed his chair further from his partner. "You know exactly where I was. I was with you, you halfwit."

"Where were you before you came to work?"

"You know exactly where I would have been."

Zuker cocked his head and raised a brow.

"I would have been at home with my wife and two girls." He stood. "This conversation is over." He powered down his computer. "When the autopsy is complete, it will show a time of death—a window in which she was murdered. And whatever that time was, I was not alone. I'll have an alibi. Not that I need one," he hastened to add. "Jaysus." He picked up his cell phone and slipped it into his pocket before heading to the door.

"Where are you going?"

"To interview an honest-to-God suspect," Ryan bellowed over his shoulder before pushing the door open and allowing it to slam loudly behind him.

12

He found Albert Petrironcalli's home less than two miles from the police department and a mere three miles from Mrs. Skovgaard's mansion. In contrast to a home that could easily be turned into apartment living for dozens, Mr. Petrironcalli's home appeared more like a starter from Sears Roebuck. It was in an older, established neighborhood with tree-lined streets and sidewalks; sandwiched in between multi-storied homes, it gave the impression of a single floor with perhaps a loft on a second floor—if it wasn't an attic. The siding looked to be original and was in dire need of replacement.

Ryan rang the doorbell and studied the porch as he waited. There was a metal glider beside the door with a ripped vinyl cushion in an orange and yellow flower pattern. The floor was wood; it had been painted with gray deck paint but was peeling. He glanced at the ceiling, which was peeling as well.

He walked to the edge of the porch, where he examined the side yard. He realized he could see to the back fence from this vantage point; he doubted that the entire lot was more than a quarter of an acre. It would probably fit in just one of Mrs. Skovgaard's gardens.

"Can I help you?" The voice was gravelly.

Ryan turned around to find a man standing on the other side of the opened screen door. He was heavyset; his belt dipped below his waist, no doubt due to his bulging midsection. As Ryan approached him, his eyes took in the soiled shirt and its frayed collar. "Detective Ryan O'Clery," he said, showing his identification. "Lumberton Police Department. I wonder if I might have a chat with you?"

~~~~~

The living room was tiny; perhaps twelve by twelve feet. The couch on which Ryan sat was brown, though he suspected the original color was closer to tan. The cushion sagged beneath him so that he remained perched on the outer frame so he wouldn't descend into it.

The man Jackie had called Petri sat across from him in a recliner that didn't look to have fared much better. A television set remained on in the corner; it had rabbit ears the likes of which Ryan had never seen before, and even then, the picture was so wavy that he didn't know how the man could determine what he was watching.

The carpet was shag with bare spots in places and reeked of urine. As he looked at the tiny Chihuahua gathered in Petri's arms, he knew he didn't have to be a detective to know the likely culprit.

"Of course I knew Annie," he was saying. "I studied under her at the University." His hair was receding, but he'd done an elaborate comb-over that reached from one ear to the other and did little to hide his scalp. His eye sockets were darkened; lack of sleep or most likely, ill health, Ryan thought. He paused every few syllables to gasp for breath before exhaling in a short fit of coughing. He was stout; his belly alone was evidence enough that he engaged in very little activity. But he was also short; perhaps not more than five-foot-four. He tried to picture Mrs. Skovgaard holding her arm up to deflect the Taser and deduced that her assailant would have to have been taller.

"You must have known her well," Ryan said.

"Well enough."

"You called her *Annie*." He smiled as if he was in polite conversation with a friend. "Even her editor called her Mrs. Skovgaard."

"We were friendly, for a time."

"Just 'for a time'?"

"We collaborated on a number of theories, some of which were published in college textbooks and academic periodicals."

"Were you an educator as well?"

He shook his head. "Never had the degrees for it."

"But you said—"

"I dropped out before graduation." He burst into a coughing fit and Ryan waited patiently for him to recover and continue. "My father died suddenly; lung cancer, back before anybody knew what to do about it. By the time he was diagnosed, he had just weeks left to live. I had to quit school and get a job to support my mother."

"I see. So after that, you didn't see 'Annie'?"

"Oh, we stayed in touch. She knew how I loved history. When I developed a theory of the Vikings in America, we discussed it in great detail."

Ryan narrowed his eyes. "*Your* theory."

Petri smiled but it was clear from the seriousness in his eyes that he didn't see any humor in it. "Yes. I did some research into the Vikings' exploration of America centuries before Columbus ever purportedly 'discovered' the continent."

"And she went on to write a book about it."

"Won the Pulitzer for it, as I'm sure you know."

"Aye."

"I gave her the information. She knew I was writing my own book about it. But when I finished it and shopped it around, I learned—to my horror, I may add—that she had finished *her* book with *my* idea and it had already been picked up by a major publisher. No one listened when I tried to tell them that she had stolen my theory."

"That had to have been very hard to take."

"Imagine if it was you. I worked two jobs to make ends meet; seasonal jobs that depended on the weather. Some years were pretty damn lean. I had the history background but no degree and no money to finish my education. I write the book of my life—the book that is going to get me noticed, recognized—*and paid*—and she's beaten me to the punch. She destroyed my career. And she knew it."

"And then she went on to win international acclaim for it."

"Plus the prize money from the Pulitzer."

Ryan held his notepad in his hand but the page remained clear. He would remember their conversation. The man had motive; that was clear. But did he have the means? "Mr. Petrironcelli—"

"Petri. Everybody calls me Petri."

"—where were you, say, night before last to yesterday morning?"

"Am I a suspect in something?"

"No. I'm just curious."

"Night before last… That's easy. Where I am every night."

"And that would be—?"

"I was working. Security guard; night shift."

"You're a security guard?"

"I couldn't do the seasonal work anymore." He rested his hand on his chest. "Emphysema. So I work at a church on the other side of town. Seven at night to seven in the morning."

"A church needs security every night, all night?"

He smiled wryly. "I'll give you the address. Then you'd understand."

"I'd like that, please." Ryan wrote it down as the man recited it. He recognized the street; it was in a drug-infested area. "Just curious; how do you manage security with your condition?"

"I sit in a chair all night and watch monitors. When I see something, I call the cops."

"And does anyone work with you?"

"No one but me." He coughed before continuing. "But if you need proof, I'm filmed while I'm watching the monitors. It'll show me sitting in the chair, hour after hour. I get up to go to the bathroom and I get coffee and snacks out of the machines. And that's all I do."

"And after you get off work, do you come straight home?"

"I live alone. My mother died some years ago. So I stop on my way home to have breakfast, every morning like clockwork. I read the paper, I chat with the regulars. Then I come home and walk my dog here. The neighbors see me every morning. We walk to the corner, where I sit on the bench outside the shop down there, and my dog does her business. I chat with folks passing by. Then I come home and go to sleep."

Ryan closed his notepad and rose. "Thank you for your time, Mr.—Petri."

The man groaned as he tried to rise to his feet.

"No need to get up."

"I'll walk you to the door," he insisted, though the door was just a few feet away and clearly visible.

Ryan made his way to the door and glanced outside. The unkempt appearance of the home made more sense now that he understood the man's condition. "It must have been very difficult for you when Mrs. Skovgaard's book was published."

Petri leaned past Ryan to push the screen door open. "The worst part about it was the research I'd done on individual families. That information was priceless. It was so unique—part of what won her the prize." He shook his head sadly. "Especially about the albino. That was priceless."

13

The coffee shop had a line nearly to the door. The two students behind the counter were kept hopping with coffee drinks Ryan had never heard of, but the non-stop foot traffic and constant clamor barely registered.

He sat in a corner as far from the hubbub as possible. His cup sat on the low table in front of him, the coffee long ago cooled. The stuffed chair was nearly as comfortable as his recliner at home and the floor lamp beside him cast a golden glow on the book he held open.

Two hours had passed and his eyes had been riveted to the pages. It had not taken long for him to find the passages he sought; Annie Skovgaard had provided a detailed index for which he was grateful; the Pulitzer Prize winning book was a hefty 620 pages.

The albino that Petri had referred to was a Viking named Gunnar; the last name had been lost to history. He was purportedly from Norway but his background, especially his early years, were sketchy at best. His story had made it into Mrs. Skovgaard's book due to his activities from the age of twenty to the age of thirty-five, during which time he traversed the Atlantic Ocean.

Greenland had been settled by Norsemen in 980 AD, some two hundred years before Gunnar entered the annals of history. By the turn of the thirteenth century, the colony was at its peak with two settlements and nearly 5,000 inhabitants. It was around that time—the exact date wasn't known—that Gunnar set sail from Norway for Greenland and then traveled further, landing in a region known today as Newfoundland.

He established quite a reputation for himself as a bloodthirsty killer. He raped a good many native women, seemingly taking pleasure in killing their husbands in front of them before having his way with them. He was also an experienced survivalist, and when many of the Norsemen abruptly abandoned Newfoundland—some say amid a hail of arrows from an increasingly hostile group of natives—he went further west to the New World.

There was evidence, according to Mrs. Skovgaard's book, that this albino traveled extensively throughout eastern Canada and even into the northeastern portion of the United States. His preferred method of murder was by knife; it seemed he enjoyed the more personal, face-to-face, eyeball-to-eyeball, method. His temper was legendary; no one knew precisely where his rage had originated or why, only that he was one of the most feared conquerors of his time.

They called him The Ghost, or Draugr, and he became known in the New World as Gunnar the Draugr. It was said he could simply appear, as if out of nowhere. He was silent, in contrast with his physique, which was two heads taller than most of the natives and even taller than his own men. Reports indicated that he was broad-shouldered and his arms were exceptionally long, making it nearly impossible for one to fight him in hand-to-hand combat. It was said that he was unscarred, never having been touched in battle, and many feared him as they would fear an evil spirit.

There was evidence that he traveled extensively, sailing back and forth from the New World to the Scandinavian countries—and even to Ireland and Western Europe.

At the age of thirty-five, he simply disappeared.

Ryan held the book in his hands for a long time, his mind moving back eight hundred years to an age that was vastly different from the modern day. Six hundred years before Rían Kelly, the uncle five generations back for whom Ryan had been named; and six hundred years before Rían lost his beloved soul mate to an albino serial killer.

It could be coincidence, he thought. Certainly not all albinos are related; everyone knew that.

But Mrs. Skovgaard had made it clear that she was working on another volume of Viking history, and she had uncovered something connected to Rían Kelly and to himself. Could she have found what happened to Gunnar after the age of thirty-five? Could she have somehow made a correlation between Gunnar the Draugr and the mysterious killer in Rían's time—or to Diallo Delport?

Delport was South African, he reminded himself. Nothing he'd read thus far had linked Gunnar the Draugr to the African continent. But if he could sail from Western Europe to the Americas, he reasoned, not once but purportedly several times, how much of a reach would it be for him to set sail for Africa?

Gunnar was a killer, he thought. It was true that Vikings had a reputation for fighting, plundering, raping and killing—how much of that was true and how much some fictional legend, he wasn't sure. Could the man have fathered a lineage of albinos who roamed the world as serial murderers? He shook his head. There was nothing that tied these Norsemen to the Kellys, or to him.

Petri had referred Ryan to Mrs. Skovgaard's book, which he said gave all the detail that he knew—his old friend had left nothing out. So if Petri's knowledge ended with this book that he held in his hands, what could the elderly woman have found out that cost her life? And why would anyone want to kill over information that was nearly a thousand years old?

It made no sense.

He began to realize that the coffee shop had grown quiet, and he glanced at his watch. He'd been there for hours. The time had flown past so quickly; Zuker must be wondering where he was. He checked his cell phone, but there had been no calls.

He picked up his cold cup of coffee and tossed it into a nearby receptacle on his way to the door. Once outside, the air felt cooler than it had the previous day. He glanced to the skies and noted the clouds were moving from the north.

On his way to the police car, he thought of Zuker's line of questioning. From a purely police point of view, he understood the need to question anyone with any type of business dealings—personal or professional—with the murdered woman. But personally, he was miffed. Zuker should have known better, he thought. He was a law enforcement officer, through and through.

~~~~~

He was still perturbed when he walked through the doors of the police station. The room seemed to quiet instantly as he entered. He had grown accustomed to that at one time, when a divorce from his first wife left him in a perpetually bad mood. Feeling the tension in the air now reminded him too much of that time—a time left behind when he met Cait.

Zuker was standing behind his desk next to Ryan's. He was on the phone but when he caught sight of his partner, he ended his call abruptly.

He waited until Ryan seated himself at his desk before asking, "Where were you?"

"I told you where I was going when I walked out the door."

"Remind me."

Ryan called up his email. "I've been interviewing the only suspect the editor gave us."

"What was his name again?"

He glanced at him. Zuker's face seemed pale and he looked at him with an intent expression. "Albert Petrironcalli."

"Albert Petrironcalli," Zuker repeated.

"Aye. Albert Petrironcalli." Growing increasingly more irritated, he turned his attention back to his email.

"And you've been there this whole time?"

"That's right."

"Interviewing Mr. Petrironcalli."

"That's what I said."

"That was a long interview."

"Sometimes, a long interview is necessary."

The room seemed abnormally silent.

"So, you left here over three hours ago, and you've been at Albert Petrironcalli's home for this whole time."

Ryan swore under his breath. "How many times do I need to tell you? Aye, I left here at whatever time I left, I went to Albert Petrironcalli's home and I interviewed him. And now I'm back here, trying to do my work if you would leave me alone to do it."

"And you didn't go anywhere else."

"I just told you where I've been." Ryan's voice rose to a roar.

Zuker remained standing and his expression hadn't changed. "So, why didn't I see you there?"

Ryan slammed his hand on the desk. "Did I not tell you that I was going to the man's house to interview him?" Without waiting for an answer, he continued, "Then why, on God's green earth, would prompt you to go there as well? Did you think I needed assistance interviewing a suspect?"

"Well, that depends," Zuker said. His voice was smooth and even, though it was loud enough to be heard throughout the room. "Was he dead before or after you interviewed him?"

~~~~~

They sat in the police car away from prying eyes. Ryan stared at the Lumber River without seeing it; his brain had gone from zero to sixty in a millisecond, and now he seemed unable to finish one thought before engaging in another.

"So do you want to tell me where you really were?" Zuker asked.

"I left the police station," Ryan said quietly. "Went straight to Petri's home."

"How long were you there?" His voice was conversational, as if they were just two friends talking, but Ryan's antenna soared upward. He'd used the same tactic in getting suspects to talk. But he had nothing to hide, he reminded himself. And he hadn't officially been declared a suspect—yet.

"Perhaps an hour; maybe a little less."

"And he was alive when you left him."

"Of course he was. If he'd been in any type of distress, I would have phoned for an ambulance."

"And where did you go after that?"

"Coffee shop."

"The coffee shop."

"That's what I said. He'd given me information that led me back to Mrs. Skovgaard's book—the one she got the Pulitzer for—and I sat in the coffee shop reading it."

"How long were you there?"

"Until about five minutes before you laid eyes on me in the office. That's how long."

"Anybody see you there?"

"The manager—Kenny—was there. He had a couple of students working; you know Amanda and Piper. They'll confirm I was sitting in the corner reading."

"Why did you lie?"

"Because I was pissed. Still am, to be quite honest about it. I'm a law enforcement officer, Zuker; a damn good one. Nothing could cause me to turn into a cold-blooded killer."

"Nothing?"

"Oh, what, are we gonna pick apart my words now? Self-defense, aye. Break into my home and attempt to harm my wife or my children, and you'd better believe I'll do whatever it takes to rescue them. You'd do the same," he added. "But to kill a historian—an elderly woman—and then a man in ill health who'd never done a thing to me or mine—absolutely not."

They grew silent. Zuker tapped the steering wheel with his hand while Ryan continued to stare at the river.

"Do you believe me?" Ryan asked at last.

"Yes. I do."

He nodded. After a moment, he asked, "Have you notified the chief?"

"I haven't spoken to him face-to-face yet." He glanced at him out of the corner of his eye. "He's in a meeting with the mayor."

Ryan groaned.

"I'm sure they have a lot of things to talk about," Zuker said in a thinly veiled attempt to reassure him, "and I don't know yet whether he even knows about Petri's murder."

"You processed the scene." It was said as more of a statement than a question.

"I did."

"Mind if I guess the modus operandi?" Without waiting for an answer, Ryan continued, "His throat was slit. From ear to ear."

"Actually, no."

"No?"

"Strangled. With a tie."

"He was strangled with a tie? His own tie?"

Zuker shrugged. "Don't know yet. We'll have to wait on a report."

"Did you ask the medical examiner to look for a Taser mark?"

"I did."

"Good."

"You taught me well, Ry. I'm looking for evidence that it was the same killer. Seems like more than coincidence that two historians were killed. I guess we can mark him off our suspect list in the Skovgaard slaying."

"I had him marked off after interviewing him," Ryan said quietly.

"Want to tell me why?"

"First, the physical evidence wasn't there. He was incredibly short. Even though Mrs. Skovgaard was a petite thing, I don't believe, when you consider the defensive Taser mark, that she was facing someone of his stature. I think she was trying to deflect the blow from a much taller assailant. Then," he continued without waiting for Zuker's reply, "Petri could barely get out a sentence or two without going into a coughing fit. He'd already stopped working his regular job and begun working at a more menial job because of his ill health. I think even an elderly woman could have easily gotten away from him."

Zuker half-nodded. "But he had motive."

Ryan shrugged. "To be quite honest about it, I think Mrs. Skovgaard may have actually taken his historical research, as Petri claimed. And he was upset about it, as any person would be. But I doubt if he would have carried it as far as to murder her."

"So, we've got two possibilities. Three, actually."

Ryan held up one finger. "He murdered Mrs. Skovgaard, in which case: who murdered him?" He held up a second finger. "The same killer murdered them both; in which case: why?" And a third: "They are unrelated, in which case we have two separate murders to solve."

"My thoughts exactly." They both stared out the window for a long moment. Then Zuker turned to Ryan. "Would you care to see the crime scene?"

14

The television was turned off and the screen was black, but Ryan stared at it from the recliner as though it was the most riveting show he'd ever seen. It felt as if scenes were unfolding in front of him: the telephone call from Mrs. Skovgaard, the conversation with Petri, the information about an albino Viking, and then the surreal investigation with Zuker of the crime scene. The two murders were related; there was no doubt about it. And though his mind did not want to wrap itself around it, he had a feeling in his gut that they were both murdered because of him.

Somehow, as Mrs. Skovgaard researched her next book, she'd taken the history of the albino further. And in some way, she had related it to his ancestors. It was the missing link, he thought, that could tie in with the murder of Rían Kelly's lover—and why, nearly two hundred years later, another albino halfway around the world found him and Cait and attempted to murder her.

But who would murder an historian—two historians—because of a past that was long gone? Even if it led to resolving the mystery of the albinos through the centuries, what difference would it make? It was ancient history, nearly quite literally.

Then the question was, he deduced further, who would have the most to lose if the story came to light? Quite evidently, the descendant of the albino and perhaps an albino himself.

His skin grew chilled, though the room was quite warm. Was it really possible that Diallo Delport survived being swept out to sea? The alternative was even more implausible: that there was a second descendent, perhaps another albino. No, he thought; he should keep his options open but pursue the possibility that Delport was indeed alive—and he was back in town.

A figure came between Ryan and the television screen, and he glanced up as Cait took his hands in hers. Her touch was electric, as though a bolt of lightning was shooting straight through him. She had always done that to him, he realized; from the first time they'd touched… to every time they touched. Without a word, she spread his arms, settled across his lap, and then embraced herself with his muscular biceps. She nuzzled her face against his neck, kissing him along a path that led up to his ear. As she nibbled on his earlobe, she used one hand to thread through his hair. Everywhere she touched, he felt charged as if every nerve ending was gloriously ablaze.

He leaned into her, closing his eyes. He was enveloped with her light floral fragrance, surrounded by her love, and he wanted nothing more than to clear his mind of everything except her presence.

She pulled back slightly and whispered in his ear, "You were too quiet at dinner."

"Hhmm."

She pulled back further. Placing her hand under his jaw, she turned his face toward her. "Is something wrong?"

"No, sweet love," he answered. She cocked her head and peered at him in obvious disbelief, and he continued, "I'm working a couple of cases, 'tis all, and it's quite like putting pieces of a puzzle together. It has me a bit… preoccupied."

"Does this have anything to do with the famous author, the one who was killed?"

"It does."

"Would you like to talk about it?"

He shook his head and squeezed her tighter. "I don't like to bring my work home with me; you know that. Our time together is too precious."

She kissed his nose and then raced her finger along the bridge, a smile creeping across her face.

He glanced past her at the playpen. "Where are the girls?"

"I put them to bed. You were so engrossed in your thoughts that I guess you didn't see me going back and forth?"

"Oh, darlin', I apologize. You know how I like to help you put the girls to bed. You should have said something."

"I did." Her eyes sparkled as she teased, "I guess your case really does have you preoccupied."

He groaned. "How can I make it up to you?"

She placed a hand on his cheek. "I'm sure I'll think of something." She drew his face toward hers. "I love how soft your skin is."

"Now that's something I'm not sure a man wants to hear."

She laughed softly. "You know what I mean. A woman likes to feel smooth cheeks against hers." Her lips wandered across his while barely touching. "And soft lips." He embraced her more fully, and she added, "And strong arms. Definitely, strong arms."

He realized in that moment, as he had countless times before, that she completely mesmerized him. Her eyes were as tumultuous as the roiling waves of the Irish Sea, set under long, curved black lashes. In those depths, he could see the same physical intensity he felt. Her brows were dark brown and gently arching; her cheekbones were high and flushed, her lips full and enticing as they parted.

Her brunette hair had been hastily pulled into an untidy bun and clipped, and now he reached to the back of her head and released it. Her long, silky tresses tumbled over her shoulders until they cupped her breasts. He threaded his fingers through it, reveling in the sleek strands, basking in the sweet aroma. There was something carnal about her hair…

She leaned toward him and he pulled her the rest of the way, tasting her lips as if it was the first time. One hand slipped to her derriere, squeezing it gently before moving along her thigh and back up again. He longed to strip her right then, right there; and he longed to savor this moment forever.

Her hands moved along his powerful biceps; she seemed to revel in the feel of his muscles under her fingers and she moaned slightly as she pressed her lips more firmly to his. Her face was intense and relaxed, forceful and soft, firm but yielding, all bundled into one magnificent package.

And she belonged to him.

He folded his arms around her, sweeping her so close to him that he could feel her heart beating against his chest. No, he corrected himself; she did not belong to him. He belonged to her. He always had. Even before they'd ever met, the dreams of his soul mate, of his eternal love, had haunted him. And since she had arrived in his life, he belonged to her—lock, stock and barrel, from the tips of his toes to the top of his head, to every thought, every moment, every breath.

"I love you, Ryan O'Clery," she whispered. Her voice was hoarse and whispered and urgent. "I love you more than Life itself."

He could not get close enough to her; he could not get enough of her. She was his soul. As he grasped her hips and then encircled her with arms that wanted to be everywhere at once, a flash of a sunrise he had wanted to forget rose swiftly in his mind's eye. Before he could stop it, he saw himself on a hurricane-ravaged beach, his eye on a smashed and desolated pier, planning his suicide. Had he not heard her cell phone in those fateful moments, they both might have perished, victims of the storm—victims of Diallo Delport.

He knew then, and he knew now, that he loved her more than Life; indeed, he would embrace Death if he knew she was on the other side.

Her breath grew ragged and she pulled back slightly. He opened his eyes to find her chest rising and falling, her lips puffy as though slightly bruised, her hair mussed and wild. "Good Lord, I love you," he whispered. His voice was low and husky and at the sound of it, her breath came more rapidly.

In the next instant, they were on the plush rug that had been beneath his feet. He felt the heat rising to the surface of his skin as she unbuttoned his shirt and raced her lips across his chest. He didn't know how she did it; her movements were slow and methodical, intent and deliberate. And yet, she was everywhere at once. Her hands kneaded his back; her deft fingers unbuckled his belt; her legs enfolded his.

He felt his passions mounting to an inferno. There was nothing else but Cait, beautiful, sensuous, adoring Cait. Nothing else mattered but this moment.

~~~~~

Ryan lay on his back as Cait folded her leg across his thighs. "You'll be the death of me, woman," he said. His statement was only half-teasing. They'd made love on the living room floor, on the couch and in their bed, and he doubted he'd ever felt so invigorated and so relaxed in his life. God bless the twins for sleeping soundly for once.

She placed her head on his chest and he absent-mindedly wove his fingers through her hair. He felt her heartbeat slowing and eventually her breathing grew smooth and soft.

He closed his eyes. In a few hours, his workday would begin and he was sorely in need of rest. But though he wanted sleep and needed it, it would not come. Each time he closed his eyes, his mind raced. In the darkness of the night and into the wee hours of the morning, he fought images of Viking invaders, of swordfights, of knife-wielding warriors, of generations of albino men who had a timeless, unending desire to hurt the women his family loved.

When Cait rolled over in her sleep, he found himself turning with her, reluctant to break the connection between them. She was everything to him. He knew that now; he had always known that. An urge began in the pit of his stomach, overwhelming his thoughts and all logic; an obsession to find the answer and solve the riddle once and for all. The compulsion was insistent, compelling him to remain awake, urging him to stop centuries of insanity. His mind argued that it was too large a task; he was only one man in a string of men targeted by raw hatred, their souls sliced open by loss.

Finally, with sunrise still a few hours away, he reluctantly pulled away from Cait and slipped out from under the covers. She murmured and he tucked the comforter around her and waited for her breathing to become rhythmic once more. Then he slipped on his jeans and made his way down the hallway.

He glanced into the girls' room to find them sound asleep, side by side, their arms intertwined, and he wondered if they'd spent nearly nine months inside Cait holding each other in the same manner. His heart went out to them. He owed it to his children to find the answer. If there was any possibility that the madness could end with him, he had to do whatever it took to stop it—including unraveling the mystery of Diallo Delport.

He moved to the spare bedroom that he'd turned into his study. When his aunt passed away nearly two years earlier, he had become the keeper of his family's genealogy. Though he'd been taught from his earliest years that the ones chosen for the task must treat it with the utmost care and commitment, he'd considered it as merely a centuries-old habit of maintaining names and dates of births and deaths. Now he realized it was so much more. Each name reflected a soul who had lived and breathed; who had felt sadness and elation, joy and depression, contentment and worry… love and loss.

He stopped momentarily to run his fingers along the bookshelves that lined one wall. There were volumes upon volumes of family history, ranging from modern-day notebooks to leather-bound journals, to Bibles and hand-woven logs of parchment. He'd begun scanning the pages into his computer months before the girls were born; and though he'd taken a break from it during these first sleep-deprived weeks of the girls' lives, he knew he would return to it. He was committed to making their family's history an electronic record.

It had not been easy or simple. But he'd arranged the records in order of date, starting with the most recent records and working backward. His heart and his soul and his mind had been engrossed in Rían Kelly's life, and he'd spent many hours and many sleepless nights reliving the events he'd documented, as if they had been his own. But once he'd moved further into the past, he'd stopped reading every entry and committed himself to simply preserving it.

He switched on the desk lamp and booted his computer. He supposed there was one saving grace that Rían Kelly had been alone and lonely for much of his life; he'd devoted it to translating documents from Gaelic to English. Otherwise, Ryan thought, he didn't know how he could possibly unravel his family's history—and find the link to Diallo Delport.

He knew Rían's lover, Caitlin O'Conor, had been murdered by an albino whose modus operandi had been identical to Delport's—except that it remained a mystery how he slit each woman's throat without the paralyzing effects of a Taser. The similarities meant, he reasoned, that when Delport arrived in America and targeted Ryan and Cait the year before, he had to have been a copycat.

At one time, he had believed that Delport was the reincarnation of the killer, and that he was the reincarnation of Rían Kelly. The similarities and particularly, the dreams that had actually been Rían Kelly's memories had shaken him to his core. But the mere idea that they were destined to live multiple lives, reliving a sordid tale of killer and victim, had proven to be too much.

Now he was settling into the theory that Delport was a copycat. He had learned of his ancestor's string of murders—for, even though he had no proof just yet, he had to assume the original killer was indeed his ancestor—and for whatever reason, Delport had chosen to relive the murders and had intended to culminate them by ending Cait's life.

But was Caitlin O'Conor's killer of 19th century Ireland the original murderer? Or had he also copied the crimes of an ancestor?

He ran searches on the folders of electronic documents and came up empty-handed before realizing that his ancestors might not have identified the killers as albinos. He became inventive, trying searches under various descriptions and multiple phrases while he battled frustration and a growing exasperation.

Finally, as the merest sliver of light began to peek around the draperies, he began to receive the results for which he'd been searching. They led him to other documents, and then to more, until he began to piece together a string of murders that stretched as far back as the thirteenth century.

The murder of Caitlin O'Conor had not been the first, as he had once believed. The killer had matched Delport's description almost exactly; the only difference was Delport had an acquired scar beneath one eye that ended in a teardrop; but Caitlin's killer had purportedly sported a birthmark of the same strange configuration.

In the sixteen hundreds, there had been another ancestor's newlywed wife slain at the hands of a serial killer, but there was no description of him. Witnesses described him as a "ghost" who appeared otherworldly. He shuddered as he recalled the description of Gunnar in Skovgaard's book: he was a Draugr; a ghost.

A hundred and fifty years before Caitlin O'Conor, two women had been murdered. His mother had been a Kelly, and as he delved deeper into her family's history, he found two brothers who had each lost their lovers to the same killer. He tried to imagine two brothers growing up in Ireland in the middle of the fifteenth century, each of them finding their soul mates only to have them snatched away before their lives had truly begun. Some witnesses' reports said the killer was Satan himself; they were convinced that he was not human.

What was it that Mrs. Skovgaard had asked him? Had he ever heard of *The White Devil?* The words formed on his lips as a tingling sensation made its way up the back of his neck. The White Devil. Of course. A man who was colorless—or completely white—a serial killer; Satan himself; the devil.

He leaned back in his chair. She had found the link between his ancestors and this white devil. And whatever she had uncovered had cost her life.

He tried to remember the dates in her book; it had been the turn of the twelfth century, he was sure of it—three hundred and fifty years before these two brothers lost their lovers to a killer described as Satan.

What could possibly have caused a lineage to seek out those of another family, generation after generation, with their sole intent to kill the women those men desired?

His lids were heavy now that the sun was rising. He wanted to remain awake, to continue digging, to doggedly pursue the clues back to the time of Gunnar the Draugr, or to the time Mrs. Skovgaard had been researching. The answer, he thought just as he nodded off, had to be on the missing laptop.

15

Duiblinn, 1171

Baldr stood in the alcove across from the orphanage as he had nearly every day for two years. With the summer solstice approaching, the air was comfortable and the sun bright. They would have some time together before she was expected home. Perhaps they could walk along the riverbank to the south of Duiblinn. His heartbeat grew rapid as he thought of her hand in his; he never tired of his time with her. Nay; their time together had only strengthened their bonds.

"Ye there!"

The tone was offensive, loud and boorish.

He looked toward the window—*her* window—and saw her face there. She no longer looked to the left and to the right; she only peered straight across the road as if to reassure herself that he was there.

"I say," the voice came again, "I speak to ye!"

He turned his head slowly in the direction of the voice. Three men approached with their eyes riveted on him.

"Ye are Hvitr Bard," one said insolently, as if the mere mention of the name he was called was vulgar.

He spread his feet instinctively, anchoring them to the earth. He kept his eyes widened, knowing the bright summer sun would further lighten them so the pupils and the irises would seem to disappear. He resisted blinking but stared back at the loutish men as they slowly approached.

All three were large men but none were a match for him. Each wore sandals with leather straps that wrapped up the length of their calves, where they were met with breeches beneath tunics. Though the weather was warm, they wore cloaks without sleeves. Belts around their midsections displayed a variety of knives, and each carried a broadsword.

Normans, he thought. Their attire was unmistakable and their attitude that of conquerors.

"Are ye not Hvitr Bard?" another asked. "Surely there are not two o' ye as ugly."

"I do not seek trouble w' ye," Baldr said, though he placed one hand on the hilt of his sword.

"Perhaps," another said, making his way further from the others to circle him, "we seek trouble w' ye."

"Ye are three boys," he said evenly, "each wishing to impress one another. Go away with ye. Find trouble elsewhere."

"Boys, he calls us," the largest one said. He was moving toward Baldr's left but Baldr remained in the alcove, where he could not be completely encircled. "We are not boys, but defenders o' King Henry II hisself. He has landed on these shores, and he claims these lands as his own."

"Let him claim what he wishes," Baldr answered. His peripheral vision caught the wiliest one attempting to position himself toward his rear. "I have no quarrel w' yer king, nor he w' me."

"Ah, but he does have quarrel with ye," the center one stated flatly. His eyes narrowed and his fingers twitched against his belt, as if he was trying to decide which weapon he would pull first. "And because he has quarrel w' ye, we do as well."

"And how could he?" Baldr asked, cocking his head. His eyes shifted from one to the other. "He does not know me, nor I him."

The door to the orphanage did not open and now he wished fervently that Maeve would not attempt to depart the safety of the building.

"The reputation o' The White Devil reaches far and wide," the one on the right said.

"So ye wish to bring me down then, do ye?" Baldr asked. "So ye may become braggarts tonight as ye drink, the three of ye together attempting to bring down one man not out for trouble."

The one on the left had moved closer. His hand was firmly on his sword's hilt. His eyes shifted between Baldr's face and his hands, clearly gauging the proximity of the albino's fingers to his sword.

"Be off w' ye," Baldr said.

"Nay," the one on the right spat. "We are to imprison ye."

"Imprison me?" Baldr asked. "For what? I have committed no crime that ye y'selves have not done as well."

"Ye are here," the one in the center retorted. "And that is crime enough."

Baldr moved his right hand to his sword. He felt it beckoning to him as if it vibrated just beyond his fingertips. "I do not wish to go to prison today." He felt his eyes flashing with growing ire. "And I do not believe any of ye wish to die today."

"It is not we who shall die. Come w' us willingly to prison, or die here as the heathen ye are."

The man on the left began to draw his sword but before it cleared the scabbard, Baldr had pulled his own. Holding it with both hands in a lightning-fast flash, he sliced the man's hand, nearly severing it from the wrist. The man's sword clattered to the ground.

As he stared at Baldr with wide, incredulous eyes, the blood draining from his face, the other two drew their swords and advanced.

"Leave now," Baldr said, "and leave w' yer lives."

"Ye die today, Hvitr Bard," the man on the right growled.

He was but a boy, Baldr thought as their eyes locked. Yet he would take a stance here upon this road and die here today.

He lunged at Baldr but his arms could not reach past the larger man's sword. With an instinct born of years of fighting, Baldr thrust his long arms toward the man's chest. He felt the metal sink within his soft torso only to reappear a moment later, covered in blood. The young man's hands moved to his heart. He stared for the briefest of moments at the bright red liquid spurting forth before looking back at Baldr with vision fogged with pain and shock. Baldr had seen it countless times before and as he turned to the third man, he knew the one on his right was sinking to his knees.

"Leave now w' yer life," Baldr said to the last man standing.

The young man ducked to the left and to the right, dodging an invisible threat as Baldr continued to stand completely still. His sword felt like an extension of his arms. It was not heavy. He could stand in this position far longer than his opponent.

With a guttural yell that was perhaps meant to disarm him, the man sprang forward, yielding his sword with one hand, swiping it back and forth. Baldr stepped backward and watched him in bemusement. He found himself just outside the alcove and as he looked beyond the man's shoulder, he spotted a larger group of Normans advancing.

This was not the day for him to die, Baldr thought. And neither would he allow himself to be placed in a Norman prison to rot.

The men began to trot toward them and Baldr swung once, catching the last of the three full in the chest. He fell atop the first, who was not yet dead but was bleeding out from his wrist as he moaned for his mother.

Then Baldr ran.

He rushed down the road to the south, the bloodthirsty cries of the second group echoing in the otherwise still air. The buildings became a blur. The sun now seemed to follow him when he wished for the darkness of night and the cloak of the midnight skies.

He found a break in the buildings and he ran between them, his bloody sword still held in his hand. His own clothing was covered in blood, but it was not his; it was the blood of the Norman invaders.

He knew he had merely defended himself, and his gods witnessed his circumstance. Yet as the shouts of the men behind him grew and others joined in, he understood that they would not rest until they'd captured him. A quick death would be too humane; he would be tortured and put on display as a public spectacle of what it meant to disobey the new invaders.

A door opened and without thinking, he rushed inside. It slammed shut behind him and he was plunged into darkness, the sun blotted out by the stone walls that now surrounded him.

A small, slight man gestured to him and Baldr followed blindly until they had reached another door and still another. The man spoke rapid Gaelic and though he tried to follow his words, he only understood that the Normans' voices had grown distant.

He did not know how long he wandered, or where he had been. He only knew that the last of the daylight hours were spent running, hiding, ducking, rushing, circling, and wondering.

Had Maeve seen what happened? Was she safe? Did she remain in the orphanage or had she attempted to get home alone, even as these invaders looked for trouble?

Long after dark had descended, he found himself at the base of the steps leading up to his room.

He stopped for the first time in hours, feeling his fast, coarse breath and willing himself to remain steady. He was Hvitr Bard, The White Devil, and the invaders had known this. There was none other with his long, white hair, his white brows and white lashes. No other had his colorless skin and eyes like blue ice.

They would come for him. They would question all those between his room and the orphanage. And none would be willing to risk their own lives to save his.

He must flee. There was no other recourse.

He reached the top step and peered down the hall. From the opposite end, he heard the familiar din of voices from the dining hall. Silently, he stepped across the narrow passageway and opened his door, ducking inside.

Though darkness had descended, his room was awash in orange and red. It took barely a moment for him to register that the horizon as seen through his window had been set ablaze. He rushed toward it like a moth to a flame, only to forcibly stop himself before making his presence fully known in the window.

From several feet away, he stared at the distant horizon, at the Irish Sea and the Viking ships set afire. A cacophony of voices, shouts and cries, reached his ears. He knew the sounds of battle and he knew them well. His fellow warriors were engaged in war.

The door opened behind him and he whirled around, his sword at the ready. Just a moment before he rushed forward, his brain registered that Maeve stood before him. She dropped the hood from her head and looked at him with wide eyes filled with fright.

"Maeve," he said, pulling her into his arms. "Ye should not have come here." His voice was soft, the emotion in clear contradiction with his words.

"I had to see if ye were well," she said, her voice trembling.

"I am unharmed. And ye? Did they—?"

"No one touched me."

"Go home, Maeve. Hurry home. Stay to the shadows and far from the banks o' the water."

"I will not leave ye."

"Ye—ye must leave me. *I* must leave *ye*," he added.

She looked at him with puzzlement, as if she was unable to comprehend what he said.

"Did ye see what happened to me?" he asked.

She nodded. "I watched from the window."

"Then ye know King Henry has invaded. Ye know I have killed. And they will come for me."

"Then we must hide ye."

"No, Maeve. My looks—they are distinct. They brand me and anyone seen with me will suffer my fate. Ye are not a part o' this. Go home to yer brothers. They will protect ye. To stay with me is—folly."

"I will not leave ye."

He shook her until her hair began to escape from her bun. "Have ye lost yer mind? I must flee here, Maeve. I will return—but I know not when. I know not how. I only know that on this night, I must join m' brothers-in-arms. I must fight beside them, or escape into the night w' them. But I cannot remain. And ye cannot go w' me."

"Baldr," she whimpered. The softness of her voice caused him to stop shaking her, but his hands remained on either shoulder. Somehow he had dropped his sword; he knew not where. There was nothing but her cloudy green eyes staring at him, nothing but her chin trembling, nothing but her tears streaming down her face.

He closed his eyes. The screams and cries of men in battle rejoined his thoughts, and he pushed everything else out of his mind.

"Go," he said. "Hurry."

He turned her around toward the door, but she swung swiftly back to face him. "Baldr," she said, "I am w' child."

Those four words brought him to his knees when nothing else could. In one flash, he knew both ecstasy and pain; his heart soared and his heart plummeted; his skin grew hot and cold; his hands shook.

The door swung open and both arms flew wide, one as if to find his sword and the other to protect his lover.

"Baldr," came an urgent, hoarse voice.

He recognized the man as one he had come to these shores with so many years ago; he was a comrade he had fought beside and one he would die beside if the gods decreed it.

"Anfeldt," Baldr answered.

He looked from Baldr to Maeve and back again. "We are leaving. The ship is to the north o' Duiblinn. King Henry has landed to the south but he will soon sweep to the north. We must hurry."

We are leaving. The words hung in the air. They would not fight. They were relinquishing this land. They were returning to the land of their births.

"Take her," Baldr said, pushing Maeve to him.

Anfeldt peered into his eyes. "She goes w' us?"

"She does. But she is not safe w' me. I am marked."

"What will ye do?"

"I will find my way to the ship. But I must go alone. She is safer with ye than with me. I will rejoin ye both."

Anfeldt wrapped his arm around Maeve. "I will take care o' yer woman."

"I know ye will."

"Hurry," Anfeldt said. Then before Baldr could hold Maeve once more, before he could kiss her or profess his love for her, they were gone, escaping down the back stairs and into the night.

16

North Carolina

Ryan knocked on the door of the hotel room and listened for movement inside. He'd already knocked once and he'd decided if Jackie didn't answer within the next few seconds, he would have no recourse but to get the hotel manager. She could be in the shower, sleeping or otherwise indisposed but he was in no mood to wait around.

"I'll go for the manager," Zuker said as if reading his mind.

He'd taken two steps away from the room before they heard the chain jangling on the other side. A moment later, the door opened to reveal the book editor in her robe.

"I'm sorry; I wasn't expecting…" Her voice trailed off as she looked from one to the other.

"May we have a word with you?" Ryan asked. He placed a hand on the door and opened it further as if the request was not up for discussion.

"Of course." She motioned for them to enter. As they moved past her, she self-consciously pulled her robe higher around her neck.

Ryan took in the hotel room: the king-sized bed, the round table with two chairs in the corner, and the stuffed chair in the opposite corner. The morning news was on the television and he picked up the remote from atop the bed and clicked it off. The bed was unmade and the aroma of strong hotel coffee wafted through the room. As he turned back to Jackie, he noticed the ends of her hair were damp.

"I tried to phone you," he said unapologetically.

"I—"

He waved off her explanation. "I've come to take you to the airport."

She blinked. "I'm not leaving."

His eyes did not waver from hers. "Yes, you are." He took a quick breath. "I spoke to Mr. Petrironcalli."

"Oh." Her face paled.

"Shortly after I left, he was murdered." The words seemed sharp and unemotional in the light of day, but then, Ryan reasoned, he'd never been one to sugarcoat it.

She inhaled sharply and paled considerably more.

"Here," Zuker said, pulling out a chair from the table. "Have a seat."

"Miss Janssen," Ryan continued once she was seated, "there is every indication that Mrs. Skovgaard's death and Mr. Petrironcalli's are related. We're connecting the dots here and it appears the only thing that ties them together is their historical work—the work that you ultimately published."

"But—why?"

"As I said, we're still connecting the dots."

She swallowed hard.

"We believe the best course of action for you at this point is to return to New York."

"Am I a target?"

Ryan thought from her expression that she might faint. "We don't know. What we do know is the killer is here, or was here, as of yesterday. And since you are connected to the historical work, we'd feel better about your welfare if you returned to New York."

"I see."

"I'm prepared to drive you to the airport. The next flight to New York departs in two hours."

She looked beyond them but her eyes were lowered, as if she was looking at the baseboard. Ryan suspected she wasn't seeing anything at all at this point, but was digesting the information he'd given her. After a moment with no response, he said, "Jackie, we must hurry."

She nodded and her back drew up straighter. "I—have to get dressed."

"We'll be right outside the door."

She nodded again and they made their way to the hall. As he grabbed the knob and began to pull it closed, he looked back to find her in the same position as if she hadn't moved at all. "Jackie," he said, his voice deep and authoritative.

She glanced up.

"You must hurry."

With that, he stepped outside with Zuker and pulled the door to, stopping it just before it clicked into place.

"You want me to notify NYPD?" Zuker asked.

"Aye. But ask them to keep it quiet. I certainly don't want to be seeing this on the evening news. Not until we have it resolved and the suspect is in custody."

"I agree." He hesitated. "Ryan, do you mind if I get back to the office? You don't need me on the drive to and from the airport, and there are things I can be doing on the cases."

Ryan nodded. "I'll drop you off at the station on our way."

They grew silent as Zuker checked his email on his smartphone and Ryan waited for Jackie. He'd never been one to remain patient for long and he found himself growing increasingly irritated as the minutes ticked by. Then the door swung open and she stood before them with a rolling suitcase and a laptop case.

"What are we waiting for?" she asked.

~~~~~

She rode up front in the police cruiser. They remained silent for much of the way, each with their own thoughts. Traffic was heavy on the interstate but he reasoned he had sufficient time to get her to the airport and get her on the plane.

"Jackie," Ryan broke the silence.

"Yes?" She turned to him with apprehension on her face.

"Did you communicate with Mrs. Skovgaard by email?"

"Oh, yes," she said, relaxing a bit.

"Was her email on her laptop?"

"Why, yes, it was. She didn't have any mobile devices."

"And she was able to utilize her email?" he pressed.

"I set it up for her myself. She was ancient, you know," Jackie chuckled. "But I came down to discuss her books with her, and I installed the software and set everything up."

"Did you communicate specifics about the books she wrote?"

"Of course. Sometimes emails were quicker and more efficient than a phone call."

He nodded and tapped the steering wheel. A moment later, he asked, "Can you send her an email?"

"Excuse me?"

"Her laptop is missing. I was wondering if you could send her an email, and request a read receipt—you know, to be notified once the email is opened."

"Do you think the killer—?"

"I don't know." He glanced at her out of the corner of his eye. "But can you do that for me?"

"Of course. I'll do it right now." She pulled her smartphone out of her bag and punched a few keys. "Anything particular you want it to say?"

"As a matter of fact, yes. The subject should read 'The White Devil' and the content should read something like 'Checking on the status of your writing.' Can you do that?"

She composed the message. "Anything else?"

"That'll do. Be sure to request a read receipt."

"Gotcha." A moment later, she said, "I marked it high priority and requested the receipt. The email has been sent."

"You have my gratitude… Will you let me know as soon as the read receipt comes to you?"

"Of course." She pulled his business card from her bag. "You'd given me your card, and it has your email address on it. I'll just forward it to you?"

"Perfect."

They took the next exit toward the airport and both became quiet once more. He had a bad feeling in the pit of his stomach, as if his insides were a chalkboard and someone was scraping their nails across it. He grew increasingly more anxious the closer they got to the terminal. Glancing in his rearview mirror, he noted there were no cars behind them, and no one had followed them from Lumberton; he would have noticed if they had. And yet he couldn't escape this sensation of eyes upon them, watching their every move.

He parked in front of the terminal. "Stay here," he directed.

He shut off the engine and climbed out. His movements were slow and deliberate as he scanned their surroundings. Everything appeared normal: the parking lot was active with people coming and going, but no one seemed out of the ordinary. No one, that is, resembled Diallo Delport.

He glanced upward but the glass that lined the second floor was dark on this side, effectively obscuring the activity within.

He would not be here, he thought. He could not know that she was leaving, or that she would leave from this airport at this time. It was simply his imagination. His nerves were on edge and it was time he got a grip on them and returned to the detective he knew he was: thorough, unemotional, rational.

He tapped on her window and then opened the door for her.

"I'll make certain you arrive at the gate safely," he said.

She chuckled. "There's no need, Detective—"

"Nonsense," he said, escorting her to the door. "It's my job."

17

Ryan tossed his keys onto his desk and pulled out his chair. Before sitting, he turned on his computer and waited impatiently for it to boot.

"You get Ms. Janssen off?" Zuker asked from the adjacent desk, his eyes remaining on his computer screen.

"I did."

"Good."

"You have anything?"

Zuker nodded and the printer behind them began to whir. "Forensics is processing a couple of strands of hair—one found at the Skovgaard scene and another at the Petri home."

"Were they white?"

"They didn't say."

"Wouldn't you be thinking that could be of importance?" Ryan asked.

His partner pulled the sheets from the printer but kept his eyes on Ryan. "Why? You said you thought it was a copycat crime."

"I'm just saying, is all, that I'd like to know the color of each hair. Can you ask that for me?"

"Yeah. I can ask that."

The computer finished booting and Ryan settled in to check his email. "Oh, this is perfect."

"What've you got?" Zuker stood behind Ryan and peered over his shoulder.

"I asked the editor to send an email to Mrs. Skovgaard."

"What for?"

"Watch this." He opened the email from Jackie. "I requested a read receipt; you know, one of those automatic emails that tell you when someone has opened the email. She must have checked her emails on the plane before departure… And the email was opened." He glanced at Zuker. "The person who stole Skovgaard's laptop—he opened her email."

"But what does that prove? That he's reading her email? It doesn't link him to the murder."

Ryan clicked a couple of keys. "Here's the source code. Look at this. Here's Jackie's originating IP address. Then there's the address of the person who opened the email. Then there's her IP address again, as she forwarded the read receipt to me." He picked up his phone and dialed an extension.

"Aye, who is this? Becky? O'Clery here. Can you find out where an IP address came from? Aye. Here it is." He read off the address. "Call me back at this extension, or on my mobile if I'm out. Thank you." He hung up the phone and turned back to Zuker. "When she runs down that IP, it will tell me exactly where this computer was located at the time the perpetrator opened the email."

Zuker whistled. "How'd you know that?"

"Detective work, mate. Detective work."

He focused on checking his other emails and Zuker returned to his desk. The minutes ticked by, and he got up to get a cup of coffee. It was stale and heavy, but it was caffeine.

His desk phone rang as he was returning, and he answered it.

"Detective O'Clery?"

"Aye."

"Becky here, from tech support. The IP address originated from a computer using the Wifi at the Fayetteville Airport."

"No, I must have given you the wrong address." He pulled up the read receipt. "There are two addresses here…" He read off each one.

"The first one you gave me," Becky answered, "is on the Verizon network. That would be one of the cell phones that subscribes to their service, or is using that tower. You say you have two the same?"

"Aye. That was the one that appears twice." He began to feel the same sensation he'd encountered earlier, as though someone was strumming his insides in a decidedly uncomfortable manner.

"The other one," she continued, "was using the Wifi at the airport; not one of the cell towers."

"Are you saying to me that the person who received the email and opened it was sitting inside the airport at the time the email was opened?"

"Not necessarily inside it. But within close enough proximity to use their Wifi… Could have been someone in the parking lot, or sitting outside the terminal…"

His cell phone rang and he checked the Caller ID. "May I phone you back?"

"You know how to reach me."

He hung up the phone. Zuker turned his attention to him, and Ryan picked up his cell phone without taking his eyes off his partner.

"What's wrong?" Zuker mouthed.

"Detective O'Clery," Ryan answered on the fifth ring. It wasn't customary for him to answer it thus; he always figured that the person on the other end of the line was telephoning him, so they should know who it was when he answered. But as the Caller ID sank into his consciousness, his gut morphed from uncomfortable into a full-blown tornado. This was about to be a very bad day.

"Yeah," the voice on the other end of the line said, "this is Detective Helgenberger, Fayetteville Police Department."

"Aye," he answered. He could feel the blood draining from his face, and he felt both heated and chilled simultaneously, as if his body was at war with itself. "What may I do for you, Detective?"

"We have a homicide at the Fayetteville Airport. The woman was carrying your card. We thought she might be part of an investigation…"

"Do you have an identification?"

"Jacqueline Janssen. New York address. Do you know her?"

Ryan continued to lock eyes with Zuker, who came to his feet.

"Detective?"

"Aye; I'm here. I know her. We'll be there directly."

~~~~~

She lay on her back across the toilet, her legs propped against the side of the stall and her head resting against the giant roll of toilet paper on the opposite side. Beneath her, a pool of blood had formed. There was no doubt where it had originated; her throat was slit from one ear to the other.

"We believe she was killed just inside the doorway," Detective Helgenberger was saying. He pointed to the paper cones with evidence numbers that trailed from the doorway to the stall. "The perpetrator tried to clean up the trail, but as you can see, there are some blood smudges left across the floor."

Ryan knelt beside one of the markers. Had there not been a body in the stall behind him, it would have been easy for anyone to miss the trail.

"The killer cleaned it up with paper towels," the detective continued. "We found them stuffed into the trash receptacle."

He peered upward. Detective Helgenberger was a stout man with blond hair that was graying at the temples, and sharp blue eyes. His mouth was set and his brow slightly furrowed, which made him appear as if he had a permanent scowl.

"Who found her?" Ryan asked.

He nodded toward the door. "She's with the Feds. We had to call them, you know; they have jurisdiction…"

"Aye."

"Traveler," he continued, "originally from Phoenix visiting relatives in Fayetteville. She walked into the bathroom, all the stall doors were closed, and she said she was looking underneath the doors to see if any were empty. She saw blood dripping onto the floor and alerted security."

"So, the killer followed Miss Janssen into the ladies' room, killed her just inside the door, and then stuffed the body into the stall."

"That's how we figured it. With the legs against the side, he was trying to prevent anyone from seeing her—probably until he could make his getaway."

"Do you have surveillance cameras?"

"In the hall outside the bathroom. Depending on the direction the killer took, it might've picked him up entering or leaving the ladies' room."

"You said *'him'*," Ryan said. "You deduced that it was a male because of the strength needed to carry the woman into the stall?"

"That's right."

Ryan rose to his feet; he towered over the other man. Helgenberger continued to peer at him curiously.

"Mind telling me how you two were connected?" he asked.

"I'm working two homicides," Ryan answered. "The first was an historian; Miss Janssen was her publisher. The second was another historian, linked to the first one."

"So obviously, there's a connection between all three."

"Aye." His eyes panned the room: the evidence technicians gathering the bloodied paper towels; the evidence cards across the floor, marking the faint trail of blood; a technician taking photographs of Miss Janssen from every angle; a federal officer barking orders. What a position to be found in, he thought. "Tell me," he said suddenly, "why wasn't she on the flight? I saw her board, and I waited until the airplane took off."

"You brought her to the airport?" Helgenberger's brows furrowed more deeply.

"Aye. It was my idea for her to return to New York. With two historians murdered, I didn't believe it was wise for her to remain in the same proximity."

"You walked her to the gate?"

A man of few words, Ryan now felt the words flood past his lips. "I carried her luggage to the counter; she checked in one bag and carried the other—a laptop—with her. I remained with her through the TSA checkpoint, and aye, then I accompanied her to the gate. I didn't have a ticket, in case you were wondering, so I showed my police ID to get through security."

"And you went to the gate with her."

"I remained with her until they began to board. As she started down the ramp, I left. But my cruiser was parked out front, and I had a view of the runway. I confirmed her plane was the only one scheduled to leave in that timeframe, so I waited until it had lifted off. Then I returned to my office. So that meant," he added, "that after I watched her walk down the ramp, she returned to the terminal. That makes no sense."

Helgenberger eyed Zuker, who had remained silent as he surveyed the crime scene. "You two are partners?"

"That's right," Zuker said.

He nodded for them to follow him. They exited the ladies' room and went into an alcove where they had more privacy. "Ms. Janssen left the airplane after she'd already been seated." His eyes seemed to become more rapt as he watched Ryan's reaction.

"Why would she have done that?" Ryan asked.

"The gate received a call for her."

"What?"

"They were told it was an emergency and to remove her from the plane to take the call."

"Isn't that a bit unusual?"

"Highly unusual. They notified the flight crew, and they took her off the plane."

"Must have sounded like a very important call."

Helgenberger eyed Ryan before peering at Zuker for a long moment. Then he turned back to Ryan. There was no doubt that he was watching the other's expression very intently as he said, "Yes. They were told it was very important for her to be removed from the plane, even if it had to leave without her. You see, the phone call came from a Detective Ryan O'Clery from the Lumberton Police Department."

~~~~~

"I can tell you exactly what I'd be thinking at this very moment, if I were you." Ryan sat in one of the chairs across from Chief

Johnston, who was perched on the corner of his desk, his arms folded in front of him and his face expressionless.

He half-waved his hand. "Go ahead."

"First, I received a phone call from Annelise Skovgaard, asking me to meet her at her home. When I arrived with Detective Zuker," he nodded toward his partner seated beside him, "we found that Mrs. Skovgaard had been murdered. Since I was—as far as we can determine—the last person she'd spoken to, and the person she'd been expecting to receive, had I not been a police detective, I would have tagged me as a suspect—or at least a person of interest."

The chief did not waver as he continued looking at Ryan impassively. Zuker remained perfectly silent.

"Then there's the possible motive. She said she had information purportedly about my family; my ancestry. I don't have positive proof that the information was contained on her laptop, but the laptop appears to be the only thing missing from her home."

He waited for some confirmation of his assessment thus far, but the chief simply cocked his head and waited for him to continue.

"Jacqueline Janssen arrived in town from New York," he continued, "and she provided one possible suspect, and only one: Albert Petrironcalli. Another historian and he happened to live within five minutes of the police department. So off I went to interview him. Within minutes or hours—it hasn't been determined yet—he was found strangled to death in the very room I'd just left.

"Now, if I was investigating the two murders and I found a complete stranger to me or the PD had connections to both victims, I'd most definitely have my suspect. All I'd be doing at this point is waiting for the conclusive evidence to corroborate my deduction."

"I have to admit," the chief said slowly, "you do offer a compelling argument."

Ryan stood and paced to the door and back. "Then I was the one who advised Miss Janssen to leave town and return to New York." He waved toward Zuker. "And he's a witness to that. He knew that I drove her to the airport. Surveillance cameras—

which I have no doubt, all tapes are being reviewed as we speak by the Fayetteville PD and the Feds—will show that I parked the vehicle, accompanied her inside, took her as far as boarding. The only thing I did not do was escort her on board and buckle her into her seat."

"And now, she's dead."

"I—" the chief began.

Ryan continued, "Not only was she found murdered by the same modus operandi as Mrs. Skovgaard, but she was removed from the airplane because someone telephoned the gate and identified himself as *me*."

"That's one reason I *don't* suspect you," Chief Johnston said.

Ryan sat down but he was feeling so anxious that he almost stood up again. "Well, I'm relieved to hear you say that, because if I was in your shoes, I'd be taking this detective off the cases and I'd be having him investigated."

"And that's why you're not the chief."

Ryan took a deep breath but before he could speak, the chief continued, "However, I am concerned. You are involved in this case. I can look at this in two ways: either the suspect has no other ties to you, other than discovering that you are the investigator for Mrs. Skovgaard's murder. That could be behind the use of your name." He narrowed his eyes as he continued, "Or it could have more to do with you than you're telling me."

"Pardon?"

"What do you know about the information Mrs. Skovgaard had on your family?"

"Nothing, really. I thought she was completely mistaken when she phoned me. She mentioned some ancestor from Norway, a country I've no connection to. But then she mentioned an uncle I do have a connection to—I was actually named after him—so I decided to meet with her and find out what information she had. When I arrived—well, you know the rest."

"Do you have any leads on the laptop that was stolen?"

Zuker spoke up. "I've been to all the pawn shops in the area. No one has attempted to unload it."

"But I don't believe it was taken for resale," Ryan interjected. "I think it was taken for the data that was on it."

"Continue," Chief Johnston said.

"There were things that were far more valuable in her home—even the jewelry she was still wearing when we arrived. Laptops have come down in price so dramatically that they're just not worth stealing anymore. Then there's the matter of the email I asked Miss Janssen to send to Mrs. Skovgaard, knowing full well she wasn't alive to receive it. She sent a read receipt—at my direction—and then forwarded it to me, so I could trace the location of the laptop." He shook his head. "I believe it's that email that led to Miss Janssen's murder."

"Why? What was in the email?"

"It wasn't so much the content of the email, as it was a connection between Mrs. Skovgaard's work and Miss Janssen as her editor. And obviously, the killer is cunning and intelligent; he had to have traced *her* email to know she was in the vicinity of the Fayetteville Airport."

"That's where she sent her email?"

"We were in the car on our way there. She used her phone, and my guess is the killer ran a search on the IP address and it somehow led to the satellite nearest the airport. He put two-and-two together, figured she was in North Carolina but was leaving, and…" His voice trailed off.

"They have surveillance at the airport…"

"Aye. I'm waiting for the footage now."

Chief Johnston nodded. "Three murders, O'Clery. Catch this guy before he kills again."

"Aye, sir." He stood, as did Zuker.

"Zuker and O'Clery," the chief said before they reached the door. "I mean it. I want this guy caught. Whatever resources you need, you've got 'em. Catch him and catch him quick."

18

Ryan's heartbeat quickened as he read the email. "Detective Helgenberger," he announced to Zuker. "He's emailed the footage from the airport."

Zuker rolled his chair to Ryan's desk. With both their eyes riveted to the screen, he opened the attachment.

The camera was trained on the ladies' room door and picked up a portion of the hallway just beyond it. It made sense, Ryan thought; if a woman was accosted in the only truly private place in the airport, the camera would at least catch the suspect coming and going.

After a moment, Jacqueline Janssen was clearly shown entering the ladies' room. Her pocketbook dangled from one shoulder and her laptop case from the other.

Seconds later, another figure entered the ladies' room. Ryan stopped the video, backed it up, and zoomed in before watching it again. Then he reversed the frames until he had the clearest image of the suspect. He leaned back, his chin cupped in his hand, as he studied it.

The suspect had his back to the camera. He was wearing what appeared to be denim jeans; they fit tight across muscular thighs that looked as though they were straining against the fabric. From the appearance of the casual jacket he wore, he was a bulky man; his shoulders appeared enormous when measured against the opening to the ladies' room. He studied the only arm that was visible in the frame; it, too, appeared to strain against the fabric.

"Weight lifter," Ryan said.

Zuker nodded. "What do you think, around two-thirty, maybe up to two hundred and fifty pounds?"

"Aye. And about six foot four."

He zoomed as close as he could and still retain picture clarity. His jacket collar was turned up, hiding the back of his neck. He wore a wide-brimmed hat that must have been pushed back from the temple, as it covered the back of his head completely. It was impossible to see more—the color of the hair, or even what race the man was.

"It looks like a cowboy hat," Ryan said.

"No," Zuker said suddenly. "You know what that is? It's an African bush hat."

"A what? How do you know that?"

"Take a look at that emblem on the side. That's the manufacturer." He pointed animatedly. "A few years ago, my wife and I went on an African vacation. One of those adventure tours; that kind of thing. Anyway, they sold hats like this there. It protects the neck from the sun's strong rays."

"Do you happen to know the brand?"

"I sure do. I think each one is handcrafted. It's called a Rogue hat."

Ryan opened a new tab and searched on the hat.

"That's it," Zuker said excitedly. "See? It's an African tin cloth bush hat. See the emblem on the side?"

"Good work," he said admiringly. "Circumstantial, but that could help to tie our suspect to Africa." He began to have a feeling along the back of his neck, as if someone else stood there and was breathing on him. If the invisible being could speak, Ryan thought, it would be shouting at him to connect the dots. "Diallo Delport was from South Africa," he said. His voice sounded almost hushed.

"It's circumstantial," Zuker agreed. "But it could be confirmation we're on the right track."

Ryan minimized the video and clicked into his past cases. "You remember when Delport was in town?"

"Who could forget?"

"I scanned his passport. There; that's it." He brought up the file. The man's face was even more jarring than Ryan had remembered. His hair was completely white and blended in perfectly with alabaster skin. His brows and lashes were white as well, and his eyes appeared to be the palest periwinkle blue. But the most startling characteristic was a raised scar that began just under his eye and ended in another raised scar halfway down his cheek that was shaped like a teardrop.

"Thirty-six years old," Ryan read, though his partner was obviously reading it over his shoulder as well. "Six feet, four inches tall. Two hundred and forty-five pounds."

"That's our suspect," Zuker said. "He didn't die in the hurricane."

"No," he answered. A chill crept up his spine until he shuddered involuntarily. "He's alive. And he's here."

They both stared at the passport picture for a long moment before Ryan regained his composure. He flipped back to the video and continued it. Noting the time the killer entered the ladies' room, two full minutes elapsed before the man exited again. This time, the hat was pulled down in the front, completely obscuring his face.

"He's smart," Zuker said. "He knew the camera was there."

Ryan nodded. "He's highly intelligent. And he's cunning."

"And he's a killer."

"Wait—what's that?" Ryan stopped the video and pointed at a bulky object under the man's arm. "I didn't see that in the other frames."

"Back it up."

They watched the man entering the ladies' room again and then exiting. Shaking their heads, they watched it again. Then Ryan began to swear.

"It's Janssen's laptop case," he groaned. "I never thought to ask Helgenberger if they'd recovered her pocketbook or the laptop."

"And now he's got it."

"Which proves my point," Ryan said. "He can't be killing women for their laptops. Makes no sense whatsoever. He could easily break into homes when no one is there and take all the electronics he wants."

His partner locked eyes with him. "He wants the data—"

"—and he thinks Mrs. Skovgaard's editor had information on her laptop—"

"Information that he either needed to corroborate the data on Skovgaard's computer—"

"—or he wants to erase all references to it, as if he wanted to make certain it would never be published." He flipped back to Delport's passport picture before leaning back in his chair. He stared into the cold, hard eyes of the killer. "But why? What could possibly be so inflammatory that he would kill rather than see it published?"

~~~~~

Chief Johnston steepled his hands as he watched the surveillance film. When it was over, he remained silent for a moment, his eyes riveted to the final image frozen on the screen. Then he swiveled his chair around to face Ryan and Zuker, who waited for his response. Their eagerness showed in their expressions but at his continued silence, their faces began to fall.

"What is it?" Ryan finally asked.

"What it *isn't*," Chief Johnston said, "is conclusive evidence that this is Diallo Delport."

"But—"

"The answer is 'no'. I will not permit you to issue an APB on Delport."

Ryan felt his cheeks begin to burn. "May I ask why not?"

"Have a seat." The chief gestured toward the empty chairs on the other side of his desk, and waited until Ryan and Zuker were seated. Ryan perched near the edge of his chair as if ready to pop back up at any moment, and though Zuker settled in, his facial expression had turned serious, his mouth downturned.

"The serial murder case you worked last year was a high profile case," the chief began. "You know it got national attention."

"Aye," Ryan agreed. "Had it not been for the national media, I would never have met Cait."

"So you'll recall when you announced that Delport was dead, it also received national attention."

Ryan's mind flashed back to the moment when he'd fought Delport within an inch of his life. It had been an act of God or Fate or whatever higher power one believed in, that the ocean swept him out to sea. He was even larger and more muscular than Ryan and easily the most formidable opponent he'd ever encountered. "I thought he was dead." His voice was uncharacteristically low. He met Chief Johnston's eyes as he continued. "I saw the waves take him out to sea. You know yourself how long the Coast Guard searched for his body. It wasn't only myself that believed he couldn't have survived; it was the professional assessment of all the law enforcement involved."

"I understand that. And I am not blaming you for what might turn out to be an incorrect judgment. But—and I need for you to listen to me closely here—I need definitive proof that he is still alive."

"The film—the modus operandi—"

"The footage shows me a large man wearing a hat, a jacket and jeans. There is absolutely nothing that serves to identify the suspect as Diallo Delport. And—" he continued, waving away Ryan's objections, "you said yourself just a day or two ago that you believed these to be copycat crimes."

"That was before—"

"I don't care. What I care about is evidence. Give me something more to go on, O'Clery. Fingerprints from the scenes. DNA. Eyewitnesses. *Something.* Until then, I will not allow you to go public with your hunch that it's Delport, and that somehow he's still alive."

"I can't be everywhere at once, Chief. I need more eyes. An All-Points-Bulletin—"

"I could be saving you from yourself. Imagine what this could do to your credibility if it turns out to be a copycat, after you've reversed yourself. Now get out of here, the two of you—and solve these cases."

Ryan sat silently for a moment. Out of the corner of his eye, he saw Zuker rise and heard him approach the door behind him. He looked up to find the chief watching him. Then he nodded and followed his partner into the hall.

He'd barely reached his desk before he was dialing the evidence technician. "Arlo," he said, "I understand you found some hairs at the scenes of the Skovgaard and Petrironcalli murders?"

"Yeah. We don't have any info on them yet, though."

"Can you tell me what color they were?"

"Hold on."

He pulled out his chair and sat down heavily while he waited. He could hear Zuker on the phone at his desk next to Ryan's, asking Detective Helgenberger if they had any other footage of the suspect.

"O'Clery?"

"Aye."

"The hairs were black."

"Black."

"That's what I said."

"Okay. Thanks, Arlo." He clicked off the phone.

He leaned his elbows on his desk and rubbed his forehead with the fingers of both hands. He had a monstrous headache. The chief was right. As much as he wanted to see Delport's face plastered on every television news station and in every newspaper, what if he was wrong? His brain argued with his gut, which insisted that Delport was alive. And though he was a trained detective and he understood evidence perfectly well, his gut was winning out.

But why? Every suspect had to have a motive.

There was something on those laptops—something Mrs. Skovgaard was researching that Delport did not want anyone to know. The motive, then, was in the data.

He clicked into his email and brought up the read receipt to the last email Jacqueline Janssen had written. It was this email, written under his direction, that had killed her.

But how could he have gotten to the airport so quickly?

Ryan closed his eyes and recalled the timeline. It was roughly twenty miles from the editor's hotel to the Fayetteville Airport.

Unlike some of the larger airports, Fayetteville had easy access, short lines, and the personnel were highly efficient. He supposed Janssen had sent the email from her cell phone to Skovgaard's address when they were about five minutes away from the airport—in fact, he seemed to recall as she was either typing or sending it, that he had been turning off the Interstate.

That meant, he reasoned, if Delport had been sitting at the computer at that very moment and had opened the email immediately, he had only minutes to react. He'd have to check the IP address—assuming he knew how, which Ryan suspected he did—and drive to the airport, have Janssen paged, and then stalk her until he saw an opportunity to kill her. Would he have murdered her, he wondered, if she hadn't been carrying the laptop?

He shook his head. It didn't matter. She was carrying it, and now she's dead.

And the question remained: how did he get there so quickly?

He opened his eyes and stared at the read receipt. The police department's computer technician said he'd read the email from the Fayetteville Airport. No, he corrected himself; he'd read it using the airport's Wifi.

It was too coincidental to believe that Diallo Delport had been sitting in the terminal when he'd escorted Jacqueline Janssen inside and to the gate. It was just too hard to believe.

Unless…

He swore under his breath.

"What is it?" Zuker asked.

Ryan clicked out of his email and switched to Google Earth. He pulled up the Fayetteville Airport and rotated the screen so he could assess it from all angles. He felt Zuker move in behind him to peer over his shoulder.

How far could Wifi reach? He wondered. He'd worked cases where suspects had logged onto open-access Wifi from as far as a mile away. So what was within a mile of the airport?

He zoomed in on a group of buildings. Of course. All airports had hotels and motels at their periphery.

"Zuker," he said suddenly. "Find out what hotels are located on this street." He pointed the mouse arrow at the street in question. "I'll find out which ones are on the adjacent street."

Zuker wordlessly returned to his desk. Still standing, he ran a search and a moment later, it was printing out. There were five hotels or motels on one street, and Ryan discovered there were four more on the adjacent street.

"Call every hotel on your list," Ryan said.

"Delport wouldn't have registered under his own name," Zuker argued.

"You're not even going to ask. I want to know which hotels have surveillance."

"You think they caught him on tape?"

"He's too smart for that. I want to know which ones *don't* have surveillance."

Within minutes, they came together at the edge of Ryan's desk. They laid the two printed lists side by side. In an instant, Ryan had scanned the handwritten notes beside each one. Then he pointed. "That's it," he said, one hand moving instinctively to find his car keys. "That's where he's staying."

19

He stopped across the street near the edge of a building and studied the motel laid out before him. It was the perfect hiding place for a killer.

Staring back at him was the entrance to the office. He used his binoculars to focus on the office personnel: a young woman and a young man, both of whom appeared to be in their late teens or early twenties. One was on the telephone while another was working at a computer.

He pulled back and angled his body so he could view the side of the motel. It was one long, narrow building with the office facing the street and the rooms facing into the side parking lot. At the edge of the lot was a chain link fence with privacy slats woven through it. A sign further down announced the hours of a junkyard.

He assumed, though he couldn't view them from this vantage point, that an identical set of rooms were on the opposite side of the building, also facing a similar parking lot. Though he couldn't see the property line on that side, he further assumed it bordered an open field, which seemed to fill the area between the motel and the airport grounds. A sign advertising a restaurant also pointed to the side he couldn't see.

"What's the plan?" Zuker asked quietly.

An airplane's jet engine broke the silence and Ryan watched as it became airborne. It flew directly over the motel before banking to head south.

Ryan set down the binoculars and picked up the printed copy of Delport's passport. "We go in together. Whatever happens with Delport, make sure you get those laptops."

With that, he opened his car door. They crossed the narrow street together with Ryan only a few steps ahead of Zuker. There was a lone car in the distance and a pair of birds circled overhead. Ravens, he thought. He heard their distinctive call like his hearing was finely tuned to them. The Irish were a superstitious lot, and though he normally didn't believe in things he couldn't see, he wasn't immune to the stories. Ravens, in particular, were often harbingers of bad fortune and evil. A wind picked up, sending a shiver down his spine as the near-naked branches of maple trees began to sway. His heartbeat accelerated as they reached the edge of the motel property.

He glanced down the side lot. There were two vehicles parked outside the rooms; one near the center and one at the opposite end. "Make sure you get those license numbers," Ryan said without breaking his stride. He felt more than saw Zuker stopping and knew he was zooming in on the cars with his smartphone's camera. A moment later, he heard the phone click and then click again.

His mind shifted briefly to Cait. He'd phoned her on their drive to Fayetteville to let her know that he was working a case and would be late getting home. Claire and Tommy were coming to dinner with their girls; he was glad Cait would not be alone.

His hand was hot and slightly sweaty as he reached for the lobby door handle. His chest was thumping with the familiar adrenaline that came before a fight. Delport would not give up easily; he would have to take him down forcibly, and he knew that. And he was ready.

The woman looked up from the computer as he entered the lobby. The man had his back to him and was still on the phone.

Ryan placed the picture on the check-in desk and reached for his police ID. Showing it to the clerk, he asked, "Do you recognize this man?"

She looked beyond his shoulder as the door opened and closed. Ryan glanced to his side to find Zuker standing slightly behind him, his hand on his belt, his weapon in clear sight. He looked back to the woman. She had a pierced eyebrow, a pierced lip and four earrings in each ear. She wore black eyeshadow, thick liner and her top was too tight. Without the tackle box and Goth cosmetics, Ryan thought, she wouldn't have been bad looking. With it, it was a toss-up whether she'd leave work to solicit sex or serve as bait for deep sea fishing.

The man turned around. Seeing Ryan's identification still displayed, he hastily told the caller he had to get off the phone. He remained a fair distance from the desk as he said, "Can I help you guys?"

Ryan held up the picture so he could see it. "You recognize him?"

The two exchanged glances.

"Which room is he in?"

"Do you have a search warrant?" The young man was clean cut. He wore a white shirt and a tie.

"I'm not asking to search his room. I'm asking if he's here."

"Last room on the left," the young girl said. "One-fourteen."

Ryan pointed to the side of the motel he hadn't yet seen. "That side?"

She nodded.

He grabbed the paper and started for the door. Passing Zuker, he said in a low voice, "Get Helgenberger. We're gonna need backup."

"The Feds—"

"I don't want the Feds."

They passed through the door and as they reached the sidewalk, he heard Zuker on the phone. Ryan wasn't waiting. He didn't remember placing the picture back in his pocket but as he made his way in front of the rooms, he instinctively flexed his hands. He thought of the police-issued Taser he carried and nearly smiled as he thought of giving Delport a taste of his own medicine.

The restaurant was located in the same narrow building, backing up to rooms on the opposite side. As he walked past them, his eyes scanned the windows but the blinds were drawn against the penetrating glare of a setting sun.

He stopped when he reached the last room. He glanced behind him to find Zuker just two steps behind. Beyond him stood the young man and woman from the front office; they remained at the opposite end of the building as they watched the scene unfolding in front of them.

He held up one finger to let Zuker know he was hesitating. He stood close to the brick as he tried to peer inside the window to the last room. The curtains were water-stained and drawn tight. He watched them for a few seconds but they did not waver; it didn't mean he wasn't inside, but it meant he hadn't been watching them approach.

He nodded to Zuker and then crossed quickly to the other side of the window, and then to the far side of the door. Zuker followed past the window and took up his position across from Ryan so they had both sides of the door covered.

Again, Ryan held up one finger. Then he stepped backward a few short steps to examine the back side of the building. There were no windows on this side and no door; just a flat wall of graffiti-covered brick. Dormant grass and dead weeds intermingled into thick brush that stretched to the airport property line; it was clear to see where one ended and the other began, as the airport was surrounded with tall fencing, beyond which the grounds were pristine.

He stepped back further to view the area on the opposite side of the motel. There, the invasive grasses had found their way into the parking lot's asphalt cracks, creating the appearance that the property was abandoned though it clearly was not. It ended at the fence to the junkyard, the tallest weeds climbing up the chain link, weaving around the slats like long, craggy tentacles.

He returned to the far side of the door. In his peripheral vision, he saw the young man and woman still standing on the sidewalk outside the office watching them with growing interest. He met Zuker's eyes and nodded once. His partner returned the nod and reached for his weapon.

Ryan stood with his back to the wall and reached out to bang on the door. "Diallo Delport!" he yelled. His voice was deep and hoarse with adrenaline. "Police! Open the door!"

He placed his hand on his weapon as he waited. There was no response. He inched closer, moving his ear toward the door as he listened intently. He shook his head and Zuker nodded in acknowledgement. Then he banged on the door again, repeating the same words as before.

When there was no answer, he studied the door. It was an old building; the exterior walls were brick but the doorframe and door were both metal. A deadbolt lock was in plain view. He imagined on the inside, there would be a metal security bar or chain.

He took a deep breath. He could kick against the door but if a deadbolt was in place and the metal was sturdy, chances were slim that he'd be successful. He could remain there and get Helgenberger or his associates to request a search warrant, but that would take time. As he weighed his options, he felt his skin grow hot as though someone was staring at him. It caused the hair on the back of his neck to stand up as if an apparition was moving into an invisible space surrounding him; the energy somehow had shifted.

He looked toward Zuker but his eyes gravitated to the figure past his shoulder. Ryan froze as he recognized the massive hulk standing on the sidewalk outside the restaurant. Their eyes locked across the distance between them. Then Diallo Delport dropped the bag he'd held in his hands and ran.

Instinctively, Ryan turned and raced around the back side of the building, hoping to head off the other man as he ran around the opposite side. He spotted him as he broke free from the building, his immense legs propelling him like pistons across the parking lot toward the junkyard. Without hesitation, Ryan rushed across the lot parallel to Delport.

For an enormous man, Delport was surprisingly agile. Ryan caught a glimpse of his faded jeans, stretched taut across his legs, below a black leather jacket that set off his white hair and alabaster skin. He reached the fence and scrambled over the eight-foot chain link, the fence bending dangerously toward the ground as if his weight would snap the metal. As his legs straddled the top, he paused only long enough to meet Ryan's eyes once more before dropping to the other side.

Ryan reached the fence several yards from where Delport had crossed. He realized he'd instinctively drawn his weapon and now he used precious seconds to return it to his waistband before scrambling up the fence as Delport had done. As his head cleared the fence, he caught a glimpse of acres upon acres of junked vehicles, twisted metal, broken glass and decay. As both hands grasped the top bar and he prepared to jump to the other side, a flash of something large and rusty sailed through the air like a torpedo. He threw up one arm, teetering dangerously on top of the fence, but his movement was too late to stop the heavy metal object from hitting him squarely above the brow.

A bright white light flashed in front of him like a lightning bolt, though he knew he'd instinctively closed his eyes. He rocked against the fence and felt it wobble beneath him as if it was on the verge of collapse. He felt more than saw the warm liquid as it gushed from his forehead down the front of his face and as it entered his parted lips, he tasted his own blood.

A voice rose within him that ordered him to open his eyes, move beyond the agony, and jump to the other side. But the pain was too great; it blinded him with an intensity that he struggled to overcome. The effort was palpable, excruciating—and dangerous. The voice grew within him, nearly screaming for him to get off the fence and get his feet on firm ground. The vision of Delport, the Taser and a scalpel loomed in his mind's eye.

With a shout that sounded more like an animal's guttural cry, he jumped wide, hoping he'd clear the fence and land on solid ground. His eyes opened just long enough to see acres of rusted vehicles and jagged car parts before he slammed into the ground. He felt the breath whoosh out of him as he rolled across the dirt. He'd barely landed before he was struggling to his feet, one arm moving to his forehead to wipe the blood out of his eyes and off his brow.

Instinctively, his other hand went to his weapon, pulling the pistol out even before he could clearly see in front of him. A jagged passageway between the fence and the first scattered row of vehicles and parts loomed before him. Delport was not there.

He whirled around, his pistol still steady and ready to fire. But the area behind him was clear as well.

He took a brief moment to yank a handkerchief from his pocket and wipe his brow. He pulled it away to reveal bright red blood. He was certain he'd need stitches but he couldn't stop to think about it now.

He moved forward cautiously, his feet silent on the dry ground. He felt the chill moving up his spine again, and he glanced over his shoulder. The passageway behind him was still clear, but he couldn't shake the feeling that he was being watched.

He spotted a metal pipe marred with blood and marveled that the heavy object hadn't rendered him unconscious. He'd need a tetanus shot, for sure. He stepped around it and moved to the edge of a vehicle, glancing around it and looking for movement before he turned the corner.

He found himself in a short corridor with junked parts on either side, some piled well above his head. He quieted his breath as he moved slowly but deliberately past them, his head turning in each direction lest he be caught unawares once more. He reached a burned out pickup, and he quickly scrambled onto the truck bed and then onto the roof of the cab to peer about him.

The junkyard appeared to be laid out in uneven rows where disassembled car doors were strewn haphazardly away from the vehicles and broken glass littered most of the ground. Everything from rusted engines to door handles lay scattered in between the vehicles. Most of the cars appeared old, the degree of rust announcing just how long they'd been exposed to the elements. Others seemed almost new but their crumpled sides proclaimed their fate; some were barely more than accordions. As his eyes landed on one vehicle in which the driver's seat was smashed against the rear bumper, he realized that many of the cars had been death traps.

He could be hiding in any of a dozen places, Ryan realized, some of them just a few yards from where he stood. He pulled his phone from his pocket; it was a wonder, he thought, that it hadn't been smashed to pieces when he jumped.

He hit speed dial and seconds later, Zuker answered. "Get a canine unit out here," he said quietly as his eyes continued to pan the area.

"Will do. Helgenberger is entering the junkyard from the front entrance. Another unit is stopped alongside the fence."

"Where are you?"

"In Delport's room."

"Get the—"

"Laptops. Yeah. I know."

A movement caught his eye and he lowered the phone, clicking it off before slipping it into his pocket. He raised his pistol as he watched something moving in between two rows of junked vehicles. It was light against the darker metal; instinctively, he knew it was Delport. If he rose just a few inches, he could get off a good shot.

The movement disappeared behind higher stacks of debris. He waited for it to reappear but when it didn't, he quickly calculated the distance. Four rows over, 50 feet down.

He prepared to jump from the top of the truck cab when another movement caught his eye. Turning quickly, he watched as Helgenberger and another officer entered the junkyard. He motioned toward the area in which he'd seen Delport, and Helgenberger nodded silently. He watched briefly as the other detective motioned to his partner. As they began moving in the direction of Delport, Ryan jumped.

He landed on the ground amid broken glass. Not wasting a second, he raced toward an opening and made his way across the four rows of debris before slowing. He estimated the distance from the front entrance. It would make sense that Delport would move further from the motel and further from the main entrance. Getting his bearings, Ryan moved craftily around the debris, his pistol ready as he rounded each vehicle, his eyes searching between the wreckage, his senses alert to any signs of movement.

The sudden caw of a raven startled him as it rose into the sky. He watched it with unblinking eyes before looking downward at the area beneath the bird. That was Delport's location, he thought. It had to be.

His footsteps were steady and silent. He picked his way around the rusted-out cab of another truck and the burned-out shell of a minivan. His breath was steady. He didn't think; he moved from instinct. He would kill on instinct.

He heard a voice as though muffled and then a hard thud. He cocked his head, listening, but was met only with silence. Even the wind had died to nothing. The sun had set, taking the last vestiges of light with it, and he found himself squinting to see through the gloom. He hadn't noticed it getting darker, and now he marveled at how quickly the darkness was setting in. A man could remain perfectly still, he realized, and he may never know he was there. He could blend right in with the rust and the metal and the rubble.

He began to move again in the direction of the last sound he'd heard. His footsteps were furtive; his mind quick.

He rounded the corner of an SUV inside which dormant weeds leaned haphazardly, his eyes trained on the area at eyelevel, before almost tripping over something large and bulky. He stumbled before righting himself and realized what he'd blundered upon was not metal and stiff but something softer.

His pistol pointed at the ground beneath him, his finger on the trigger, before he realized it was Helgenberger.

Ryan quickly knelt, his fingers moving to the pulse in the man's neck. He was alive. His eyes were wide; the white surrounding his irises were clearly visible all the way around. As he continued to lie in front of him, Ryan realized the only body part that was moving *were* his eyes. They stared beyond his shoulder, causing him to whirl around, ready to fire, but there was no one behind him.

Ryan rose and moved so his back was against the undercarriage of a vehicle lying on its side. Groping for his cell phone, he hit speed dial. Zuker answered on the first ring. "Helgenberger's down," Ryan said. His voice was barely over a whisper but it sounded loud in the encroaching silence. "Tasered."

"Dead?"

"Negative. How many officers are here?"

"At least four."

"We need more."

"I'll get 'em."

Ryan pulled his bloodied handkerchief from his pocket. "I'm tying my handkerchief to a vehicle antenna," he said as his eyes landed on a vehicle opposite him. "Helgenberger is directly beneath it. Get a helicopter out here. We need lights and eyes from above."

"Roger."

Ryan clicked off the phone. He waited momentarily as his eyes grew more accustomed to the dusk. He could detect no movement around him. A glance at Helgenberger showed his eyes still wide, still staring.

He moved cautiously to the vehicle across from him. Slipping his pistol into his waistband, he stepped onto the running board and tied the handkerchief onto the antenna, then ran it as high as he could. He couldn't shake the sensation that eyes were boring into his back and as quickly as the cloth reached the top, he was down and his pistol was back in his hand.

He could no longer see light on the distant horizon; the sun was long gone. Dusk had turned to blackness. He glanced upward. There were no stars; no sliver of a moon; only an inky darkness that moved like a shadow around him.

20

Duiblinn, 1171

The clamor of discordant voices had risen to a crescendo that descended upon Baldr from all directions. The night sky was set ablaze as ships and homes and businesses were torched, the crackle and clatter of wood and possessions caving in amongst the flames dwarfed only by the screams and shouts. The accents and languages varied but as Baldr tried to avoid the growing din, he knew that on this night, history was changing. The Vikings were being forcibly expelled with the full onslaught of the Norman invasion.

The Norman forces were overwhelming. Those Ostmen who had Celtic wives were retreating inland; those that did not were fleeing to the north shores to the ships that waited there.

He fought off one warrior after another; he wanted only to be reunited with Maeve, to leave Eire and return home to the north, home to his people—but one after another attacked until Baldr's sword dripped blood and his arms, as muscular and formidable as they were, ached with a weight he could not shake.

His steed was gone, freed from the stables as they'd been set afire. He had no recourse but to run, walk and scuttle down one street after another, winding his way on foot, hoping and praying that Maeve was safe, the ship remained and they both awaited him.

When at last the noise grew muted behind him, the crowds had grown sparse until he was alone in the darkness, stumbling forward, peering through the night in an attempt to see the north shores. He kept his eyes staring straight ahead, trying to make out the outline of the ships, to spot activity that could only mean that they were preparing to set sail.

But when he spotted movement on the horizon, it was an orange-red glow that danced and swayed. It began as something small and barely discernible but soon separated, growing higher and broader as a new chorus of voices reached his ears.

As he continued toward the shore, he realized the lights were torches held aloft—and they stood between his ship and himself.

He hesitated as he gauged the distance. He was less familiar with this landscape than he was Duiblinn itself, but he moved perpendicular to the crowd that approached the sea as he kept one eye on the men and the other on his escape.

He was a short distance away now. He could see movement on one of the ships; men were shouting to one another as they rushed to set sail. A lone figure sat near the center, huddled against a chill that had pervaded the summer night like the frigid hand of a god was falling atop them. Was it Maeve? He narrowed his eyes in a futile attempt to see her better. It had to be her—and he was almost there.

He hurried his stride, his eyes set upon the lone figure.

He'd grown near enough to the ships to recognize the voices of his men when a group stepped in front of him, blocking his path.

They were all black-haired and fair-skinned; men larger than the invading forces but not as sizable as the Ostmen. And he recognized them.

There were four: Daegan, Stiabhan, Keegan and Royan.

Royan was the largest one, both taller and broader, and from his stance among the others, Baldr had no doubt that he was the eldest. He stood in the center of them, his eyes narrowed and his expression grim. Daegan and Stiabhan flanked each side, while the shorter, slighter Keegan hung back a short distance as if there more to observe than to participate.

"I have no quarrel with ye," Baldr said.

"You are Hvitr Bard," Royan spat. He lifted his head as if defying Baldr to deny it.

"Aye," Baldr said in the Irish fashion. He pointed toward the shore, which now seemed further away than it had just a moment ago. "And I am leavin' Eire, ne'er to return."

Royan used his sword to point to Baldr's. "An' whose blood be that on yer weapon?"

"No Celtic blood, I assure ye that. I have fought the invaders."

"Ye are runnin' away from the invaders."

"I am leavin' Eire to yer hands or the hands o' Henry the Second, whiche'er prevails."

Royan began stepping sideways in front of Baldr, his hand flexing and straightening around the hilt of his sword. Daegan and Stiabhan spread apart, each moving toward Baldr's peripheral vision.

"I do not wish to fight ye," Baldr said.

"I do not recall havin' asked ye."

Baldr lowered his sword to the ground. "I know yer family, and I will not raise m' blade against ye."

Daegan scoffed. "Ye know not who we are, nor who our family may be."

Baldr motioned toward Royan, who had spread his feet wider apart and was fingering the hilt of the sword. "Ye are Royan." He nodded at each of the brothers in turn. "Daegan, Stiabhan…" He pointed toward Keegan in the rear. "An' the youngest, Keegan."

Royan's eyes narrowed to a slit. "And why would Hvitr Bard, The White Devil o' Duiblinn, know the likes o' us?"

"It matters not." He motioned toward his sword as it lay on the ground. "I have laid down m' weapon. I want only to board that ship. A' ye will ne'er see me again."

Royan sneered. "Or ye will join yer brothers and all yer kind will descend upon us like mad dogs until e'ery last Irishman is dead in their graves."

"I give ye m' word. I will not raise arms ag'in ye."

Royan sliced through the air and Baldr jumped back as the blade came close to his abdomen. "Yer word is worth nothin'. Pick up yer sword. An' fight like a man."

"I will not."

"Fight like a man or die like the weasel that ye are."

Baldr looked from one to the other. Royan, Daegan and Stiabhan each eyed him with blood in their eyes. When he looked to Keegan, the boy peered at the ground and shuffled his feet.

"Do ye attempt, then," Baldr said, "to teach the boy how to kill? Then go to the south where King Henry's men are burnin' yer city. Ye'll find many a man who will fight ye there." He tried to step around the men, but they moved closer in silent unity, blocking his way. He raised his chin. "Would ye kill a man who bears no arms?"

Royan swiped at him again and again as Baldr dodged the blade.

Would his men hear him if he called out? Baldr wondered. He gauged the distance to the ships but realized with a sinking heart that the torches were continuing to grow in number as the Celts drew closer to the shore. He understood in a flash of insight what they intended: the Ostmen had conquered their island, had fought their men, had taken their women; they had subjugated them. And now, with Henry landing on their shores, they planned to fight them all. They would drive the Ostmen from Eire, and then they would battle the Norman invaders.

Nay, Baldr corrected himself. They did not intend to drive out the Ostmen. They clearly planned to kill them all.

Royan took another swipe and still another, backing Baldr up a step at a time. The brothers advanced as well, tightening their circle around him until there was scant chance of escape.

"I will not raise arms ag'in ye," Baldr said again. "Why do ye want to murder me, when I am leavin'?"

"Did ye not kill our men in battle after battle?" Stiabhan derided. "Is there more than one Hvitr Bard? Or is there just one w' the blood o' many a Celt on 'is hands?"

Baldr backed up again and again as one sword after another attempted to reach him. He was fast on his feet despite his bulkiness, but he knew he could not hope to outdistance them indefinitely.

Fire burst into the sky as the ships were set alight. The sound of his men fighting against the Celts reached his ears. Somewhere in the noise and the mayhem, he heard the sound of a woman's voice screaming. His head jerked toward the shore, his body tense as he readied himself to rush to Maeve's defense. Surely the gods who kept him unscarred throughout his lifetime would continue to protect him, his love, and his unborn child.

Royan rushed toward him as Baldr tried to sidestep all the brothers at once. This was not his day to die. It could not be.

When the axe sliced through his back, his mind burned in a thick, red haze. He fell to his knees as a myriad of thoughts raced through, jumbled, disjointed and climbing atop one another. There were the four brothers in front of him. They had not touched him. Yet now they stood with their swords at their sides, watching him fall like a great oak. He had been unscarred. And now, with one movement, his back was sliced open. The air felt chilled and sharp as it found his open wound; every nerve along his back screamed with a devastating torture that threatened to completely overwhelm his senses.

He toppled face-first into the dust, despite his determination to remain on his feet, regardless of the voices that cried out within him insisting that he rush to the ships, and in the face of a growing panic that he could not protect the only woman he had ever loved.

It was then that he saw the other men; they had come from behind and had struck him—defenseless, with his back to them. He saw one dusty boot and then two planted beside him. Then one came down upon his shoulder with such force that Baldr wanted to cry out in agony. It was only then that he realized from the moment the axe had become embedded in his back, he had filled the air with an unadulterated, guttural shriek.

Now the man held his body in place with his foot while he ripped the axe from him, cleaving his back further until Baldr was certain his insides lay exposed like a gutted animal.

Then they were gone.

He thought he saw the torches moving, swaying, dipping, rising, as they wandered away from him and closer to the ships. But then the night sky surrounded him. He struggled to raise his head but faltered only inches from the ground; the struggle was too great. As his cheek landed on the ground once more, his eyes settled on the distant stars. There was a full moon rising, he realized in an odd moment of peaceful clarity. It grew in size and brilliance as it parted the black, roiling clouds until it was all he could see.

He labored vainly to bring himself to his knees, but the bottom half of his body seemed disconnected from his torso. He could not will himself to move either foot or either leg... It was then that he realized his long, white hair had grown crimson. And as he lay in the dust of a road a world apart from his own, his blood continued to pool around him.

The voices grew faint and the fires paled and the moon continued to expand until it seemed to envelop him in a cocoon of dazzling white light. "Valhöll," he breathed, his voice gurgling with the taste of his own blood as he surrendered to the end that awaited him.

21

Ryan quietly closed the door behind him as the sound of voices reached his ears. He hesitated in the front hallway, half-listening to Claire, Tommy and Cait. He didn't remember when he'd felt so tired.

Pure adrenaline had propelled him for hours as he scoured the junkyard with dozens of other officers, aided by a helicopter that lit the area with a blinding intensity. Then as the FBI and the Fayetteville Police Department took over the search, they'd insisted that paramedics arriving on the scene to transport Helgenberger look at Ryan's forehead. He might have argued against it, had the pain been less; but he knew it was bad from the expressions of those around him.

He drew the line at going to a hospital, however. His work was not finished there and he wouldn't be spending the rest of the night in an emergency room shivering under some thin sheet because someone forgot to adjust the heat. So they'd cleaned the wound and taped it together with instructions not to remove the bandage—and to get a tetanus shot as quickly as possible.

Despite the pain, he'd returned to the motel. There he found a team of evidence technicians going through Delport's room with detailed precision under Zuker's watchful eye. Ryan learned that once the chase had begun, his partner had persuaded the motel staff to open the door and allow him access, thus granting permission for a search and seizure.

Zuker had also completed the necessary forms for the chain-of-evidence, which allowed them to keep two laptops in the Lumberton Police Department's possession. It had been done before the Feds had arrived and Zuker had promptly removed them to the police vehicle.

Ryan now held one of those computers in his hands as he stood in the hall. One had been an older model, bulky and heavy, while the other was thin and light. He assumed the older model had belonged to Annelise Skovgaard; if she hadn't been technologically savvy, it would make sense that she wouldn't have required the latest and greatest. Jacqueline Janssen, however, would most likely have desired a lightweight model if she frequently traveled. He had taken the older model and Zuker had received the newer one, each ready to perform independent searches and compare their findings the following morning.

As he debated whether to turn toward the living room where the voices continued or move quietly into his study, which was what he truly desired, his thoughts were interrupted.

"There you are!" Cait stepped toward him, leaning in to kiss him. At her lingering touch, he felt the last vestiges of tension seep from him like a storm suddenly ceasing and with it, the last of his energy. He felt utterly and completely depleted.

"I thought I heard the door," she continued. "You said you'd be late, but… Are you okay?" Her last words were spoken as her eyes traveled to his forehead.

"I'm fine," he managed to mumble as she leaned past him to turn on the light.

"You are *not* fine," she said, her brows knitting. She brushed dirt from the back of his shirt. "What happened to you?"

"I thought I'd be hearing himself come in," Claire's voice rang out.

"Ryan's hurt."

"I am not hurt."

"I'd say you are hurt," Claire said as she joined them. "I'll be taking that gadget so Cait can see what's what." She started to take the laptop from Ryan, but he held onto it doggedly.

"I said I'm not hurt."

"Well, I don't recall either of us asking you," his sister said, tugging the laptop out of his hands. "I distinctly recall stating the fact that you are."

"Christ."

"Don't be taking the Lord's name in vain with me," she said, her voice assuming the distinctive quality she used when the girls became too rambunctious. "Now get along with yourself and allow your wife to properly inspect your injury."

"The computer—"

"I'll be putting it in the study, which is where I suppose you were heading?" Without waiting for an answer, she stepped around them and strode down the hall.

As she disappeared into the bedroom he'd turned into his study, Cait took his hand. "Off to the bathroom with you," she ordered, "so I can take a good look at you."

~~~~~

"Good Lord in heaven," Claire said, leaning back in the chair. She dabbed at her eyes. "What a beautiful love story, it is—and tragic all the same."

Ryan sipped coffee that had long ago grown cold. The caffeine coupled with aspirin and whiskey had done wonders to take away his throbbing headache. As a result, he'd been able to concentrate on locating Mrs. Skovgaard's research files and with his sister's help, they'd honed in on the story of an albino in twelfth century Dublin; one they called The White Devil.

"Re," Claire was saying, "this woman—Maeve—I've never known of that name in our family records."

"Neither have I," he agreed. "And I've been scanning them for the better part of the past year. I would have remembered a story such as this."

"What of the others? Daegan, Stiabhan, Keegan and Royan?"

"I do remember them. I'll be locating those records to refresh my memory of who's who. But I'm certain there were just the four brothers—no sister at all."

"Oh, Re." She dabbed at her eyes again. "He was leaving, Re. He meant them no harm."

Ryan stood. His back ached and he realized when he'd jumped from the fence and fallen on the ground, he might have injured his back. Now it seemed petty compared to the fatal injury Baldr had sustained. "It seems absurd."

"Oh, it's more than that. It's cruel. It's—it's murder, is what it is."

He shook his head. "That's not what I meant."

She looked at him with emerald green eyes made more vivid from her tears. "What, then?"

He cracked his knuckles. They were covered in grime that he was just now noticing. He'd nearly forgotten the hours of clambering over junk and debris as they'd become engrossed in Baldr's story. He glanced at his cell phone. It had lain on the desktop, its silence proclaiming that there had been no additional news—which meant they had not found his suspect.

"This occurred over eight hundred years ago," he said, his eyes narrowing.

"It's still cruel."

"But eight hundred years? How could a family carry a grudge for eight hundred years?"

"I'm not certain I'm following you."

"This—Baldr guy—he's a dead ringer for Diallo Delport."

"Oh, that's a poor choice of words."

Ryan half-waved his hand in dismissal. "There must be some relation."

"Do you think so, Re? Or wouldn't you be thinking that every albino on the face of the earth bears the same description? White skin, white hair, light eyes?"

"Tall, short. Fat, thin. Black, white, Hispanic, Asian…"

"Alright, already. But are you supposing that this Diallo Delport is Nordic?"

He shook his head. "South African. But that doesn't mean he isn't a descendant… But nearly a thousand years of hatred? I wouldn't be understanding that."

"It isn't so far-fetched, Re. Think of the Arabs and the Jews. That goes back several thousand years."

"But—there have been things that have continued to occur over the centuries that kept that hatred alive."

"And are you suggesting this is the only clash between our families? How would you know that until you've combed through all the records that happened since?"

He sighed and ran his hand through hair that felt in dire need of washing. "I suppose."

"So," she continued, "Was it Baldr Delport, then?"

"I doubt it. Twelfth century… I don't know if the Vikings were using last names at that time."

"I can answer that."

They both turned to find Tommy and Cait in the doorway.

"How much did you hear?" Ryan asked, his eyes moving to Cait. She looked tired as she leaned her head against the doorframe. There were dark circles under her eyes and she was uncharacteristically subdued.

"Just something about Viking names in the twelfth century," Tommy said, stepping into the room. "You might've forgotten my ancestors were from Norway?"

Ryan chuckled. "With a name like Ericson, how could I forget such a thing?"

"Well, that's just it. In the twelfth century, the Nordic people weren't passing down their surnames. Their names literally meant 'son of'. Ericson meant 'the son of Eric'. My sons would have been 'Thomason' –son of Thomas."

"And our daughters?" Claire asked.

"Dotter," he answered. "Thomasdotter. The daughter of Thomas."

"So, a son and a daughter would have had different last names?" Ryan pressed.

"That's right. And depending upon whom they married, their children would have carried different last names as well."

Ryan started to ask about the specific name of Delport but spotting Cait leaning against the doorframe, he stopped himself. "Cait, my love, you're tired."

Claire glanced at her watch. "Well, it's no wonder. It's closing in on midnight."

"No."

"Yes," Cait said. "And if you all don't mind…"

"Go to bed," Claire said abruptly, standing. "And it's time we should be going home as well."

"I'll help—"

"No, you won't," Ryan said, coming to Cait's side. "Go to bed, darling. I'll help Tommy get the girls in the car, and I'll be back in directly."

"Re's right," Claire said, moving past them into the hall. "You need your sleep, Cait. Those girls of yours will be awake in just a few hours."

Ryan kissed her softly. He wanted to remain there with his lips on hers but reluctantly, he pulled away with a sigh. "Go. And I'll be just a moment."

~~~~~

Ryan snapped Erin into the seat as Tommy finished doing the same with Emma. Both girls had been fast asleep on the sofa in the living room, and neither so much as batted an eye when they were picked up and carried to the minivan. Ah, to be so secure, Ryan thought.

As the back doors closed, he watched as Claire settled into the front seat. Just before she closed the door behind her, he grasped it.

"Claire," he whispered hoarsely.

She glanced at him with startled eyes. "Aye, Re?"

"Don't be telling Cait what we were up to this evening."

"It's not a good idea to keep secrets from your wife, Re."

"You remember what she was like after Delport tried to kill her." His voice caught and he fell silent. He was somewhat surprised that the memory was still as raw and fresh as the day it happened.

"Aye, Re," Claire said quietly. "Long after her body healed, I suspected the emotional trauma had remained."

"The physical pain was but a mere fraction of the suffering she endured." They were happy; he knew they were. But sometimes he discovered Cait looking off into the distance, her eyes clouded and her face ashen, and he knew without asking that she was recalling her ordeal.

Claire's warm hand caressed his cheek, and he realized that his mind was racing through all that had gone before. He met her eyes as he shoved the memories deep into the dark recesses of his mind.

"You can't keep this from her," Claire said gently.

He nodded.

"You'll tell her then?"

He closed the door and looked down the street as she rolled down her window.

"Re?"

"Don't tell her, Claire. Allow me to do it… at the right time."

Her lips parted as though there was more she wanted to say but as Tommy started the engine, she simply nodded. Then her window was rolled up and he was left to watch their taillights disappear into the darkened street.

~~~~~

He thought Cait was asleep when he turned out the light in the bathroom. He'd remained in the shower longer than he'd intended but once the hot water began to pound his shoulders and his back, he'd realized how tense he'd become. Long after he'd cleansed the grime and the blood from his body, he'd lingered, reluctant to leave the warmth, reveling in the way the streams of water caressed his tired muscles.

But as he pulled back the covers and climbed into bed, she rolled over to face him.

"Are you okay?" she asked.

He leaned in to kiss her and smooth her hair away from her face. Her lids were heavy and as she waited for him to respond, she closed her eyes.

"I'm fine, darlin'."

"How did you injure your head?"

"Chasing a suspect."

"Oh, Ryan."

He waited for her to open her eyes before answering. "Don't worry, sweetheart. You can't worry, really; if you concerned yourself every time I left for work… Well, I couldn't do what I do. And you couldn't function, either."

"I know."

He snuggled in beside her, drawing her against his chest.

"Is there anything you want to tell me?" she asked.

He weaved his fingers through her long strands as he kissed her atop her head. "No, darlin'."

He could have sworn he felt her tense against him but she didn't respond. He glanced at the clock on the nightstand; it was nearly one o'clock. In a few short hours, the girls would awaken and another day would begin. A wave of exhaustion rolled over him and he heard his own deep breathing lulling himself to sleep.

22

Ryan tossed his keys on his desk in frustration. "I don't understand it," he grumbled for the umpteenth time. "How could he have gotten away?"

Zuker poured a cup of coffee before returning to his desk across from Ryan's. "We don't know he's not there."

"But they said——"

"——that they hadn't found him yet. But the Feds haven't given up. They still have officers and agents combing the junkyard. In the light of day, he might just turn up."

"I have a feeling he's gone." He pulled out his chair and sat down heavily. "You saw the size of that place; it's several acres. There is no doubt in my mind that while we were searching for him last night, he escaped. There were enough holes in that fence line for an army to march through."

"So where do you suppose he's gone?"

The voice came from across the room. Ryan looked up to find Chief Johnston walking across the detectives' office toward them.

"You know it's Diallo Delport," Ryan said flatly.

"I heard."

"We positively identified him."

"I know."

Ryan drummed his fingers on the top of his desk.

"Let's start at the top," the chief said. "I take it that he's your prime suspect for the murder of three people?"

"That's correct. I'm awaiting forensics but I've no doubt he killed all three."

"And what's his motive?"

Ryan took a deep breath. He glanced at Zuker, who nodded silently. They'd discussed their individual findings on the drive to and from the motel and junkyard and both had arrived at the same conclusion. "Realizing this does not sound logical," he began, "but we believe Mrs. Skovgaard had uncovered information about an ancestor of Diallo Delport's; a man known as The White Devil. I don't know why it should have mattered to him now, as the ancestor lived nearly a thousand years ago—"

"But we believe he killed all three in an effort to stop the publication of the book," Zuker interjected.

"You're right," Chief Johnston said. "It isn't logical."

"But then we realized," Ryan continued, "that we were attempting to apply logic where there was none."

"Go on."

"Logically, it shouldn't matter to anyone living today what their ancestor might have done a thousand years before. Obviously, time marches on and bloodlines survive; otherwise, none of us would be here. But when you view it from a purely emotional level, there could be a strong urge for a man to want to protect his family's… reputation."

Chief Johnston raised one brow quizzically. "Delport's a serial killer. And you're saying he wants to protect his family's reputation?"

"I admit it makes no sense to a reasonable person. But a serial killer has to be a bit warped, wouldn't you think?"

"Did you uncover something about this ancestor?"

"Aye… He was a Viking doing what Vikings did…"

"Meaning," Zuker added, "plundering, raping, fighting, killing—but also discovering new lands, and falling in love in the process."

"Well, I'm sure it's not the falling in love part that Delport would want to hide," the chief said. "So where is Delport now?"

"The FBI and Fayetteville PD spent all night combing through the junkyard but they didn't find him," Ryan answered reluctantly.

"So the FBI's involved?"

"They have jurisdiction over the airport homicide."

"Go on."

"They processed his room and should have gotten some good DNA. Hopefully, it will tie in with forensic evidence from the three crime scenes."

"Any ideas on where he'd go from here? What he'd be planning?"

Zuker and Ryan shook their heads. "We placed a call to the publishing offices in New York," Ryan said. "We're waiting for a return call. What we don't know is how many others might have known the story of The White Devil. But if his motive was to stop the story from being published… well, I'd say he succeeded. The author is dead; so is her publisher and so is the only other historian that might have known something about it."

Chief Johnston glanced around the room. Two detectives were in the far corner conferring quietly, but no one else was within earshot. "O'Clery," he said, turning back to Ryan, "you stated that Mrs. Skovgaard phoned you the night before her murder. She said she had information about *your* family."

"Yes, but—"

"How does Delport's ancestor tie in with you?"

"I don't believe he does. There was mention of a lover he had but she's not in my family tree, that's for certain."

"Dig deeper."

"Pardon?"

"Here's the way this is going to play out. Zuker's the lead on this case. You might be somehow connected." He waved away Ryan's protest. "But whatever happened a thousand years ago doesn't interest me nearly as much as this: Delport tried to kill your wife one year ago. He's committed a string of murders, then and now, and your place is with your wife right now."

Ryan leaned back in his chair. "I want to get this man."

"I know you do. But I'd wager you also want to protect your wife."

"I can protect her by getting him."

"We can protect her by getting him," the chief corrected. "Go home. I'll get a detail assigned to Zuker; the best men I've got."

"But—"

"If you want to help, find out the connection between Delport and you—or his family and yours. Establish a firm motive."

"I'll go bonkers if I'm relegated to my house while someone else is chasing after this guy."

"Just for a day or two. Watch over Cait. We'll keep you informed." He glanced at Zuker. "Won't we?"

23

Though it was early afternoon, the skies had turned a mottled gray and black as the clouds swirled angrily overhead, heralding the approach of a storm. As Ryan climbed out of the police car, a bolt of lightning grazed the skies. Rain would not be far behind.

Zuker assured him once again that they would keep him informed of any new developments. As Ryan closed the car door and watched him drive away, he felt his emotions conflict: he wanted to be there with Cait, and he wanted to protect her and the girls. But he also wanted to get on the street, hunt down Diallo Delport, and stop this insane rampage. He was a man of action, not one to be sent home as a case heated up.

He started up the sidewalk as a single drop of water fell on his shoulder. Instinctively, he moved to brush it off, his eyes roaming from his shoulder to the street beyond. Autumn had arrived quickly. With the approaching storm, the winds had kicked up, sending the red, orange and yellow leaves of fall cascading downward onto dormant brown grass. The world seemed awash in the colors of autumn; gone were the bright greens of summer, along with its multicolored flowers and colorful bushes.

As he glanced down the street, one color caught his eye precisely because it seemed out of place with the hues of the season. It was deep blue and shiny. He stopped and stared at the object, narrowing his eyes to see it better. It was a Ford Mustang parked a block away, the unlit headlights appearing like darkened eyes watching him. He felt a chill race along the back of his neck.

His mind flashed back to a year earlier when he'd seen a Mustang of that exact description; Diallo Delport had been driving it.

"Ryan!"

Cait's voice broke his concentration and he whirled around as she opened the front door a bit wider and stepped onto the stoop.

"What are you doing out here?" he demanded, his voice gruff and strained.

"What are *you* doing out here?" she retorted.

"Get back in the house!" he ordered.

She stopped outside the threshold and stared at him as if he'd gone mad. He took several strong strides toward her as her eyes continued to widen. Another drop fell on his shoulder and then another.

"It's about to storm," he said, forcing his voice to soften. He reached her and placed one hand on her shoulder, turning her back toward the house.

"The mail—"

"I'll get it. You'll get wet."

He nearly pushed her into the foyer. "Shut the door," he ordered before turning back around.

He started down the sidewalk toward the mailbox, his eyes scanning the street. The car was gone.

Startled, he stopped to peer in the vicinity where he'd seen it, but there was no sign it had ever been there. He turned to look in the opposite direction but the street was perfectly clear. It had been facing him, he thought. Had the engine been running at the time? If it had been turned off, he should have heard it start. Wouldn't he?

"Ryan?"

He turned to find Cait standing in the doorway, her expression clearly displaying how baffled she was as she watched him. Before he could turn back around, the skies opened in a torrent.

He dashed to the mailbox and retrieved a bundle of junk mail before rushing back toward the house. He was soaked as he reached the open doorway. Cait had disappeared but once he was inside and the door was closed securely behind him, she reappeared with a towel.

"What are you doing home?" she asked.

He tried to buy some time as he accepted the towel from her and shook the raindrops out of his hair. He wrapped his shoulders in the terrycloth but even as he attempted to dry his clothing, he realized his efforts were futile. Glancing up, he caught Cait watching him. "I'm soaked," he stated flatly.

"I can see that."

"Now aren't you glad you weren't caught in that?"

"Are you home because it's storming?"

He started to retort but realized he would only dig a hole for himself. Instead, he pointed at his head. "I told the chief it was nothing," he said.

"Do you have a headache?" she asked, peering at the bandage which was now soaked through. "Are you dizzy?"

"Of course not," he found himself saying.

"Then why did he send you home?"

He hesitated. "Maybe I have a tad of a headache."

"Oh, for heaven's sake," she said, her tone softening her words. "Get in there and change your clothes." She nodded toward their bedroom. "I'll get some aspirin."

"I don't need aspirin."

"Fine," she said, pushing him toward the bedroom. "I suppose you want your Connemara Irish whiskey then?"

"Wouldn't be a bad idea come to think of it."

She rolled her eyes. "Go. Dry off. And I'll get your drink." She chuckled as she started in the opposite direction toward the kitchen. "Truth is," she called over her shoulder, "I'm glad you're home. I could use some company."

As she disappeared through the doorway, he pulled the sheers away from the window closest to the door. The rain was driving hard as it pounded against the glass, and he was hard pressed to see anything beyond it. But as he allowed the curtains to drop back into place, he knew he had not imagined the bright blue Mustang.

~~~~~

Dee screamed as if the devil himself was after her. She was balanced against Ryan's broad shoulder, her hands bunched into the cloth he'd positioned beneath her. Amazed at her powerful lungs, he stopped in the middle of the living room to observe her expansive mouth, her toothless gums in full view as she shrieked. Tears poured down her face.

"Good Lord," he said, though he was certain that Cait could not hear him above the ruckus, "if I came across a child like this screaming like a banshee, I'd be convinced the parent was guilty of child abuse."

Cait pulled back the seat cushions from the sofa. "Where is that pacifier?" she demanded, her brows knit.

"It can't be far," he insisted as he scoured the playpen. "It's never far from her."

Darcy remained propped up in her baby seat, happily smacking her own pacifier and appearing oblivious to the frenzy around her.

"Here it is," Cait said as she turned over a baby blanket. She hurried to the kitchen sink to rinse it off, peering at them across the island that separated the kitchen from the living room.

Ryan joined her. As she popped the pacifier into Dee's mouth, he said, "If I didn't have a headache before, I certainly have one now."

Cait began to laugh.

"Seriously," he said, "we're going to have us quite a problem once this thing wears out."

"Hopefully, that won't be any time soon."

"Good God."

"So coming home might not have been such a good thing for your headache?"

As his daughter pressed her face against him, contentedly sucking the pacifier, he looked down at Cait to find her chuckling, her eyes twinkling. "Will she sleep now?" he asked. "I need a break, I do."

"I'm surprised at you," she giggled. "You usually aren't so easily rattled."

He carried her to the playpen and laid her down on the soft mat. As he gently covered her legs with a baby blanket, she closed her eyes. A moment later, Cait deposited Darcy beside her. The girls each grasped their pacifiers as though to shove it against their mouths while their free hands found each other.

Cait handed him a glass of amber liquid. "Here. You look like you could use this."

~~~~~

"So what do you have?" Ryan asked. He cradled his cell phone between his chin and his shoulder as he continued to study the document on his laptop screen.

"Not much," Zuker answered. "Ernest and Kiesha are working your neighborhood; they've driven every street all afternoon but they haven't seen any Ford Mustangs—blue or otherwise."

Ryan swore under his breath.

"We also ran a DMV check and there are no Mustangs registered anywhere in your neighborhood. You sure that's what you saw?"

He closed his eyes and visualized the vehicle sitting against the curb just a block from his house. "Positive."

"But you didn't see anyone inside it?"

"I didn't get a good look. I—was interrupted."

"I see. Well, we'll check with the rental car agencies also."

"What about Fayetteville PD?"

"They've got all their officers alerted. They want to make an arrest for that murder at the airport."

"Aye. I'd be supposing it isn't good for business to have a murder in the airport ladies room."

"No. I'd suppose it isn't."

"And forensics?"

"Yeah… About forensics."

Ryan waited for his partner to continue but the silence dragged on. He cocked his head and listened for any sign that Cait was awakening from her nap. "What about forensics?" he asked.

"They'd like to know if you could stop by tomorrow for a DNA swab."

"Pardon?"

There was an awkward silence followed by, "Well, you know they picked up a hair at Mrs. Skovgaard's home and another at Petrironcalli's."

"So?"

"They're both black."

"And they think they're mine?" His voice rose.

"Calm down, O'Clery. They just want to know if they are yours. If they're not, then we could be looking at another suspect."

"We have our suspect," he insisted.

"I know that and you know that. But we can't go into court on a hunch. We need solid evidence."

"But Delport doesn't have black hair."

"You think?"

Ryan exhaled sharply. "So what does it prove, these black hairs?"

"Are you refusing?"

"No. I'm not refusing. I'm just—"

"Pissed. Yeah. I get it."

"I'll come by in the morning."

"What did you tell Cait?" Zuker asked.

"About what?"

"About you being home. What did you think I was talking about?"

He thought he heard the recliner pop back into place and he hesitated while he listened. "I told her I was sent home with a headache."

Zuker guffawed. "That's something a *girl* would say."

"Oh, for Christ's sake."

"Don't tell me she bought it. Cait's smarter than that."

"Yes, as a matter of fact, she did. And you're giving me a worse headache than I've got." He heard light footsteps on the hardwood floors. "Listen, Zuk, I've got to go. Call me if you get anything?"

"Will do."

Ryan clicked off the phone and rotated his desk chair to find Cait standing in the door. "Did I awaken you?"

She shook her head sleepily. "What awakened me was reaching for you and not finding you there."

He rose and stepped to her, pulling her to him. "I'm sorry, love. This case I'm working; it's just on my mind, is all."

She pushed back slightly to peer up at him. "Is there anything you want to tell me?"

"Aye. I want to tell you how very much I love you."

She tilted her head and raised one brow. "Is that all?"

He feigned surprise. "Isn't that enough, my love for you?"

The sound of a baby fretting broke their standoff, and Cait backed away. "How's your head?" she asked as she entered the hall.

"Oh… Still hurting."

"Must be a hell of a headache for the chief to send you home."

"Oh, it's massive."

Her response was lost amid the baby's cries. He listened for a moment but satisfied that Cait had everything under control, he turned back to Mrs. Skovgaard's computer.

24

Duiblinn, 1172

Maeve's scream pierced the night air. It was borne of wrenching pain and tapered off to an exhausted cry that wracked a body swollen with child. Her long hair was soaked and clung to her skin. The bedding on the narrow cot was as drenched as if the storm that raged outside had breached the roof over her head.

There was barely enough room for the two women who attended her; the home that Maeve shared with her family was tiny, consisting of two bedrooms and a cooking and eating space. The four boys shared one bedroom and her parents another. Being the only daughter, Maeve occupied a rearranged pantry which had been furnished with a small bed and a diminutive chest of drawers.

She was vaguely aware that her father and brothers were just on the other side of the wall, most likely seated at the table next to a stone fireplace. But while the outside air was chilled and turbulent with the deepest and darkest of winter days, the room in which Maeve labored felt oppressive, hot and stifling.

"The babe is breeched," the midwife stated, her flat voice confirming her own exhaustion. "Do not push and I will try to right it."

Maeve's mother soaked a piece of linen in a bowl before wringing it out and wiping her daughter's forehead. She worked with pursed lips and lined eyes, avoiding Maeve's pain-filled, inquisitive eyes. It had been this way since her belly had begun to round; after that first night of accusations, of her mother's tears and her father's wrath, of her brothers' indignation and raucously expressed disappointment, they had all avoided looking in her eyes, as if they went through the motions but no longer felt anything for her.

"I say, do not push," the midwife said again.

Maeve spoke through gritted teeth. "I do not push. But the child does. I cannot stop the babe from strugglin'."

The child felt as if it ripped her in two, and she screamed as the midwife attempted to right the shoulders. She heard the woman mumbling but only when the labor pain ceased for the briefest moment did she hear the words. "It is a boy, and he is a large one. His shoulders are so broad…"

Maeve collapsed against the thin, straw-filled mattress, exhausted and spent. Labor pains had begun the previous evening as the sun set and a massive storm moved in. They had continued throughout the night, her moans cloaked in the growing winds and pounding rains that arrived with a vengeance. The morning dawned with skies a bright red, heralding another day of unrelenting squalls. Both the storm and her pains continued without respite. The sun had long ago set once more; but with no end in sight from the cruel misery and the harsh tempest, she realized she could die here giving birth to Baldr's son. Her lips moved in a silent prayer, a prayer she had mouthed incessantly. She loved this child. He was Baldr's child. Despite the difficulties, despite the torment, despite the storm that raged inside and out, she prayed that he would be born soon, and he would be healthy. He was all she had left in this punitive, unsympathetic world.

"Ah," the midwife breathed.

The pain began again, but this time she shouted to Maeve, "Push, Maeve. Push with all ye 've. The babe is righted now. Push 'im out."

With a guttural, agonizing scream, she leaned forward on her elbows, bending nearly double to push the child out of her. He felt as though he was completely stretched out from her hips to her breasts, and giving birth to him felt more like her own insides were turning inside out.

Then with a final torturous wail, she felt the relief of her child slipping from her. The midwife caught him in her hands. "Oh," she breathed.

Maeve wanted nothing more than to lie back upon the mattress and sleep the sleep of the dead with her babe in her arms, but at the woman's hushed voice, she rose higher still to look at her. The woman's face had blanched, her mouth open in a small, round "o", her eyes wide.

"Does he live?" Maeve asked.

The woman did not look at her, as if she was unable to tear her eyes away from the babe.

"Does he live?" Maeve demanded.

At that moment, the child cried out. His voice was strong, loud, insistent. It was the most beautiful voice she had ever heard.

She reached her hands out to take him, but Maeve's mother seized the child from the midwife. The pursed lips had grown tighter, the eyes filling with tears, the cheeks twitching. She did not turn toward Maeve but removed the babe from the room, the thin door slamming shut behind her.

"M' child," Maeve wept. "Bring me m' child."

Mere moments passed before the door from the kitchen flung open, banging against the opposite wall. Royan strode in, despite the fact that Maeve was still situated in a birthing position. He pushed past the midwife to come to Maeve's side. With narrowed eyes and a convulsing jaw, he struck her full in the face.

She was slammed against the bed, the shock of her brother's assault intermingling with the physical trauma of the birth and the emotional upheaval that threatened her sanity. He struck her again across her right cheek and again across her left, until her head was lolling back and forth.

The midwife began to cry and pulled at Royan's outstretched arms. "She is not done," she pleaded with him. "Leave her be until she is done. I beseech ye, Royan, do not do this!"

The door to the home flew open, allowing a blast of frigid air and sheets of rain to spread through the kitchen into Maeve's room, and she realized that with Royan's entrance, the door remained open to her birthing. Then the outer door closed just as suddenly, leaving the chill of the night swirling about them.

"Ye whore!" Royan shouted, striking her again. "Ye bedded Hvitr Bard, the devil hisself!"

"Give me m' child," Maeve cried. "I want to see m' babe!"

"Ye'll ne'er lay eyes on the monster," Royan spat. "Keegan 'as taken it."

"Keegan—why?"

"I have ordered Keegan to kill the bastard."

"No!"

"It is the devil's spawn. How could ye?" He wiped his forehead as if a headache had formed.

Through the nightmare that surrounded her, Maeve had a sudden vision of clarity. Royan stood beside her, his face contorted with rage and despair. At the foot of her bed stood her mother, tears streaming down her face, her head shaking in resignation. Beside her was her father, his face ruddy, his lips twitching as if he wanted to speak but the words would not come. Daegan and Stiabhan stood in the doorway, their bodies shoulder to shoulder. None seemed to care that she was bloodied and raw. It was as if they had all caught her in the act of having sex with Baldr at that very moment. Their faces reflected a myriad of emotions: gross disappointment, distress, anger, sadness. But all love for her was gone; there were none who inquired about her welfare; none who cared about her babe.

"Keegan has left with m' child?" It was both a question and a statement; her voice sounded disembodied.

"Aye," Royan said, clenching his fists. "The child is dead now."

She no longer felt the pain searing through her body. She sat straight up and when she spoke, her voice was deep and dark, the words coming from her as if she had been possessed.

"This is the day," she said, her voice rising and strengthening with each word, "that each one o' ye is cursed. From this day forward, every woman any one o' you shall love shall forcibly be taken from ye." She raised her chin in defiance. "Ye shall raise yer children w'out their mothers, and they shall inherit the same curse as ye. The sins o' their fathers—o' each one o' ye—shall be upon their heads, and their children's heads."

As they stared dumbstruck, her voice continued as if it was controlled by another being, one stronger than any of them. "Ye and yer descendants shall always know the hell ye brought upon yerselves this day."

Her voice had continued to rise with each carefully enunciated word, growing stronger and louder. It had not registered on her anguished mind that the storm was continuing to grow in intensity, but with her final words the door flew open in the outer room of its own accord. Sheets of rain breached the outer room, spreading into her tiny bedroom and pelting them all with sleet that pounded them like an angry beehive. "Each o' ye," she spat, her words blending with the unforgiving, vicious winds, "is cursed forevermore!"

25

North Carolina

Ryan wiped a tear from the corner of his eye and then studied it pensively against his fingertip. He didn't know when he'd last cried; it might have been the morning he found Cait on the Outer Banks, unconscious and barely alive. It might have been on one of the seemingly endless nights he held her in his arms, soothed her fears and rocked her to sleep. Or it might have been the day he held both his children in his arms and thanked God that he'd not only been reunited with his eternal soul mate but he'd been given the gift of two beautiful baby girls.

He could not imagine the anguish Maeve endured.

But Diallo Delport was not Baldr. They were as dissimilar as he, Ryan O'Clery, and either of the two men.

Baldr might have been a marauder but in the light of historical reference, he'd done what Vikings did. He might have fought and killed but he was also a man who loved deeply. He'd found his soul mate in Maeve, and she'd found hers in him.

What if something had befallen himself? Ryan wondered. What if Cait had been forced to continue living without him in a family that had replaced love with hatred, acceptance with condemnation?

And then, what if his child had been born, only to be wrenched from her mother and murdered?

It was unimaginable.

How does a woman continue living after that?

He stood and walked to the window, where he stared outside without really seeing. How could his ancestors have murdered an innocent babe?

He knew from his study of his ancestry that Keegan was a grandfather eight hundred years back. Keegan, the youngest of the four brothers, had been ordered by the eldest to murder his sister's child.

No wonder Diallo Delport wanted him to suffer.

Wait, he thought, catching himself. He, Ryan O'Clery, had not murdered Maeve's child. He had nothing to do with that barbaric decision. Had he been placed in a similar situation today, he would have physically fought Royan and protected the child. He would have defended Maeve the same as he'd protect Claire today; she would have always had a roof over her head, food in her belly and love from his heart. He was not Royan Kelly.

And Diallo Delport was not Baldr.

He heard the faint cries of his girls down the hall, but he wasn't yet ready to tear himself away from his thoughts. He felt immersed in Mrs. Skovgaard's manuscript, Maeve's star-crossed love, in her ill-fated life. He felt her pain as if it had been his own.

He forced himself to step back. Assuming the detective's role and attempting to shed his emotions so he could think more clearly, everything seemed to come together. Maeve lived. He didn't know how long her life had been or if she had found another love and had other children. But somehow her story had been passed down—not through Ryan's lineage but through Delport's.

Wait. He cocked his head as if listening to the voice of an ancestor speaking to him from the spirit world. He didn't want to absorb what his mind, his heart and his soul was shouting for him to hear:

He, Ryan O'Clery, was related to Diallo Delport.

His skin began to crawl and his blood felt as if it was turning to ice.

It couldn't be.

But it was.

Maeve had been removed from his family records, eliminated as though she had never existed. And yet, he thought as he glanced back at Mrs. Skovgaard's computer, the noted historian had not only discovered her story but also had connected her lineage with Ryan; both had led back to Keegan's and Maeve's father.

Ryan didn't believe in curses. He didn't believe that Maeve had gone from a loving woman to an accomplished sorceress. But what did make complete and total sense was that she had passed down her hatred—a hatred that, he had to admit, was completely understandable—and she had also passed down the words she'd uttered at the time her babe was taken from her.

More than six hundred years later, Rían Kelly was unwittingly the victim of Maeve's descendent—for surely she must have had another child—and almost two hundred years after Rían, he would have fought the battle of his life to keep Cait from falling prey to another descendent.

How many others might there have been? He gazed at the volumes of family history that lined his bookshelves. Would he find one after another, dating back nearly a thousand years? Could her suffering have morphed into torment for nearly every generation since the twelfth century?

What possible reason might Diallo Delport have had to keep this secret from the world? Maeve had done nothing wrong— except, perhaps, love the wrong man. But one loves the person who is meant for them, he thought. The fact that she'd fallen in love with a Viking made no difference. He was her soul mate.

If anything, bringing her story into the light would be a type of vindication. Would it not? Delport could have shined a bright light on a dark past that even Ryan had never known existed.

Then why kill the historian—two of them, in fact, plus an editor—who was ready to tell the world of her love story?

He crossed back to his desk and picked up his cell phone. He would have to consider all of this some other time. Right now, he needed to think like the detective he was. He now had a motive for Delport's slaying of the three people—and the murders that had taken place a year before, *and* his attempted murder of Cait.

His finger paused above the speed dial. He would notify Zuker of his finding. It would place a direct connection between Delport and himself. The notion sickened him but it couldn't be helped. They had to be such distant relatives anyway, he tried to assure himself, that the blood connection really didn't matter beyond Delport's warped senses.

He looked up to find Cait watching him from the doorway.

"Did you hear me?" she asked.

He crossed the room in long strides, taking her into his arms and burying his face against her soft shoulder. He caught the briefest glimpse of her widened eyes and when he drew back, he avoided her quizzical gaze as he pressed his lips against hers.

"What's gotten into you?" she managed to whisper when they at last stopped to catch their breath. "Are you okay?"

"I'm fine, my love. I will always be fine with you by my side."

She placed an open palm against his cheek and rubbed her thumb against his skin. "I love you, Ryan O'Clery. I love you more than Life itself."

He held her tightly and tried to exorcise the vision of Maeve in Baldr's arms, of the soft-spoken Irish lass deeply and passionately in love with the White Devil of Dublin. Finally, he pulled back.

"What was it you were saying?" he asked.

"What—oh, when I came to the door." She laughed softly. "I'd almost forgotten. See what you do to me? I'd planned to go to the grocery this afternoon. Since you're home, I was wondering if you felt like going with us?"

26

"Ryan, are you sure you're okay?"

Cait's voice should have jolted him back to the present but Ryan's mind was so deeply entrenched in the implications of what he'd read that her prodding was barely a nudge.

"Ryan?"

He realized she had a package in her hands, and he interrupted his thoughts long enough to take the box of disposable diapers from her and add it to the shopping cart. "That it?"

She glanced over her list. "That's it." She began to push the double stroller down the aisle. He hesitated briefly before catching up to her with the cart.

"Thank you for doing this with me," she said. "Your head must still be hurting?"

"I'm fine," he said. "Just a bit preoccupied."

"Is that what it is?" she asked, smiling slyly.

"Besides," he continued, forcing himself out of his thoughts, "I enjoy spending time with you and the girls. To be quite honest, I can't imagine how you manage the shopping by yourself."

"Oh, I have a system when I'm alone." She chuckled. "I put one of the girls in the sling on my back and the store has baby seats that I use for the other in the front of the cart. You do what you have to do."

They stopped behind an elderly woman with a handful of coupons. Ryan glanced at the other registers; his height gave him an advantage of almost a bird's-eye-view of the length of each line. Realizing they'd selected the shortest, he settled back to wait his turn. With the girls both asleep in the stroller, there was little to do but people watch.

Law enforcement officers were trained to look for trouble, he realized. He glanced down the aisle behind him and watched two teenagers giggling as they looked through massage oils. There was shoplifting, for example. The quick movement that deposited an item into an open pocketbook or bag… the coat that seemed a bit too large, especially in one particular area… or the person whose eyes were shifty as if they were memorizing where each of the employees were and what they were doing.

The teenagers selected two massage oils and joined another line.

He turned his attention to the register as the lady in front of them finished. He dutifully pushed the cart into the open area where the cashier passed each item across the scanner. Cait had moved to the other end of the register, where she was pulling out her wallet. He moved to her opposite side, which had him facing back toward the register.

Above the cashier was a security mirror. At first, he thought it was strange because it should have been facing the store's interior. But as a woman paused outside to look at some sale items, he realized the mirror faced the sidewalk sale in front of the store.

He looked beyond the woman to the skies. It had remained overcast. The trees at the edge of the parking lot swayed and bowed as substantial gusts caught them. His eyes continued to roam across the mirror; it was rectangular and provided a good view of the sidewalk. Someone had paid attention to security details, he thought.

His eyes landed on a man standing on the other side of a table piled high with autumn flowers. He noticed the boots first; they were large work boots meant for a sizable man. As his eyes moved lazily up the figure, he took in the jeans; they did not appear to be work jeans, faded and worn, but these actually had a crease in them, which he found interesting. The man stepped beside the table and Ryan registered massive thighs that seemed to strain at the denim.

By the time he got to the man's chest, he realized the man was facing him as if he might be returning Ryan's scrutiny in the security mirror. Keeping his eyes veiled as only law enforcement officers seemed able to do, he quickly moved upward to his face.

He felt the blood drain from his head and an icy sensation rushed through his veins. The man had locked eyes with him. His brain did not want to accept what his eyes saw. Ryan leaned into the mirror, his eyes narrowing and his brows creasing.

Diallo Delport.

He whirled around, but the man was gone.

A part of his brain registered Cait's voice as she spoke to the cashier. Another part quickly gained control, pushing him to act purely on instinct. He approached the front windows with great strides, his eyes darting from the table to the sidewalk to the parking lot. He was there. He could not have simply disappeared.

He started toward the door.

"Ryan?"

At the sound of Cait's voice, he half-turned. "I'm getting the car."

"But—the cart—"

"I'll come back in and get it." Then he stopped and turned back to look her in the eye. "Stay here."

Her eyes widened and her brows furrowed. Undoubtedly, he'd used a tone of voice she didn't like but there was nothing to be done with it now. He hurried through the door and stopped on the sidewalk. His eyes took in the sidewalk from one end to the other; there were several shoppers going through the sale merchandise, but no sign of Diallo Delport.

He stepped to the curb. The parking lot wasn't packed but it was full enough; he could be there, inside any of the vehicles—or crouched alongside one.

He heard the automatic doors behind him and he whirled around to see Cait pushing the stroller through. "I said, stay inside!" His voice was a roar and several of the ladies shopping turned to glare at him. Cait stopped. Stunned, she hesitated only a moment and then backed into the store. She waited on the other side of the glass. Even from this distance, he could tell she was biting her lower lip.

He cursed under his breath as he made his way to their parked vehicle. The driver's side was opposite to the store and as he approached it, he peered not only at each side but at the cars surrounding theirs. For an enormous man, Delport was swift and he knew he could easily jump him with his Taser ready.

He hit the *Unlock* button on his key fob. As he got into the vehicle, he glanced back at Cait. He didn't see her, and his blood began to pump more stringently. He had to assume she was remaining just inside the door. Certainly, Delport would not attack in plain sight of so many witnesses.

The girls. His blood grew cold and then hot and then cold again. Christ Almighty, his girls were with Cait.

He was inside the car and had it started in record time. He thrust the vehicle into reverse and slammed his foot on the gas pedal. Behind him, the loud, rude sound of a honking horn caused him to smash his foot to the brake. He cursed again as a slow-moving car rolled behind him, the driver eyeing him as if he'd lost his mind.

He whipped out behind him, passing the other vehicle in the parking lot, before shifting into the pickup lane in front of the store. Almost before the car had come to a stop, he leapt out. He was inside the store in a flash. Cait remained just inside with the stroller in front of her and the cart beside her.

"Get behind me," he ordered, grabbing the stroller.

"What are you doing?" Cait hissed, the blood rising to her cheeks.

He didn't respond but pushed the stroller through the doors. He was feet from the vehicle and feet from Cait, who followed with the cart. As she joined him, he remained beside her, his eyes panning the sidewalk in front of them.

"Get in the car," he said.

As she climbed in, he handed Darcy to her.

"Ryan, you know we don't—"

"Don't argue with me," he snapped as he shoved the child onto her lap. He slammed the door before quickly opening the back door directly behind her. As he deposited Dee into her car seat, he said, "Lock the doors as soon as I close the door. Are you understanding me?"

"I understand." She didn't turn around but her voice was strong and steady.

He closed the door and heard the pop of the locks.

He grabbed the empty stroller and the cart and hurried to the back of the car. He worked quickly, his head feeling as though it swiveled in all directions as he tried to keep an eye on his back as well as the trunk of the car. He folded the stroller and slid it inside and then rapidly tossed each of the grocery bags in behind it. He left the cart behind the car as he approached the driver's side. Once even with the door, he hit his key fob once to open only the driver's door. Then he hastily opened the door and slid inside, locking it behind him.

He took a deep breath. He kept one hand on the steering wheel as he peered into his rearview mirror. Then he started up the car.

He was quiet as he moved through the parking lot. In his peripheral vision, he registered that Cait was sitting silently beside him. Darcy fretted in her lap and she tried to appease her with a pacifier. Behind them, Dee fretted as well, as if she realized her sister was not in her customary seat.

He wanted to drive back through the parking lot, perhaps up and down the aisles of parked cars, but he thought better of it. He wasn't in his police car. He had his wife and children with him, and the most important task was to get them home safely.

Once he'd made the decision, he sped through the neighborhood. He could feel tension growing in the small confines of the vehicle. He spotted their house ahead and didn't slow as he swerved into the driveway. He hit the remote to open the garage door and only slowed long enough to avoid hitting it as it glided upward. Once inside, he hit the remote again, waiting for the door to close behind him before he turned off the ignition.

"Stay here," he ordered. "Lock the doors. If you need me, hit the panic button on the remote."

Cait nodded silently.

He didn't have time to see whether she still bit her lip, or if her eyes were narrowed in that you've-done-something-inexcusable look that women could effortlessly attain. He slipped out of the car, waited for the pop of the lock, and then entered the house.

He moved from room to room, checking closets and under furniture. His weapon was above the refrigerator and he grabbed it along with the clip as he moved through. He loaded it as he walked, his eyes sweeping through each room, expertly clearing it before moving on to the next.

Finally, he returned to the garage.

He realized he still held his gun in his hand and he shoved it into his waistband. He unlocked the doors with his key fob and walked around to Cait's door. Opening it, he reached inside and pulled Darcy into his arms. As he drew the small child to him, he realized that his heart was pounding and adrenaline was rushing through him.

"Are you alright?" he asked as Cait stepped out of the vehicle.

She nodded wordlessly as she moved to unbuckle Dee.

He followed her into the house. They deposited the girls into their playpen, where they grasped at one another.

"Do you mind telling me what that was all about?" Cait asked. She cocked her head and peered at him as if she was trying to read his mind.

"My apologies if I alarmed you," he said. He tried willing his heart to beat more slowly. "And my apologies if I snapped at you."

"Apologies accepted. But I still want to know what all that was about."

He moved toward the kitchen. The door into the garage stood open in the laundry room and he stopped at the island between the kitchen and the living room. His eyes remained on the open door, and his ears were tuned to the girls cooing behind him.

"I spotted a suspect in the parking lot," he said.

"A suspect."

"Aye." He turned to look at her. Her eyes were the color of a stormy sea; they stared at him now with an intensity that was difficult to deflect. "That's right. A dangerous suspect."

"You might have told me."

"I didn't have time to explain."

"I see."

He nodded toward the living room. "Stay in here, Cait. Keep your eyes on the girls. And I'll empty the car."

He moved more methodically as he approached the garage. He'd checked the house; it was clear. There was no way Delport could have beaten him there.

He grabbed two bags from the trunk. How did he disappear so quickly? He'd been staring right at him in the store mirror. In the split second it took to whirl around, he was gone. Had he imagined it?

He deposited the bags on the kitchen counter and returned to the car for two more. He couldn't have imagined it. Not a chance.

Gunnar the Draugr, his brain seemed to mock. *The ghost*.

He could feel Cait's eyes on him as he moved back and forth from the car to the kitchen. She remained on the other side of the island, only a few feet away from the playpen.

He finished with the last bag and closed and locked the door leading into the garage.

"I have a call to make," he said, brushing past her. "Are you fine with unpacking the groceries?"

"Sure," she said.

He moved rapidly through the living room. Entering the front foyer, he checked the deadbolt on the front door before moving down the hallway toward the bedrooms. He slipped into his study, and he hurriedly dialed Zuker's cell phone.

His partner answered on the second ring.

"I just spotted Diallo Delport," he stated.

"Where?"

"The grocery."

"He was buying groceries?"

"Outside the store."

"Which one?"

Ryan rattled off the name and the cross-streets.

"Did you attempt to pursue him?" Zuker asked.

"I couldn't. Cait and the girls were with me."

"Are you still there?"

"Negative. I came home."

"You came home and then you called me?" Zuker's annoyance was palpable.

"Don't get cheeky with me," Ryan retorted in defense. "My first priority was to get my family to a safe place."

"And you couldn't have phoned while you were driving?"

"You're wasting time," he snarled. He exhaled sharply. "I apologize. It's just—"

"Hold on."

Ryan ran his hand through his hair as he approached the front window. While he waited, he parted the slats in the blinds and peered down the street in one direction and then in the other. There was no sign of Delport or the blue Mustang. He forced himself to take several deep breaths while he waited. Finally, his heart rate appeared to be slowing.

"O'Clery," Zuker said.

"Aye."

"I'm on my way and I've notified Dispatch. We'll have the area covered. How long ago was it?"

"Ten minutes."

Zuker swore. "He could be nearing the South Carolina state border by now."

"But he isn't," Ryan insisted. "Delport is here. He's in this town and he's watching me and my family." Aggravated, he pushed his fingers through his hair again as he turned around.

Cait stood in the doorway. Her eyes met his coolly.

He clicked off the phone.

"A suspect?" Cait said.

"I didn't want to alarm you."

"I have a right to know, Ryan. Delport tried to kill me, in case you've forgotten."

"I'd never forget that."

She pointed down the hall. "Those are my children," she said, her voice trembling. "If there is any threat to their welfare, I have a right to know."

He stepped toward her.

She held up her palm as if to stop him. "I have a right to know, Ryan."

"I understand. I only meant to protect you."

She abruptly turned and walked back toward the living room.

"Don't walk away from me," Ryan called as he followed her into the hall.

Her stride didn't slow as she turned into the living room.

In a few quick steps, he had caught up with her. He reached out and grasped her by the arm.

As she whirled around, she said, "You had no right to keep this from me."

"I had every right," he countered. "You and the girls are my responsibility."

"No, Ryan. The four of us are *our* responsibility. Ours as a team, a partnership."

"I didn't want to alarm you—"

"Stop treating me like I am some delicate flower that's going to fall apart in the first stiff wind." He started to speak, but she held up her hand to quiet him. "I've been through a lot. *We've* been through a lot. And the one thing you should have learned about me is I'm tough. I'm resilient."

"My intentions were good."

"They were misplaced. Put your detective's cap on, Ryan. Would you advise a victim to keep something like this secret from their spouse?"

He leaned back on his heels. "No, but—"

"Then why on earth would you try to keep it secret from me? Don't answer that," she hastened to add. "I can't help to protect our children if I don't know of the threat."

"Don't be angry with me, Cait."

She wrenched her arm away from him and continued through the living room to the kitchen. Without speaking, she slid a footstool in front of the refrigerator and climbed onto it, opening the cabinets above the appliance.

"What are you doing?" he asked as she pulled a pistol from the cabinet.

"It's my gun," she said unapologetically. "I had it long before I met you."

He watched as she pulled out a box of ammunition. Then she brought both to the island and began loading the clip.

"But what are you doing? Surely, you don't think you can find him yourself—"

She whirled around to face him. "No, Ryan, I don't. But I do think he'll find *me*. And when he does, I won't be caught unarmed."

"But—" He waved his hand toward the girls. "You can't be toting a pistol in one hand and a babe in another. What if it went off? What if one of the girls—"

"Accidentally fired it? Look at them, Ryan. They can barely hold their heads up by themselves. You think they're going to grab this gun and pull the trigger?"

"But…" His voice faded and he stood silently watching her. She loaded one clip, inserted it into the pistol, and then loaded a second clip. "Do you know how to use it?" he asked.

"I wouldn't own it if I didn't know how to shoot."

"But—could you shoot to kill? It isn't like the movies, Cait. You don't shoot a pistol like a Sig Sauer once and the bad guy falls back dead. He'll keep coming and injuring him could only enrage him."

"Like he's not enraged enough as it is?" She laid the pistol and the spare clip on the countertop. "I want to know everything that you know, Ryan. And don't pull that crap that it's a case you're working. This isn't a *case*. This is us we're talking about."

He nodded in resignation. "I'll show you what I've been piecing together."

"Catch this guy, Ryan. Put him away for the rest of his life." She looked at him with wide, moist eyes.

"I will, Cait. I won't rest until I do."

Darcy began to fret. As he watched her make her way to the playpen and lift their daughter into her arms to soothe her, he knew he would do much more than simply put him in prison.

First, he had to find Diallo Delport. And then he had to kill him.

27

Ryan closed the front door behind him as he stepped onto the front stoop with Zuker. The stormy skies had given way to an early dusk, casting the neighborhood into the final vestiges of red and orange. The street lamp at the corner had begun to flicker on and he found himself seeking out the other lights and determining their proximity to his house.

"So," Zuker was saying, "obviously the chief has made this case the department's highest priority. When the second shift came on, every officer was briefed on Delport. Everyone is looking for him."

Ryan nodded. "And the stake-out?"

"Ernest has the front," he said as he acknowledged the marked police car in front of the house. "Kiesha is at the corner where she's got a view of the back. Nothing's going to happen to Cait and the girls here, O'Clery. The whole department's got your back."

"I'm not understanding how he does it," Ryan said quietly. "He seems to appear out of nowhere and then he disappears just as quickly—without a trace." He narrowed his eyes and scanned the block. The trees were twisting and weaving in the growing wind and every movement put him more on edge. "It's as if he was an apparition—a ghost." At the sound of his own words spoken aloud, he felt a wave of apprehension flow through him. Gunnar the Draugr, he thought. The ghost.

"He won't get away this time," Zuker said.

"How many has he murdered?" Ryan contemplated. "Three women last year—"

"Three people this year," his partner finished.

"Fayetteville is also on full alert, I suppose?"

"Absolutely. In fact, there are alerts on all the electronic Interstate signs. State police have him as a top priority, also. The evening news programs are doing stories on him tonight."

"And when the shifts change?" he asked, nodding toward Ernest's police car.

"We'll have you covered all night."

"How long can this go on?" He didn't expect an answer; he knew it couldn't continue indefinitely. There would be other cases. Eventually, he'd have to return to work where he'd have busy days and a growing list of assignments. Sooner or later, Cait would be left alone to care for the girls. She'd want to sit in the back yard and soak up the sun's rays, run errands around town and do what mothers do—without the fear that a killer was waiting for the right opportunity to strike. It couldn't go on for long, he reasoned. He wouldn't allow it to go on for long.

"Try to get some rest," Zuker was saying as he started down the sidewalk toward his waiting patrol car. "Let us do our jobs, and you just take care of Cait and the girls."

"Aye," Ryan said. "I'll be doing just that." He watched as his partner started his car and drove off slowly with a slight wave of his hand. I'll be taking care of my girls, he thought, to the last breath I take.

~~~~~

Ryan placed each of the girls into their individual plastic baby tubs and left them on the floor beside him as he knelt to fill the bathtub with water. He poured a generous amount of liquid baby soap under the faucet and monitored the temperature as he allowed an inch or so of water to accumulate before turning off the faucet and covering it with a soft plastic mermaid. Though the girls were too small and too young to move outside their miniscule tubs yet, he felt more relaxed knowing the brightly colored mermaid would keep them from hitting their tiny heads against the hard metal faucet.

It brought back memories of Emma and Erin when they were this small, though he quickly realized that his own girls had been born much smaller than his nieces. Still, he'd babysat them from the time they were a week old, giving his sister and brother-in-law much needed breaks. Soon, Claire and Tommy would do the same for him and Cait.

Satisfied the water was the right temperature and depth, he placed Darcy into the water first, plastic tub and all. She began to fret as soon as her sister was out of view and Ryan soothed her as he turned to lift Dee. As soon as the girls spotted each other once again, they began kicking their plump little legs and cooing to one another.

He always placed them so they faced each other and as they made sounds only the other twin understood, he splashed some water across their bodies and gently cleaned them. He'd removed his shirt before beginning and as always, it was only a matter of time before his chest was as wet as they were.

He spoke to them as he poured a teaspoon of shampoo into his large hands and lathered up. Then he softly brushed his hands over their heads. Darcy did indeed look just like him, he thought, with her head full of black hair and her large green eyes. She was Irish through and through. Dee resembled her mother except for those startling blue eyes. They almost always disarmed him with their alertness, like there was an adult in there somewhere. He raced his thumb over the birthmark on her cheek; it might have appeared round except for the little dip at the bottom. It was almost like a tear. It was beautiful, he thought. *They* were beautiful.

He was so engrossed in washing them that he didn't notice Cait moving in behind him until she placed a hand on his shoulder and knelt beside him. He paused in his work to kiss her, his eyes sweeping over her long brunette hair, damp from her shower.

"Thank you for taking such good care of them," she whispered.

"I love them," he said. "You've made me happier than I ever thought I could be."

"Good," she said as she reached for the baby towels. "That's the way it should be, don't you think?" She smiled coquettishly but there was something in her eyes that made him pull back a bit to look at her.

"Did you have a relaxing shower?" he asked.

She shrugged and moved closer to the tub to lift Darcy out. "It was a nice break."

"But you're worried."

He lifted Dee out and toweled her off while Cait quietly dried Darcy. Just when he thought she didn't plan to answer him, she said, "Of course I'm worried, Ryan. I'll be worried until he's locked away for good."

"They'll catch him soon."

"It was nice of them to post a couple of cars to watch the house."

"Nice?" He chuckled wryly. "It's their job. But," he hastened to add, "They're just as committed as I am to catching this bastard."

"Don't swear in front of the girls," she chided with a soft smile.

"Why? You'd be thinking their first word will be 'bastard'?"

She laughed and he realized how much he loved the sound of her laughter. It was soft, feminine, melodious.

She handed him Darcy until she managed to stand and then she took the baby from him. The twins were almost instantly subdued as their lids grew heavy.

Ryan chuckled as he diapered Dee and slipped her nightie on her. "They're so predictable."

"They'll be asleep as soon as their bodies hit the mattress."

And they were asleep before their parents had tucked them in and reached their bedroom door. Ryan paused in the doorway as he turned around once more to observe them in their crib, their hands grasping one another even in sleep. Muted light from the lamppost outside made its way around the pastel yellow curtains, providing a soft glow to the room. It hadn't been that long ago that this room had been empty, the door closed; now the crib with its little mobile descended from the ceiling gave him a warm feeling in the pit of his stomach. This was what he'd always wanted: two little girls to call him 'Daddy' —once they began talking, that is—and as he watched the idyllic scene in front of him, he realized he didn't want to leave. He wanted to remain rooted to the doorway, taking in the diaper changing table with its pattern of pink and yellow ribbons decorating the plastic coverlet; of the white chest that housed their clothing; of the crib itself with the twins entwined in each other's arms.

~~~~~

Ryan inhaled the sweet honeysuckle scent of Cait's long hair as he listened to rain hitting the window pane. The weather had turned cooler and with the dramatic change had come a fierce thunderstorm as cool air met warm. The sounds of the thunder had been an intense backdrop to their lovemaking. He'd found his emotions uncharacteristically diverse; he was usually stable and steadfast. But tonight they'd ranged from gentle lovemaking as he savored the life partner he'd always imagined but never thought was possible… to heights of passion that left him spent and their lips bruised… to a powerful release of the pent-up tension that had unmercifully accumulated over the previous days.

Once they had finished, he thought they would slip quickly into the slumber they both craved, but after a brief respite he found himself wide awake and the anxiety returning tenfold. They talked deep into the night as he told Cait the story of Baldr and Maeve. He told her of the three murders, of finding Delport at the motel and how he'd almost had him but he'd slipped through his fingers…

They talked until both their voices had become slow with drowsiness, their lids heavy with sleep. Finally, Cait drifted off and he thought he would, too, only to find himself wide-eyed and wide awake just a few minutes later. He tried not to toss and turn because each time he did, Cait moaned something unintelligible and turned with him. Now he lay snuggled against her back, his arm thrown over her in a protective embrace and his face nuzzled against her shoulder and her long brunette hair. He vacillated between wide-eyed contemplation, convinced he would not sleep this night, to fitful dozing.

While awake, his thoughts raced and while asleep, they turned to nightmares that awakened him. He heard every sound until the patter of rain against the windows turned to footsteps in the hallway and the cooing of the girls' voices over the baby monitor had morphed into startled cries against an unseen enemy.

He tried to remind himself of the police officers watching the house and many more on the lookout for Diallo Delport. He attempted to convince himself that Delport would be insane to attempt to harm his family. And when his other self reminded him that Delport must already be insane, he sought to ignore the voices altogether and focus on something mundane… until the cycle began all over again.

His hand swept across Cait's rounded hip, feeling its way to her stomach and then to her soft, yielding breasts. He had everything he'd ever dreamed of. How many men, he wondered, managed to meet their soul mate? How many were convinced they'd met the perfect woman and actually have that woman feel the same way about them? Yet from the moment he'd laid eyes on Cathleen Reilly he'd known she was the one he'd waited his whole life for, and within minutes, he'd known she felt the same spark for him. Their love had only grown deeper and stronger, the adversities they'd suffered reminders that they did not tread this life alone, and their future lives were solid and permanently interwoven. He gave her what she craved: security, love, commitment; a muscular man ready and willing to protect her. In return, she gave him everything he needed: a sanctuary, tenderness, love and devotion; a woman who gave him purpose.

Their two girls were a constant reminder that their lives were forever connected into an eternal cosmic braid.

They were one.

Whose voice was it, he wondered, that spoke up to remind him that Maeve and Baldr had felt the same way? That they had both been drawn to the other with equal devotion and love? That she had carried his child just as Cait had carried Ryan's?

It was that star-crossed love, that relationship that seemed doomed from the start, the insurmountable fate of time and place that ultimately killed all three: Baldr and his infant child as well as Maeve's spirit.

So who the hell was Diallo Delport?

He sighed audibly and rolled onto his back. The man was flesh and blood; he was born approximately the same time as Ryan but half a world apart—Ryan in Dublin and Delport in South Africa. Each would live, if they were fortunate, for eighty or ninety years on this earth. Each would be faced with doing the best they could with whatever they were dealt. Each would find opportunities for love, passion, adversity and hopefully the ability to overcome whatever stumbles they made.

Then why, he wondered, would this man who had every opportunity to live his own life, be so obsessed with ruining Ryan's? He had done nothing to Diallo Delport; he hadn't even known he existed until he'd arrived in this town a year before and began killing innocent women.

He squeezed Cait's waist as he recalled Delport targeting her. He'd come close to killing them both. And why? Who appointed him the avenger for Maeve and Baldr? How could a hatred run so deep that more than eight hundred years after a star-crossed love, a boy is born who would grow into a cold-blooded killer?

He was incensed that this man would interject himself into his and Cait's lives; livid that he would come to these shores to hunt him down and destroy what happiness he deserved; furious that he would anoint himself a vengeful god capable of devastating innocent lives.

He turned onto his side and leaned onto one elbow. Stop, he ordered. This isn't getting us anywhere.

I'm a detective, he thought. Think like a detective.

I've established motive. The motive was the murders of Baldr and his infant son. Aye, it's a stretch to consider a motive that reaches back hundreds of years… But it needn't go back that far—only to 1839 and Rían Kelly.

All that Diallo Delport needed to do when he arrived on American soil one year ago was reenact the serial murders Rían Kelly was investigating nearly two hundred years earlier. And that was precisely what he did, right down to the specific women he selected and then targeting Cait. The final piece of the puzzle had been locating Ryan, which would not have been difficult given his family's custom of naming their children after an admired relative. The icing on the cake for Delport was discovering that Ryan had even followed in the family's law enforcement tradition—a tradition that might have begun with Royan Kelly in the 12th century.

The thought now of Royan becoming an officer of the law and responsible for apprehending criminals was reprehensible now that Ryan knew Royan himself had ordered the murder of an innocent infant. And to think his own direct ancestor, Keegan, had actually been the one to carry it out…

There was something that continued to gnaw at him, churning him inside out. The minutes ticked by sluggishly and there were moments in which Ryan thought dawn would never arrive.

He'd moved to the far side of the mattress so he wouldn't awaken Cait now that she seemed to be sleeping peacefully. When she awakened, there would be stress enough to contend with; she certainly didn't need to be wide awake as he was.

Each time he closed his eyes, he saw Baldr and felt his deep and committed love toward Maeve. His heart broke with the heartache he knew she was forced to endure when he was murdered, especially as close as they were to leaving Ireland. Undoubtedly, her brothers—or other Celts—found her, preventing her escape, and they'd kept her in their own home until she'd given birth. Had they planned the child's murder all along?

His inner detective's voice cried out once more. He'd established the motive for the slayings one year before. But what was the motive for killing the two historians and the editor?

It couldn't be the story of the star-crossed lovers. No one would have blamed Maeve and Baldr for their love; they were clearly victims, regardless of what Baldr might have done as a marauding Viking.

So Baldr was the White Devil of Dublin, he thought. Hvitr Bard.

He sat straight up in bed.

Then who was Gunnar the Draugr?

28

Belfast, 1173

Maeve closed the book and managed a smile for the children, though her green eyes had lost their vibrancy. "That is all for today," she said softly. "Tomorrow each of ye shall recite a passage from the book." She rose and brushed non-existent lint from her dress. "Now get ye ready for yer supper." She clapped her hands. "Quickly, children."

She watched as the orphans dutifully gathered their school work and filed out of the room. They were often hushed; though Maeve was always full of compassion for them, the others who worked in the orphanage were often not quite as accepting. It made her sad to think of their plight, and she often wished they could grow up more quickly so they could be rid of this oppressive place and able to make their own way in the world.

She followed them to the door, where she spotted James O'Braoin, the headmaster of the Duiblinn orphanage, as he ushered in a new group of children. She had not seen him since the day she rushed after Baldr, the day the Norman invasion began in force, and the day her life had ended in so many ways.

Now she caught his eye and he lifted a finger in a silent request that she remain where she was.

After the transferred children were left in the care of the staff, he stopped to whisper to the Belfast headmaster, who looked first at him and then at Maeve. His cheeks grew flushed but he nodded before backing away, calling out to one of the female staff.

James strolled down the hallway toward Maeve, a ready smile on his face. "Maeve," he said, grasping both her hands in his. "I thought I should ne'er see ye again."

"What are ye doin' in Belfast?"

He nodded toward the door through which the children had been escorted. "We must speak."

She spread her hand toward the empty classroom. "I would love to find out all that has happened. It has been so long since I was in…" Her voice faded and she bit back the tears that suddenly threatened.

"Maeve," he said, gesturing for her to be seated. "I am sorry for all that ye have endured."

"'Twas nothin'," she said, arranging her skirts as she sat. "I have heard the invasion has been brutal."

"Aye, and it has." He sat across from her. "The Normans… Some of 'em are as wicked as the others who seem intent on invadin' Eire. Maeve, I did not see ye after—after that night, the night King Henry first landed."

She nodded briefly.

"I know how much ye loved 'im."

She glanced up, startled by his words.

"It was right there on yer face," he said softly. "When ye were w' 'im, there was a peace about ye."

She nodded silently, averting her eyes to stare at her hands in her lap.

"I heard he did not survive that night."

"I do not know what happened," she said. "I inquired but had to remain discreet." She took a deep breath. "All that I know for certain is he made it out o' the city proper. He was not far from where I awaited him. The Normans, they had not come that far north yet, so it had to have been the Celts..." She brushed a tear from her eye.

"I am sorry, Maeve. Truly I am."

She tried to smile. She had buried the pain long ago, she thought; but here, with a man from her past, her insides seemed to be shredding as if the agony was fresh and new.

"I know," James continued, "that ye bore a child."

"I do not wish to speak o' him."

"Is that true, Maeve?" He placed a finger under her chin and lifted her face to his. "Is that really true?"

She gazed into his eyes. They were blue; not the ice blue of Baldr's eyes but a deeper sapphire. They were wide and inquiring. His lips were slightly parted; his tongue flicked over them a couple of times as if he was readying to speak, but he was unable to find the words.

"What is it?" she asked. Her voice was hushed and trembled slightly.

"It was a dreadful storm," James said. He cupped her chin in his hand. "I remember it well. I almost did not hear Keegan poundin' on the door..."

"What are you sayin'?"

"He carried a babe in 'is arms, a babe who had quite obviously—" he cleared his throat "—just been born to this world."

The questions froze on her lips. She did not want to hear more, and she wanted to know everything.

"He did not end yer child's life, Maeve. He said he could not."

"He—brought m' child to ye?"

He nodded. "We found a wet nurse. He is a strappin' child, Maeve. Big and strong and—so gentle and intelligent."

"Is," she repeated.

"We've taken good care o' him, Maeve. I wanted to get word to ye, but yer family—they told us ye were gone. No one knew where."

It had seemed like a lifetime ago and now it seemed like yesterday. She had not yet healed from birthing. Within a day, the entire family had left the house and left her alone, and she had risen from bed, dressed, and started walking. She knew not where she journeyed; she only knew that she followed the stars northward. For days she walked, and then weeks, and then she lost track of time. Until finally, she found herself in Belfast. No one knew her there. It was a decent place to start again; a place where those she had turned her back on forever could never find her.

A knock came at the door and the headmistress poked her head in. "Shall I—?"

James rose. Taking both of Maeve's hands in his, he said, "He is here, Maeve."

"My—my son? He is here?"

He nodded. "Do ye wish to see 'im?"

She choked on the words as they rushed out. "O' course I want to see 'im," she cried. "O' course!"

The headmistress opened the door wider and reached into the hallway to pull a child into the room.

"There was ne'er any doubt as to who the father was," James said, smiling softly.

He was eighteen months old; yet he looked like a boy of five years. His shoulders were broad, his arms long, and his head large. His skin was completely colorless, almost transparent. His hair was long and white, the same color as his father's. As she rushed to him, going down on her knees in front of him, he met her eyes with an inquisitive stare. His eyes were the color of blue ice, the color of the coldest winter skies; the color of the frost along the shores on a midwinter morn. They were rimmed with long white lashes above which brows so pale that they blended into his skin were barely noticeable.

And he was the most beautiful child she had ever laid eyes upon.

~~~~~

Norway was beautiful in the wintertime, just as Baldr had said. The snows reflected the sun so the entire country seemed awash in light. The people were friendly, kind and accepting. It seemed they had all heard of the legendary Hvitr Bard and when Maeve landed on their shores with her child, they recognized the connection instantly.

She was given a small home in a mountain village in which to raise her son; it was the village where Baldr had been born and where he had grown to manhood. She taught the village children how to read and write and in return, she received food and skins and all she needed to survive.

She called her son Gunnar Baldrsen, which the villagers told her meant *Baldr's son, a fighter*. True to his name, he grew to a strapping young man, a giant among giants, quick with the sword, strong in the back and shoulders, his legs like solid oak trunks.

Eventually, he would leave his mountain home for coastal living as if drawn there by a magic hand. When he stood behind the head of the dragon that graced the Viking ship's bow, he appeared as if he'd been born to the sea. His travels would take him around the world. Yet he always returned home, bearing gifts for the woman who adored him as she had his father.

Maeve never married. She was content to live with the memories of the greatest love she could ever have imagined. And she made certain that her son understood his father's legendary status as intensely as he knew himself. For he was part and parcel of Hvitr Bard, The White Devil of Dublin, just as the continuing line of his albino children would be. She would never let him forget the injustice that had been intended for him, of the angels that had intervened, and of the family that would forever be cursed for their hatred of the man she loved.

29

North Carolina

It was mid-morning but the skies were as dark as dusk. As the sheets of rain pounded against the windows, Ryan peered between the blinds at the police car stationed in front of the house. It sat beneath a street lamp that had remained on throughout the morning, the sensor never recognizing it was daytime as the darkness had never fully departed. He knew another police cruiser sat along the side street with a full view of the back yard; though the shifts had changed, the position of the cruisers had not.

"I have mixed feelings about her son surviving," Cait said. He half-turned to see her sitting at his desk, her eyes still riveted to Annalise Skovgaard's laptop screen.

"As do I."

"As a mother," she continued, "I am happy for her that she had her son and he reminded her so much of Baldr."

"Aye. Yet, the son grew to become Gunnar the Draugr."

"His reputation was fiercer than his father's."

Ryan stepped toward the desk and opened the top drawer, where he retrieved a flash drive. He inserted it into the side of the laptop and reached across Cait to copy the files.

"What are you doing?" Cait asked.

"It's part of the family history," he said quietly. "Maeve should never have suffered the way she did."

As the files began to copy, she turned toward him. "But do you realize what this means, Ryan? It means," she continued without waiting for his response, "Keegan is not a murderer. He could not follow through with Royan's order. He was a good boy, and he did what he thought was right."

Ryan's eyes met hers. They were nearly the color of the tumultuous rains just outside their window, yet they were filled with compassion—the empathy, he realized, of a mother. "I am glad to know that my ancestor did not murder his infant nephew. Regardless of what Gunnar became or the legacy he left, every life is precious."

She reached for his hand. At her touch, he felt the connection he knew he would always have with her. It went deep and was strong; she was his soul.

"Why do you suppose Delport didn't want this story told?" she asked.

He shook his head. "I don't know. But it's motive enough that he killed to keep it silent."

"You're talking like a detective now," she said with a gentle smile. "I'm asking the man."

The files finished copying and he took a moment to unplug the flash drive and set it beside his desktop. Then he powered down the laptop and unplugged it. "I wonder if part of the thrill of killing was the mystery. Imagine Rían Kelly losing Caitlin O'Conor to a killer and never knowing why she was targeted… Or how close he came to destroying us before we ever truly began."

"There's no telling how many times the story played out," Cait added. "Different centuries, different people…"

"But always Baldr's descendants targeting the Kelly family."

"They played judge and jury."

"Well," Ryan said, standing to his full height, "the tradition stops here. It *must* stop here."

"What are you going to do?"

He took a deep breath. "I have to go into the office," he said. "I hate to leave you, but you'll be safe with the police officers here. We can even ask one of them to come inside, if you'd like."

"How long will you be gone?"

"An hour or two, at the most. I just need to talk some things over with the chief."

"Care to share?"

"Not yet. I don't know what he might agree to, or if he has ideas of his own… But I have to make certain that this insanity stops here, with Delport and me. Speaking as a man and not a detective," he added, "I can't allow this to continue through future generations. It should never have gone this far."

He tucked the laptop under his arm and made his way into the hall. As Cait followed, she said, "I wish you didn't have to go."

"I promise I won't be long. I'll be back by lunch. How's that?" He stopped in front of the nursery. Stepping inside, he set the laptop on top of the changing table and made his way to the crib. The girls were taking their mid-morning nap. Their bellies were full and now they both contentedly sucked on their pacifiers. They looked almost like mirror images of one another; each had a diminutive hand against their pacifier, ensuring it did not leave their mouths, while their free hands were intertwined. "I hope they will always remain this close," he said softly.

"We'll make sure they do," Cait said, joining him. "Our home will always be filled with love."

"Our first big battle will be when Dee must surrender that pacifier," he chuckled.

"I can see her starting college with it still in her mouth," Cait laughed.

"God help us if anything happened to it. It's so unique—I don't know where we'd find another just like it."

"It was a gift from my sister," Cait said. "I'll have to find out where she bought it."

"Oh, and that's all we need is a house full of purple and pink paccies." He bent over the rail and tenderly kissed Dee on her forehead. She murmured contentedly and he moved to Darcy, planting a moist kiss on her forehead. Then he straightened. "I don't want to leave," he admitted. Then with a heavy sigh, "But I must. Shall I call one of the police officers inside?"

Cait picked up the laptop and handed it to him. "Let them know you're leaving?"

"Of course."

"And ask them if they think I'm alright if they stay where they are… If not, then, yes. I want to make sure we're all safe."

"You're my highest priority." He walked down the hallway to the living room. His eyes fell on the island that separated the living room from the kitchen, where Cait's pistol sat. He didn't like this idea of having to ensure a weapon was nearby for defense. But if the chief bought into his plan, it would all be over soon.

And after nearly a thousand years, soon wouldn't come soon enough.

30

The police department was uncharacteristically quiet. Every available officer was on the street, but even the telephones were silent as the chief finished reading the most relevant chapters in Annalise Skovgaard's manuscript before spinning his chair around to face Ryan and his partner.

"So you see," Ryan said, "I believe the only way to stop this insanity from continuing into the future is to go public with everything we know about Maeve and Baldr."

"Convince me how this will stop a serial killer."

"Their story was one of ill-fated love. Captured in the context of the time in which they lived and the backdrop of history, I'm certain their story isn't unique in the annals of time. But what is unique," he continued, "is the so-called 'curse' Maeve placed on her brothers and their descendants."

"I don't believe in curses." Chief Johnston leaned forward.

"Nor do I. But what I do believe happened is the story was told to the son who survived, Gunnar the Draugr. He passed the story to his children, and they to theirs. I don't know yet how often this scenario of an avenging serial killer has played out over the centuries. But I do know it happened at least three times and it's led to Diallo Delport's latest crime spree."

"So your strategy——?"

"——is to get the media involved to tell the tale that Delport sought to suppress. I suggest we contact the publisher; with one of their highest profile authors and her editor victims of the killer, I would think they'd be agreeable to releasing Mrs. Skovgaard's book."

"I don't know much about publishing," Chief Johnston said, "or I should say *anything* about publishing. But it seems to me that it would take time to get a book into print."

"I thought of that. So we get permission from the publisher to have excerpts printed in the local newspaper, and we contact television and radio across the country. With Mrs. Skovgaard's nearest living relative still in Norway, we may be able to get international coverage—not only in Norway but in South Africa as well."

"And if the publisher doesn't agree?"

"We do it anyway. Let them challenge us; I would think the public's safety would trump a publisher's bottom line in any court."

Chief Johnston stood and stepped to a window overlooking the parking lot. He remained silent for a long moment. Ryan glanced at his watch; the minutes were ticking past and he was anxious to get back home to Cait and the girls.

Finally, he turned around. "Supposing we were able to get the local newspaper to run a story in tomorrow's paper," he said, leveling his eyes at Ryan. "How would that help us catch Diallo Delport?"

"It's a two-pronged strategy. The long-term strategy is to get this story into the light of day. With enough media exposure, it could stop this madness from happening again. The short-term strategy is to enlist the public's aid in locating Delport."

"Every network in North Carolina and many in South Carolina ran stories on last night's news. We made sure they had Diallo Delport's passport picture and all the information they needed to alert the public. It's also on the front page of today's paper."

"And," Zuker said, "It's also been broadcast along the eastern seaboard. His information is on all the electronic interstate signs."

"And the state police?" Ryan asked.

"They've been notified. Every police department in two states is on alert. Luckily for us, Delport is so unique in appearance that if he shows his face at a service station, a restaurant, or just driving down the road, someone should see him and hopefully alert us."

"This storm isn't helping," Ryan said thoughtfully. "We have to do more."

"We've divided Lumberton into grids," Zuker said, "with officers assigned to each square."

"Can we get them to go door-to-door, at least to the businesses in town?"

"We can do that," the chief said, returning to his desk. "We also have officers visiting each motel and hotel in the county; the sheriff's department has joined in the search as well as Cumberland County and Fayetteville PD. And of course, the FBI is involved due to the airport murder."

"And the buses, airlines, trains?"

"All alerted. He's been placed on the watch list so whether he travels domestically or attempts to leave the country, he should be apprehended."

"I feel like I'm leaving something out," Ryan said. "This man is highly intelligent and incredibly resourceful."

"Then think like him, O'Clery," Chief Johnston said. "Anticipate his next move."

A polite knock turned all their heads toward the door to the chief's office.

"Arlo," the chief said in greeting the evidence technician.

"Sorry to disturb you," Arlo said as he entered the room. "I heard Detective O'Clery was here, and I was hoping to get a DNA swab."

"Of course," Ryan said, rising.

As Arlo opened the kit and Ryan quickly swabbed the inside of his cheek, Chief Johnston asked, "What's this all about?"

"A couple of black hairs found at two of the crime scenes," Arlo said, carefully placing the swab into the container. "We want to cover all the bases. If they don't match the detective's DNA, we know we may have two suspects."

"Do what you have to do," the chief said, "but I'm sure we're looking at a lone killer."

"I don't mind telling you," Ryan said as he seated himself again, "that it's a bit disconcerting to be asked to do this."

"Well, it should be obvious what Delport had intended."

"I'm not sure I follow you."

"He wanted to frame you for the murders—at least Skovgaard's and Petrironcalli's. Think about it."

Ryan took a sideways glance at Zuker, who was watching him intently. "Aye," he said. "I suppose that was his plan."

"So," Chief Johnston said, "what's next for you two?"

Ryan glanced at his watch. It was already noon. "I'd like to work the phones," he said. "I'd like to follow Delport's trail back to South Africa and speak to the police there. Perhaps he has family members who can shed some light on his next move. But if you don't mind," he added, "I'd like to do it from home. I'm concerned about leaving Cait and the girls until he's captured."

"Are they alone now?"

"Negative. Ernie is inside the house with Cait until I return, and Pepper is watching the exterior."

"Good. Yes, by all means, work this case from home."

Zuker rose. "And I'll get with O'Clery to find out what else I can be doing."

Ryan joined him as they made their way to the door. "I wanted to thank you," he said, turning back to the chief, "for the officers watching my home."

"Don't mention it. You're family. And you're targets."

~~~~~

"I'll get the forensics report from each crime scene," Zuker said as they walked the hall back to the detectives' room. "And I'll see whether the autopsy reports are available yet. We'll want to build ironclad cases so we can lock Delport away forever."

"The only way Cait will ever feel safe again," Ryan admitted, "is if he's locked away someplace where he could never escape."

"She still having nightmares?"

"They stopped a few months ago, but quite frankly, I expect them to start again at any time now that she knows he's not dead…"

"And he's back in town." They reached their office and stepped inside. "We'll get him, O'Clery. Every officer on the force has their adrenaline revved up to catch him."

Ryan stopped at his desk as Zuker moved to his. He was still speaking but his words sounded far away to him now; no more than whispers on the wind. Somewhere in the back of his mind, he registered that his partner was shuffling papers, and opening and closing desk drawers.

But his blood had turned to ice and he felt completely frozen as he stared at his desk top.

"You hear me, O'Clery?" Zuker said. His voice had grown louder and Ryan realized on a distant level that he had stepped to his desk and was standing beside him. "O'Clery?"

When he spoke, his own voice sounded disembodied and far away. "Where did that come from?"

"Where did what—?"

Like a jolt of electricity striking his body, Ryan felt a blistering heat begin deep inside him. It poured through his extremities like liquid lava until it heated the surface of his skin and caused his head to pound in his temples. His hands felt thick and swollen and his senses screamed into full alert as he stared at Dee's unique pacifier sitting in the center of his desk.

~~~~~

"Answer the damn phone, Cait!" Ryan roared. His tone echoed down the hallway like a pinnacle layered atop a myriad of voices. The department had roared to life in the last few seconds and now officers were on their radios or hurrying to their patrol cars.

"Ernie's in the house," Zuker said from somewhere behind Ryan.

Before he could respond, Cait's phone was answered, her voice drowned out by a baby bawling.

"Cait!" Ryan said, coming to a full stop as he leaned his ear into the phone.

"I can't talk right now," she said.

"Why is Dee crying?"

She didn't answer immediately, and his words hung in the air, the demanding tone sounding even to himself as rude.

"Cait!" he said, his voice just below a bellow.

"I can't find her pacifier." Her voice was low and subdued.

Damn it, he thought. "Where is Darcy?"

"In her crib."

"Can you see her?"

"Yes. Of course. I'm looking right at her."

"Ernie wants your orders," Zuker said, coming to stand beside him.

"Cait, listen to me. Get out of the house."

"Get her out of the house," Zuker said on the phone to Ernie.

"Units on their way," another officer announced as he filed past them. "The first cars are less than a minute out."

"What's going on?" Cait asked.

Ryan looked into Zuker's eyes. "Cait, Ernie's going to put you into the patrol car. You and the girls." As Zuker repeated the instructions to Ernie, Ryan began walking toward the front door. "I'll be there in two minutes."

"He's here, isn't he?" Cait's voice was eerily calm.

"I'll explain everything when I get there." He clicked off the phone and whirled around to see several officers waiting for his instructions. "Get the evidence technicians. I need the pacifier on my desk processed, especially DNA." To their quizzical expressions, he added, "I'll explain later... And I need evidence technicians at my house." He stopped at the door and pointed to the closed circuit cameras. "And I want to know who put that pacifier on my desk and when—and how he got in."

31

Both babies were wailing at the top of their lungs and when Ryan looked at them sitting side by side in their baby seats, he thought their mouths were open wide enough for him to see clear through to their tonsils. He glanced toward the kitchen to see Cait checking the temperature of their formula. Despite the officers waiting for further instructions, he stepped past them and lifted his girls into his arms.

"Every window and every door has been checked and rechecked," Zuker said as he entered the room. "There is no sign of forced entry."

"I checked everything when I came inside," Ernie added. "Everything was locked tight. No one came in and no one left."

Ryan bounced his girls gently as he watched the German shepherd making its way around the room. "No one else is here now," the canine officer said. "We've cleared every room in the house."

"What's about here?" The distinctive Irish voice caused Ryan to turn around. "Re?" Claire's brows were knit together. "There are a dozen police vehicles surrounding your house," she continued. Her eyes scanned the babies. "Is everyone alright? Cait——?"

"We're all fine," Cait said, squeezing her shoulder as she brushed past her.

Ryan spotted Emma and Erin behind their mother. "And there's my favorite ladies," he said in a voice that he hoped did not betray his anxiety. "Would you care to feed Dee and Darcy for me then?"

"Sure, and that's what we're good for," Emma said, hopping onto the couch. "Hand me a babe, why don't you, and a burpy nappy?"

As Erin settled in beside her, Ryan knelt in front of them and handed them each a baby. "Be sure to hold their heads up," he said gently.

"And of course we will," Erin answered. "We're experts at this, you know."

"I know," he smiled. He stood as Cait handed them each a bottle and cloths. When he turned around, he came face to face with Claire, who was watching him intently with large green eyes. When Cait joined them, he nodded toward the island separating the living room and the kitchen.

As they gathered in a small circle, his height afforded him a clear view over their heads. When he first began renting the house, he was told the original kitchen had been small and enclosed. The owners had knocked out the wall separating the kitchen from a formal dining room and living room. They'd doubled the length of the kitchen, removing the dining room altogether and they'd installed the island where the original wall had once stood. The effect was an open floor plan where anyone standing in the kitchen could see through to the living area. In place of a dining table, there were now bar stools at the island.

"Cait," he said as his eyes panned the room, "I need to know where you were the whole time I was gone."

Ernie and Zuker joined them as Cait answered, "The four of us—Ernie, me and the girls—were right here."

"In this room."

"That's right."

"And you didn't leave at any time?"

"Well, I went to the bathroom for all of five minutes."

"And that's it?"

"That's it."

He turned to Ernie. "When Cait went to the bathroom, where were you?"

"I had a couple of calls to make—checking in with the office. Your girls were asleep and I was afraid my voice would wake them. So I stepped outside. But," he added hastily, "I couldn't have been outside for more than two minutes, tops. It was storming and your stoop doesn't provide much protection from the rain."

"So you went outside the front door?"

"I stood right at the door. I had a clear view of the front of your house. Pepper was parked on the side with an unobstructed view of the side and the back."

"Get Pepper in here," Ryan said to Zuker.

Zuker radioed for Pepper and requested another officer remain in her original position.

"That side," Ryan said, pointing to the door off the kitchen, "is the laundry room and the garage. I'm assuming the garage door was closed and the laundry room door was locked."

"That's correct," Ernie said.

"And we verified it was locked when we got here," Zuker said. "To manually open your garage door, someone would have to be inside already, and they'd have to disengage the electric door opener."

"That leaves the front of the house—" Ryan continued.

"—where I was standing," Ernie said. "And I guarantee you, nobody got past me."

"Two bedroom windows are on the front of the house," he mused aloud. "The girls' room and my study. And you had a clear view of those." It was said as a statement but Ernie vehemently verified it.

Pepper made her way through the room toward them. She was tall and stout; Ryan had seen her tackle suspects and knew she took her job seriously. She rarely smiled and she was always professional and focused.

"Pepper," he said, "from your position, what could you see of the house?"

"On the side facing the cross-street, there's only one window."

"That would be to the master bath."

"And on the back side," she continued, pointing to the wall behind them, "there's another window besides that plate glass window and the back door."

Ryan had to admit, the house wasn't a tough one for surveillance. It was only one story, and the window they couldn't see from the island was in the master bedroom; it was the window that greeted him each morning as he awakened. He glanced across the room through the large plate glass window. "And those hedges?" he said. "You could see through those?"

"There's a break in the hedges. I parked the cruiser where I could see through the break to the back of the house."

Ryan turned to Zuker. "Get some officers in the back to look through those hedges."

"O'Clery," Zuker said, dropping his voice, "the back door was locked when the officers came in. The deadbolt was in place."

"But—"

"Your bedroom window was locked; in fact, it's painted over. I doubt you could open it even if the house was on fire."

Claire turned to Cait. "Do you know what's about here or am I the only one they've cared to keep in the dark?"

Cait's eyes met Ryan's. "They haven't filled me in," she said quietly. "But I think Ryan is just about to."

His eyes moved from Cait's to Claire's and then to Emma and Erin, who were burping the babies like they'd been nannies for a decade. When he turned back to his sister and wife, they continued looking at him expectantly, nearly shoulder to shoulder.

"There was a pacifier on my desk at work."

"Ooh," they both said in unison.

"So do you always get half the police force out when you find a soother on your desk?" Claire demanded.

"Cait," Ryan said, "it was Dee's pacifier. I'd know it anywhere."

"Are you sure you didn't accidentally take it to work with you?" Cait asked.

"I am positive. I would never do that."

"It wouldn't be the first time," Zuker added quietly, "that a brand new daddy did something like that."

"Not me," Ryan insisted.

They all turned away, each looking in opposite directions.

"You had me scared half to death," Cait said. "I thought Delport was here in this house."

"I thought he was, too." Ryan turned to Pepper. "Thank you. You can return to your vehicle."

"Anytime," she said with a bemused smile on her face. Quickly masking it, she made her way past the other officers toward the front hallway.

"O'Clery, the canine unit wants to leave. They didn't find anything… No one found anything," Zuker said.

~~~~~

Chief Johnston stood on the sidewalk as he directed the officers. "I heard what happened," he said quietly to Ryan and Zuker. "The evidence technicians have the pacifier." His eyes twinkled. "You know if they find no DNA other than yours and your daughter's, you'll never live this down."

"I swear—no matter what everyone else thinks—that I did not bring it to work with me." He had a wrenching headache.

"We'll keep two officers here for the time being. Regardless of PacifierGate, we do have the very serious matter of a killer on the loose—and one who has targeted you. Let's not forget that."

The rain had mercifully stopped, leaving behind gutters filled to overflowing. The sidewalk on which they stood was soaked with enough puddles to make walking it difficult without stepping into one. Though it was barely afternoon, the skies above resembled dusk. The clouds were black and ominous and though they were fast moving in a brisk wind, others quickly took their place. Ryan surmised if he were to look at a weather map, there was a band of storms stretching for miles on end. He once thought of storms such as this a great excuse for remaining indoors and sexually engaged, but now they just seemed to further frustrate him.

"I would have been here sooner," the chief was saying, "but I stopped in to talk to the editor of the paper, Bobby Baxter. He said they'd be very much interested in running a series of articles about the murders, Diallo Delport, and his motives."

The front door opened and Ryan turned to see Emma standing in the doorway, gesturing to get his attention. He held up a finger to let her know to stay put as he listened to the chief.

"I want you to fully understand, O'Clery," he continued, "that this could bring some unwanted attention to you and your family. You'd be airing your dirty laundry right there on the front page of the paper."

"I realize that," he said. "You're fully aware that I'm a private person. But I don't see any other way of ending this."

"Very well. I'll ask Bobby to start the ball rolling."

Something jerked at Ryan's shirt and he turned to find Emma standing beside him.

"Young lady, where are your shoes?" he asked as he looked at her bare feet.

"I wouldn't have needed them had you come to the door," she answered.

Zuker and Chief Johnston chuckled.

"Don't get cheeky with me, young lady. Wouldn't you be seeing that I'm in a conversation with adults?"

"Yes, but—"

"Then go along inside and I'll be there directly."

"But—"

"Is the house on fire?"

She shook her head.

"Is there otherwise an urgent emergency?"

She shook her head once more.

"Then off with you, darlin'." He turned back to the men, adding over his shoulder in a softer tone, "I'll only be a moment."

"Fine," he heard her mumble as she started up the sidewalk. "I'll ask your cousin to wait then."

There had been moments in Ryan's life which he knew would remain with him forever, though he usually didn't know it at the time. Sometime later, though, when he reflected on the circumstances and where the moment had led him in his meandering path through life, he'd realize its significance. But as he turned around to watch Emma skipping past the puddles on her way back to the house, every nerve in his body felt completely on edge. It was as if every hair on his skin from the top of his head to his calves had turned into finely tuned antenna. His tongue felt thick and his mouth was dry and his eyes suddenly became incapable of blinking.

"What did you say?"

Emma did not turn around. "I wasn't trying to be cheeky, Uncle Re," she said over her shoulder.

In two long strides, he was beside her. "What did you say?" he demanded. He'd instinctively reached for her shoulder to spin her around so he could look in her face when something akin to a shriek reached their ears. He caught a glimpse of Emma's wide eyes before he leapt from the sidewalk onto the top step and rushed through the house.

"Where is she?" Cait was demanding.

"Where is Emma?" Claire's voice chimed in.

Ryan reached the living room door. "Emma's with me," he said. "What's the screaming about?"

Cait nearly flew to Emma's side. She grabbed her by both shoulders, her hold so urgent and forceful that Emma sought refuge under Ryan's arm. "Where is she?"

"Where is who?" Ryan asked.

Emma's bottom lip began to quiver.

"Dee," Cait said. "Where is Dee?"

"I told you," Erin piped up from the couch.

Ryan's mind felt as if it was on fire. Emma was hugging his leg, seeking protection from Cait's hold. Claire was picking up Darcy from Erin, who had begun to cry. Claire's face, normally pale as Irish skin can be, was positively ashen. Cait's face was so pallid that she appeared likely to faint. He registered Chief Johnston and Zuker on his heels. When Emma began to cry out, he scooped her into his arms. In a few short strides, he was beside the couch, one long arm reaching out to touch Erin's head.

"Tell me," he said in his gentlest voice, "what happened to Dee. You won't be in trouble. I promise you both."

"Re, don't—" Claire began.

"Stop." He fixed Claire with his glare. Turning back to the children, he sought to quiet his voice once more. "Tell me where Dee is. Did she get up and walk away?"

"Of course not," Erin chuckled through her tears.

"I was feeding Dee, Uncle Re," Emma said, wiping her tear-stained cheeks on his shirt. "When all the sudden, the door just opened up behind us."

All eyes went to the back door, which now stood just short of closing.

"And who was there in the door?" As he asked it, he sought to steady his legs as he set Emma on the couch beside her sister.

"That's exactly what I said," Emma said. "I said, 'who is that in the doorway?' And the man said, 'why, it's your cousin Dee.'"

"And then I said," Erin picked up, "'we haven't got a cousin Dee, but we have a niece Dee.' And then he said, 'well, isn't that a fine thing for my cousin Ryan to name his girl after me.'"

"Then he asked which one was Dee," Emma said, "and I showed him. And he asked to hold her. And then he said for me to come and get you and let you know he was here."

Ryan knelt in front of them so he could look them in the eye. "And what did cousin Dee look like?"

"Why, he looked just like Auntie Cait's boss," Erin said.

"Mary, Mother of God," Claire breathed as she sat heavily in the chair adjacent to the couch.

Ryan looked at her. "I don't understand."

"When Delport followed Cait to the Outer Banks," Claire explained, her voice shaking, "we were watching her news reports on the telly. Emma and Erin saw Delport in the background in nearly every shot. They thought he was Cait's boss. I—I even phoned the police department to tell them—"

Her last words hadn't escaped her lips before Chief Johnston was on his radio, ordering every available officer to set up a perimeter around the neighborhood. His voice was urgent and as he spoke, he demanded a physical description of Dee as well as reiterating Delport's description. His words blended in with Cait's and Claire's as well as Emma's and Erin's cries as they picked back up. In the back of his mind, he registered Zuker going through the back door as he also hit the radio with orders and instructions. He wanted nothing more than to rush after him, but something held him back. It was as if a quiet calm was sweeping over him. *You're a detective*, a tiny voice said. *Do what you're trained to do.*

"It's okay," he said, squeezing both Emma's and Erin's shoulders. "Don't cry. I need you to be strong and help me by staying quiet and calm. Can you do that for me?"

Before they'd even answered, he was standing and turning toward Cait. Her face was completely gray. Her eyes were wide and though they stared straight at him, they didn't appear to register that he was there. "Sit down, Cait," he said gently as he reached for her.

"I will not." Her voice was strong and forceful, in direct contrast to her appearance.

"Erin," he said, turning back around, "did cousin 'D' leave the house?"

"Aye, and he did," she said through her tears. "Right through that door." She pointed toward the back door. As his eyes followed, he spotted Zuker walking the perimeter of the hedges. Pepper was standing at the break in the hedges saying something about not having seen anyone, her voice carrying strangely over the din.

He was at the back door before his brain had even registered that his feet were moving. Behind him there was nothing but voices; officers questioning, officers ordering, Claire and the girls crying. He turned back only long enough to register that Claire was rocking Darcy as she sobbed. Darcy was safe.

Dee was not.

He stepped onto the concrete patio. Chief Johnston was beside him in an instant. "I want officers going from door to door," he spoke into his radio. "Issue an Amber Alert. He can't have more than two or three minutes' jump on us."

Two or three minutes, Ryan thought. How far can a man get in two or three minutes?

His eyes roamed above the hedge line. Though his home was only one story, he was surrounded by houses taller than his. He pointed toward their second story windows. "See if anybody saw anything," he directed Zuker. "Someone had to have seen something."

Zuker's voice seemed a million miles away as he repeated Ryan's instructions to officers appearing on the scene. Everyone's voices seemed disjointed, their words no longer coherent. Every instinct told him the answer was right in front of him. His eyes traveled downward to the hedges, to the bare areas scattered throughout.

"He left through a break in the hedges," he heard himself saying. "He went to the street behind us."

He was across the lawn and to the hedges in record time. A grown man could easily move through these breaks, he realized. Why wasn't Dee crying? She always cried without her paci; why wasn't she crying now?

His eyes moved upward to the house directly behind theirs. An elderly woman had lived there when he moved in. He'd rarely seen her and when he did, she was barely able to stand on her own. His eyes moved to the window as officers moved past him through the hedges, fanning out on the street behind his.

The window had no curtains.

His eyes moved to the next window. It, too, had no curtains.

His brain and his eyes moved faster and faster like a movie sped up to warp speed, registering that each window contained no window coverings.

The house was vacant.

His eyes catapulted back to one window. A round metal object peered back toward his house; it was barely discernible in the darkness but as he turned to follow its trajectory, he heard his own voice, hoarse and urgent. "Jesus Christ."

~~~~~

"I'm going in with the team," he stated flatly. His eyes darted past Chief Johnston to the *For Sale* sign in his neighbor's front yard, and then to the front door itself. The SWAT team was in position, evenly divided between the front door, the garage door and the back door. Two officers were on the roof, one facing forward and one backward. Behind him and across the street, he knew other officers had also taken to the roofs for a better view of the area. The State Police helicopter along with a hostage negotiator had been dispatched and would be there in minutes.

The chief nodded silently and motioned to the team.

The men at the front turned as one toward the front door. As Ryan stepped toward them, Chief Johnston said, "Let them go in first, O'Clery. You're not suited up."

He heard the chief but he did not acknowledge his directive. Before his feet touched the bottom step of the wide front porch, he heard the front door splintering. Voices came from everywhere at once as the side and back doors were similarly broken open.

He'd seen enough SWAT missions to know that they usually tossed in flashbangs before entering; so-called because they contained a flash grenade of blinding intensity as well as an ear-splitting noise. They were non-lethal but temporarily used the body's own reflexes to disorient the suspect, enabling the SWAT members to enter while the suspect was incapacitated.

But as the men swiftly moved inside, each with their weapons positioned against their shoulders and ready to fire, he knew why that had not been used here: there was an infant involved. A flashbang could permanently damage the frail membranes of an infant's eyes and permanently damage their hearing.

He rushed up the steps to enter behind the team. They fanned out as if they'd had a blueprint of the home, moving forward through the house as another team progressed from the back to meet in the middle. Half the men broke away and moved upstairs. As Ryan followed them up the steps, all he could see in front of him was a sea of black—black helmets, black uniforms, black packs filled with weapons and ammunition…

In his mind's eye, he pictured the telescope in the back room and as the team fanned out again, clearing each room in turn, he made his way to the back of the house.

There were so many shouts of "Police!" that his mind tuned them out. There was danger in going into a home where a man could be holed up with an infant as a hostage. In any other situation, they would have waited for the hostage negotiator.

Except this time, they were dealing with Diallo Delport.

A serial killer would kill again and again until he was stopped. He would not make demands and surrender an infant when they were met. The best case scenario would be that they'd reach him before he'd done harm to his child. The worst case was Delport would want an audience assembled before killing her.

He reached a back bedroom and peered inside. It was empty except for a candy wrapper on the dusty hardwood floor. How long had the house been vacant, he wondered, and he hadn't noticed?

He moved to the next room as a member of the team reached it. They entered together but stopped immediately.

The room was approximately twelve feet square. Closet doors were open, revealing an empty closet with a few wire hangers forlornly gracing an aged wood rod. A miniscule, old fireplace looked cold, the grate empty. The hardwood floors were worn, the walls scattered with picture hooks but no pictures.

And in front of the solitary window sat a telescope on a tripod.

~~~~~

Ryan sat on the simple stool. He felt the warmth move from the tips of his fingers upward through his arms even as the same heat began in his feet and traveled through his legs. They met in his chest, causing his insides to feel as though they would burst into flames at any second.

He felt the skin on his face blazing and he knew he must be beet red. His breath came deep and hard, the sound echoing in the close confines of the room.

He did not have to touch the telescope. He was nearly the same height as Diallo Delport; all he had to do was lean forward and his eye was positioned exactly where his would have been. He fought to keep his hands from angrily throwing the metal object through the window by grasping his pants legs and alternately flexing and straightening his fists.

As his eye neared the telescope, he looked through the plate glass window directly into his living room, where Emma and Erin sat on bean bags in front of the television screen. He could even identify which program they were watching. Cait sat on the couch with Darcy in her lap, rocking her gently as she fed her from her bottle. Claire alternated from Cait's side to the window and back, nervously pacing. An officer stood at the island, one hand resting on his belt and holster, his head cocked toward the radio clipped to his shoulder.

Everything made sense now. His keys had gone missing when he'd known where he'd placed them—where he'd always placed them. Sometime before they knew Diallo Delport was still alive, when their doors remained unlocked because they thought they were safe, he had walked across their back yard, entered their house and taken his keys.

He'd made copies of them and sometime later, returned them.

He knew when to enter simply by watching the house.

His eyes moved to his bedroom window. It was covered with blinds but atop the rectangular shape of the main window was a half-moon window he'd never bothered to cover. Why should he have covered it? He'd thought no one could see in. But now as he looked through to his bedroom, he realized Delport had known when Cait was in the bathroom or when she—and he—were engaged, and he'd known how much time he had.

Like a ghost, he'd entered their home and left it and they'd not been the wiser.

He rose from the stool, silently making his way past officers who had declared the house empty, from the crawlspace to the attic. He moved down the stairs like a sleepwalker, through the main floor and onto the front porch. The figures of Chief Johnston and Zuker and a myriad of officers were all a blur of uniforms and radios.

Without thinking, he walked down the sidewalk to the first cross-street and then to his own street rather than take the shortcut through the hedge. He barely registered the police cars with their lights flashing, the neighbors standing in front of their homes watching, or the helicopter that had arrived and was circling the neighborhood despite the heavy clouds overhead.

His feet felt heavy and slow, though before he knew it, he was standing on his own front steps.

Somehow Cait had known he was coming and before he reached the door, it was opened. He didn't look at her face until he had entered the house. When their eyes met, he could not hold back the tears. He grasped her, pulling her into his embrace as he sank his face against her soft shoulder. He wouldn't allow her to see him cry. He couldn't. All his upbringing and all his police training were at war with his emotions; he wanted to remain strong and in control but he felt weak and out of control, like someone else had taken over and was steering his course.

He almost didn't hear his cell phone ringing. When he did, he considered not answering it. But as Cait pulled away, her own face tear-stained, and grappled for it, he wiped his eyes and reached into his pocket.

"Aye."

"Come to the top of the water tower." The words were clipped but distinct. The caller clearly spoke English but was not American; his voice was melodious, not quite Irish and not quite Australian. It was South African, and the caller was unmistakable. Ryan realized he was holding his breath as Delport continued, "Come alone or the child dies."

He switched it to speakerphone. His eyes dried instantly and his chest felt as if it had turned to stone. He looked up to find Chief Johnston and Zuker just feet away, their eyes riveted to the phone.

"How do I know she's okay?" he asked, though he could hear her fretting.

"Would you like for me to make her cry?" he asked smoothly.

"No," he retorted instantly.

He chuckled. "Listen carefully, Ryan O'Clery. Your child's life depends on it."

His eyes met Chief Johnston's. "I'm listening."

"I can see for miles from here," he continued, his voice like silk. "I'll know if you leave your house alone. If any cars follow you or meet you here, she gets thrown from the top of the tower."

"No one will follow me."

"Come unarmed. And bring your police radio."

"When?"

"Now. You have twenty minutes."

32

A sea of eyes encircled Ryan. "It could be a diversion," he stated. His words were rapid-fire; though the water tower was just a few minutes' drive, there were plans to be made and made quickly. "Claire," he said, turning to his sister, "where is Tommy?"

"He's at work, Re, at Fort Bragg."

"Call him. Tell him I want you, the girls and Cait to check into the BOQ at Fort Bragg until this is over."

"Aye. I'll ring him up straight away."

He turned next to Chief Johnston. "Can you get them a police escort to Fort Bragg?"

"Consider it done."

"Claire, tell Tommy to have MP's meet you at the gate."

He turned to Cait. She remained silent though her eyes spoke volumes. They seemed enormous as they locked onto his. Her chin was set and the color blazed in her cheeks. "Cait, darlin', don't worry about Dee. I'll get her home safe and sound. I promise you that."

"I know, Ryan. I have faith in you."

Her simple words caught at his heart like nothing else could.

Though he was filled with doubts, he knew he had to appear as though he was in complete control. "Hurry and get your things packed; I want to know before I leave..." His words faded into the air that encircled them and they were left staring into each other's eyes. A myriad of emotions passed between them: pain, trust, anguish, trepidation.

"O'Clery, there are things we need to discuss." The chief's voice urged him back.

Ryan reluctantly broke his gaze from Cait, nodding toward the front door. The chief, Zuker and a few officers joined him as they made their way outside. Two officers remained inside the house to watch over Cait, Claire and the three girls as they prepared to leave.

"The water tower has been getting repainted," Zuker said. His words came quickly. "There's scaffolding surrounding the top of the onion."

In his mind's eye, Ryan pictured the water tower. They were either known as spiders or onions; a spider was one in which there were multiple supports, where an onion resembled a green onion with one central support and a more bulbous top.

"The ladder is bolted to the tower itself," Zuker continued. "It isn't going to sway or come loose from the tower. Just don't look down."

"Let's move on to what I do when I reach the top," Ryan said curtly.

"Whatever you do, don't look at the hostage," Chief Johnston said.

The hostage. The words sounded cold.

"That's what she is, O'Clery," the chief continued. "She's not your daughter. Not today. It's a hostage situation and the suspect has requested you."

"You're going to telephone us before you leave here," Officer Connelly said. Ryan turned in his direction. He hadn't worked much with Connelly; he was a negotiator with the State Police, and had arrived around the same time as the helicopter. Though he'd anticipated assisting with the situation in the vacant house, he found himself instead advising Ryan as he readied to leave. "Keep your phone on speaker. Ours will be on mute. That way if there's any background noise here, the suspect won't be able to hear it." He clipped a second radio mike to Ryan's shirt. "I'm turning on this mike so everything that's said will automatically be picked up. Do not turn it off, regardless of what happens. Use your regular radio if Delport wants to communicate with us."

Ryan nodded.

"Your job is to get the child in your possession. Once you do, hit the flooring."

"Understood." His own voice sounded disembodied to him as he wiped the sweat off his brow.

"We'll have snipers positioned around the water tower. We're dispatching them now from headquarters. They'll be in place before you arrive. Once the child is separated from the suspect, the snipers will have authorization to fire. You'll want to take up the lowest profile possible. Every second will count."

He had an instant image of shielding Dee with his own body while bullets flew over his head. Delport wouldn't be taken down quickly. "Shoot to kill," he said simply.

Connelly nodded. "Of course."

"You know why you don't look at the hostage, right?" Chief Johnston interjected.

"To prevent my emotions from gaining control," he said. He waved his hand as if brushing away his concern, but Dee's tiny face was imprinted on his mind. It was one thing to remain calm and cool and logical when it was somebody else's loved one. It was quite a different thing when it would be his own child.

"That's right. Stay focused on the suspect."

"Don't go armed," Connelly continued. "Anticipate the suspect disarming you immediately; he'll have the upper hand because he'll have the hostage. Any weapon you take could be used against you."

"Any ideas on how I'll defend myself?" One brow shot up.

Connelly averted his eyes. "Keep him talking. Act like you're there to help him."

"Ooh, yeah. Right." He knew his sarcasm wasn't lost on the officers. He started toward his vehicle. "I'll be leaving now. I won't be arriving late to find…" He didn't finish the sentence.

His car was parked at the end of the sidewalk and now he opened the door. He paused before getting inside as he took one last look at the house. "You'll make sure Cait and my family are protected?"

"Don't worry about a thing, O'Clery." Chief Johnston put his hand on Ryan's shoulder. "As soon as you leave, I'm going inside to make sure they get on the road to Fort Bragg. I'll make sure they're well taken care of."

"A couple more things," Zuker added as Ryan climbed inside and started the engine. "Because of the work being done there, expect super bright lights. We won't be able to get close because he'll see us coming from any direction. You can see half the city from there."

"So I'm on my own."

"Not quite. Remember the snipers. They don't have to be close. They just have to be accurate."

Ryan leveled his eyes at his partner. "Under no circumstances are they to put my child's life in further danger."

"We know that, Ryan. Trust us."

"Anything else?"

Chief Johnston leaned toward the window. "Your code word. It's 'Jesus'."

"Are you serious?"

"It's a hostage situation, O'Clery. I can't have you say 'apples' or 'oranges' without it raising suspicion. We have to maintain the element of surprise."

He let out a tense breath. "And what happens when I say it?"

"Duck."

"My child—"

"We know. Be careful, O'Clery."

With one more glance at the house, he nodded silently and put the vehicle in gear. It wasn't until he was half a block away that he realized he hadn't hugged Cait or told her he loved her. A chorus of voices sprang up inside him, begging him, ordering him, coaxing him to return. It would only take a moment to turn the car around, speed up the driveway, get out and hug her and Darcy.

But even as the voices continued, he moved further away from home and closer to the outskirts of town.

~~~~~

The heavy rains had stopped more than an hour earlier but the skies were a peculiar shade of steel blue. Angry clouds roiled and tumbled overhead and though it was barely three o'clock in the afternoon, they obstructed any sunlight. As Ryan got out of his vehicle, he realized it may as well have been midnight.

The water tower stood before him, surrounded by a chain link fence. It appeared vastly higher than he remembered. As he climbed the fence and made his way toward it, he decided it was easily 120 feet tall, the height of a twelve story office building.

How could Diallo Delport have possibly known that he was terrified of heights? And yet he did know. *He knew.* And he was exploiting his fear to lure him to the worst possible place imaginable.

It was all part of the game to him, Ryan reminded himself. While his own emotions churned inside him at a sickening pace, he knew Delport had no such feelings. He moved his hand to the cell phone clipped to his belt. Though it was silent, he knew several officers and probably the chief himself were gathered around, listening to his breathing. The Bluetooth device in his ear had once seemed miniscule and unobtrusive; now it felt thick and clumsy and obvious.

In his mind's eye, he went over the last minute instructions they'd provided as he'd driven to the south of town. Theoretically, the plan was simple, consisting of separating Dee from Delport so the snipers could eliminate him. How he was to get his daughter away from a killer was anyone's guess; he would simply have to improvise, a task that now felt unobtainable.

Once he'd turned off the road and parked, he'd notified the officers and they'd muted their end. Now his phone began to ring. He looked at the Caller ID; it was Delport. "The suspect is phoning me," Ryan said. "I'll have to place you on hold." Without waiting for the police officers' response, he clicked over to Delport. "Aye?"

He thought the bright lights that illuminated the water tower were those Zuker referred to, but as soon as he answered the phone, a set of blinding beacons turned the area into broad daylight. He instinctively threw a forearm in front of his eyes to stop the sudden pain that pierced his retinas.

"Hello, Detective O'Clery," came Diallo Delport's unruffled voice. "Take the ladder up to the scaffolding. Keep your phone line open to me. If I don't hear your breathing, I'll assume you don't care what happens to your daughter."

"How do I know she's up there?" he asked.

A sudden cry pierced the air; he could hear it from somewhere above him as well as through the phone. The stereo effect intensified his anxiety and he tried to force himself not to focus on what Delport did to cause her to cry out.

"Did you hear that?" Delport said calmly. "Or should I try something a little more—"

"I heard her."

"Then what are you waiting for? Get started."

He kept his arm above his brow as he sought to see past the blinding light. Once he found himself underneath the onion-shaped top, he was relieved to find it provided some shadow. He found the ladder easily. He adjusted the telephone on his belt, felt for the police radio Delport had demanded, and placed a hand on the ladder. Though the officers were no longer able to hear him through the cell phone, he was thankful Connelly had considered redundancy and he had the radio mike open. He caught himself before he spoke to them; undoubtedly, that was one reason Delport had demanded the open phone line. He clicked the phone onto speaker so they would hear both sides of any conversation.

The ladder was soaking wet from the heavy rains. He pulled his hand back as his gut churned. No one had mentioned what to do if the metal rungs were slippery. He had no gloves and now as he glanced down at his shoes, he realized he was woefully unprepared for the climb. Even discounting his fear of heights, his shoe soles were smooth, which would create challenges even on a dry day.

"What's keeping you, Detective?"

The voice was taunting. He closed his eyes as he clenched and then straightened his fist. "I'm on my way," he forced himself to say. He hoped his tone did not betray his trepidation. He's a friend, he told himself. Think of him as a friend. I am going to throw up, he thought. "I'll be there straight-away."

He grasped the ladder and attempted to jerk it away from the water tower. It held firm. At least he didn't booby-trap it, he thought. But as he placed another hand on the ladder and added first one foot and then another, he couldn't dismiss the thought that he was climbing into a uniquely bizarre ambush.

Don't look down, he told himself. But the more the refrain pounded in his ears, the harder it became *not* to look down. He glanced upward instead and immediately regretted his action. It was dizzying to look straight up the metal ladder; it appeared to go on forever, right into the roiling clouds themselves. One tiny slip and there would be nothing to keep him from falling.

His palms grew sweaty, adding to the slickness of the rungs as he tried to force himself to get a grip on his emotions. He clung to them for a moment, trying vainly to slow his heartbeat through sheer willpower. Just look straight ahead, he told himself; focus on the metal tower.

Painstakingly, he lifted one hand and grasped the next rung. One foot followed and then the other. As each shoe hit the rung, the sole slipped backward. He involuntarily gasped as he righted his feet.

"Having a little difficulty, Detective?" Delport mocked.

"Not at'al," Ryan said. "I'll be there directly."

"I hope so. I'm losing patience."

Steady, he told himself. He forced himself to place one hand after another, one foot after another, as he stared at the red and white paint in front of him. It seemed as if he was climbing Mount Everest; the rungs felt as though they would never end. They felt greasy as he ascended but he would not allow himself to consider that Delport had placed something on them to impede his progress. He has to get back down, he told himself.

Unless, he thought, he wanted the police radio so he could have a helicopter transport him out of here.

In which case, he argued, he'd have to get to the police radio first. Which meant he had to reach the top.

"Not bad," Delport said, a soft chuckle in his voice. "You don't have much further to go."

Ryan glanced upward before he could stop himself. Peering over the side of the water tower was Delport's disfigured face. The scars that made their way down one cheek seemed even more grotesque than he remembered. He seemed to be leaning over the chasm with no fear—and in one arm casually rested Ryan's infant daughter. It appeared as if he was holding her over thin air to frighten him. His other hand held a Taser that, from this angle, appeared as large as his child.

He would gladly give his soul to the devil if an angel could somehow, in that very instant, gather his daughter in their wings and whisk her away. He took a deep breath but it did nothing to stop his heart from pounding in his temple. As he fought to erase the image of his child before it drove him over the edge, his attention turned to the feat in front of him. He wanted nothing more than to press himself flat against the ladder and wait for someone to get a damn cherry picker and pluck him off this thing. His hand shook as he grasped for the next rung but he was beyond caring if Delport saw it. He told himself the only way off this thing was to reach the top. Once he was at the top, he would not be coming down this fecking ladder; that was for damn sure. He'd sprout wings and fly off before he'd place a foot on this thing ever again.

The wind picked up as he neared the top, buffeting him sadistically. His hair fell across his brow but he did nothing to push it back from his eyes. He was too intent on keeping his hands moving from one rung to the next.

Finally, a rickety set of wood rails came into view. He'd hoped that scaffolding meant something solid to prevent a person from diving off the edge of this blasted thing, but now they looked like nothing more substantial than matchsticks.

"So tell me, Diallo," he said, trying to force his voice to sound casual, "how do I know I won't reach the top only to have you kick me right off this thing?"

"You don't know."

One more rung and his head would be exposed. He tried not to think of Delport standing there, waiting patiently, with a steel-toed boot ready to kick him in the head. The image of the board sailing across the junkyard and hitting him just an inch from his eye now loomed large. He had to think of the possibilities. And he had to be prepared for them.

He tilted his head back and peered upward. Thank the Good Lord that the ladder extended beyond the top; now that he was nearly there, he was scared as hell to take his hands off the damn thing. If Delport attempted to kick him or step on his hands or otherwise torture him, he had to concentrate on one thing: holding on. If he could hold on, he had a chance of reaching Dee.

"So tell me," he said, "what made you choose this location for our little get-together?" Despite his efforts, his voice wavered under the physical and emotional strain.

"I like the view."

"Oh? And what is it that you like about it?" Sweat poured off his forehead into his eyes, stinging them. As he heard Delport take a breath to answer, he propelled himself upward. The sudden movement caused one foot to slip and he grasped the railing so tight he thought a crowbar couldn't pry him off it.

"We're so high up here," Delport was saying, "that you can see all of Lumberton from here. I can even see the Interstate clear to South Carolina."

Ryan knew if he reached the top, he was promptly going to throw up.

His head cleared the landing and he found himself looking squarely at Diallo Delport.

He was not standing at the top of the ladder as Ryan had feared. He was about two yards away. In between them were paint cans and a painter's tarp that fluttered in the growing wind, exposing brushes and supplies. In an instant, his mind had inventoried possible supplies and discounted them all as potential weapons. Still, he reminded himself, he had to use something to destabilize Delport. And he had to consider how he would pry his daughter out of the killer's hands.

As one foot and then the other found something solid underneath, Ryan forced his vision to remain on what was right in front of him. If he looked beyond the water tower, it would bring him to his knees. He just knew it.

"You see," Delport was saying, pointing with one long arm that extended past the edge, "Twenty miles away is the border of South Carolina. Imagine being so high up, you can see that far. I bet I could see all the way to Florence from here."

He knows I am terrified of heights and he's talking like this to further disorient me.

Ryan's eyes moved from the tarp to Delport and back again. He had hoped for a wide, flat surface with substantial barricades to keep one from catapulting off the side. Instead, he found himself on rickety, temporary painters' scaffolding. It was narrow, approximately six feet wide if that; on one side was the onion-shaped top, which extended for several more feet above their heads. On the other side was the flimsiest railing Ryan had ever seen, consisting only of two-by-fours nailed to vertical two-by-fours, all of which appeared to be recycled junkyard material. A man would have to be mental to work up here.

Delport turned toward him. "You wouldn't be stupid enough to come up here armed." It was said as a statement but it had a threatening connotation.

Ryan held up both hands. "Of course I'm unarmed."

"Take your shirt off." Delport pointed at his clothing with the Taser.

He cocked his head. He didn't have time to figure out his motive. He held his child too close to the edge for him to argue. Dee stirred in his massive arm but Delport seemed not to notice. He began unbuttoning his shirt. His fingers were still wet from the ladder and perspiration and they felt thick and clumsy.

"Down to the skin."

He discarded his shirt on the wet scaffolding, momentarily glimpsing the second open mike before slipping the undershirt over his head. He tried to wipe the dampness from his palms onto the material but it was already thick with moisture.

"Take off your belt."

He fixed Delport with his eyes as he slipped his belt off, along with the radio and cell phone. "Can I disconnect the cell connection now that we're face to face?"

"No."

The wind was much stronger at this height than it had been on the ground and it bit at his exposed skin and rustled through his hair. The dark clouds seemed to be reaching toward him with fiendish fingers that disappeared only to reappear seconds later, morphing into tentacles before withdrawing once more.

"Put the belt, the radio and the phone right there." He gestured at an area on the tarp. As Ryan complied, he added, "Then remove your shoes. Socks, too."

In any other circumstance, their conversation would have ended with the directive to remove his shirt. He would have been starting the brawl of his life, and Delport knew it. Only one thing kept him from tearing the man apart: the bundle he held in his arms. Ryan knew it was also the only thing that kept the snipers from eliminating him right then and there.

As he bent to untie his shoe, he glanced outward for the first time. There were no buildings in site. With a sickening feeling growing in his gut, he realized there was nothing that came close to the height of the water tower. Certainly snipers could not be several stories below them and half a mile away and still hit their target.

"Throw your shoes and socks over the edge."

"Come on."

Dee began to fret and he instinctively stepped toward them, his eyes going immediately to his child. He regretted it instantly; his emotions began to whip and churn. He wanted nothing more than to take his daughter securely in his arms, hold her as tight as humanly possible, and never let go of her again. He'd never felt so helpless in his life.

His eyes moved to Delport's face. He knew what he was thinking; he could tell by the smirk that crept across his ugly mug. His skin looked pale and sickly against the black clouds, though the braided cords in his neck held the promise of brawn beneath his clothing. "Throw the shoes and the socks over the edge." His voice was icy and calm; he knew he was in control.

Ryan tossed a shoe over the edge, followed by the other one. The socks seemed to catch on a wind current before they dropped out of sight.

"Now the pants."

"Do you really think I'm hiding a weapon in my pants?"

"I won't know until they're off."

Ryan fought to keep his anger down as he unzipped his pants. He had to hold onto the inadequate scaffolding as he stood on one foot and then the other, and with the increased wind gusts, the weak framework began to rock. The tarp fell away from the supplies and began to ruffle and weave toward the edge. When the pants were off, he held them away from his body. "Surely you don't think I'm carrying a weapon in my boxers."

"Turn around."

With a deep breath, he turned around. With his feet firmly planted on the scaffolding, he forced himself to look beyond the tower. As far as he could see in any direction, there were no buildings higher than two stories. Where could they have possibly dispatched the snipers?

"All the way around."

Ryan obeyed his order as he fought to keep his growing anger from destroying his composure.

"Put your pants over there." He nodded toward an area a few feet away from his shirt. As Ryan complied, he added, "Now back up."

His blood turned to ice. Certainly he did not force him to climb that damn ladder just to disrobe and jump off. "I read about the white devil of Dublin," he said. He hadn't intended to blurt that out and now his words seemed to hang in the air.

After what seemed an eternity, Delport said, "Did you now?" His South African accent sounded for the slightest moment to be almost Irish. He stepped toward him but he was still too far away for Ryan to attempt to seize hold of Dee. He motioned with the Taser. "Back up."

He rested his hand along the scaffolding nearest the tower. He took a step backward and then another. As he circled the tower, he said, "Royan Kelly was not my ancestor."

Delport kicked the police radio toward him. "Keep going." As Ryan moved past the point where the ladder reached, he kicked the radio again and then twice more as they made their way in a circular fashion to the other side of the tower.

He was getting dizzy with the change in scenery against the horizon, and he tried to keep his focus on Delport's face. At the same time, he knew he had to memorize whatever he could discern in the landscape beyond them; Dee's life could depend on him knowing the direction from which the snipers would shoot. But as he trained his eyes to lock onto Delport's and took in their surroundings in his peripheral vision, his heart sank lower. They were isolated. Completely isolated. "Keegan was my ancestor," he continued. "I can show you the records myself."

Delport hooted with a loud, boisterous laughter, splitting the air with the sudden noise. "We can all sit around cups of tea and bring out the family albums." He spat the words as his eyes narrowed.

"Keegan didn't murder Maeve's babe."

"Oh, didn't he now?"

"You know he didn't," Ryan said, trying to force his voice to remain calm. "The babe was Gunnar the Draugr, wasn't he? And wasn't Gunnar your direct ancestor?"

"You think you're a clever one, don't you?"

"Why the scar?" Ryan gestured toward Delport's cheek.

The large man stopped and ran his thumb over Dee's cheek, never taking his eyes off Ryan. "Gunnar was born with a birthmark just below the eye," he said, his voice low and rumbling. "It resembled a tear."

Ryan swallowed and forced his eyes away from the man's hand as it cupped his child's cheek. "So it was in solidarity with Gunnar."

He cackled. "I *am* Gunnar."

"What I didn't quite connect," he continued, his voice sounding breathless to him, "was where the name 'Delport' came from?"

"Same way as you got the O'Clery name."

"So your mother married a Delport. And was she a Kelly?"

He sniggered. "You know what she was. She was a Baldrsen."

"Ah, and of course."

"The Kellys can all go to hell."

A drop of rain fell on the top of his head. *Shite*. Now, God? You're going to rain on me now?

Think. Where the hell would the snipers be positioned? He dared to look beyond the tower, narrowing his eyes in the hope that Delport could not follow his line of sight. He thought quickly, trying to consolidate his scattered assessments. There was nothing as high as this tower in all of Lumberton; the snipers would not only have to be far enough from their position that they wouldn't be noticed, but they'd also have to be below their position. That eliminated rooftops, as it would be too easy for Delport to spot them.

He locked his eyes on the other man; if he could maintain eye contact, he could prevent Delport from studying their surroundings. A small voice inside him told him he'd been up here before; he'd scoped it all out, and it was part of his plan. He would know the vulnerabilities, and that was why he'd ordered him to the other side of the tower. He wondered if the snipers were frustrated now; whether they'd moved beyond their view, and they were waiting for them to reappear.

"Do you realize," Ryan said, "if it weren't for my grandfather Keegan you wouldn't be standing in front of me now? He saved your grandfather Gunnar all those centuries ago."

"Stop there."

Ryan stopped. They might have gone completely around the tower for all he knew. His line of sight registered only Delport's face, the bundle in his arms, and in his periphery, more tarp and more paint buckets. The wind had continued to increase, causing the tarp to billow. It had come off the cans and supplies in several spots, and seemed dangerously close to flying off the water tower altogether.

Delport shifted Dee in his arms. She began to fret and he stuck the Taser in his back pocket before inserting his thumb in her mouth. Her tiny head looked so frail, especially in his arms. *Look away.*

He didn't hit her when she cried, he realized. He didn't curse at her. She was sucking his thumb. Ryan looked instead at the other man's face; it had softened as he watched Dee quiet in his arms.

"So you think that's what it's all about?" Delport asked. His voice was both menacing and chilled, in contrast with the image of a babe in his arms. "Getting together to compare branches of the family tree?"

"Had I been Keegan, I'd have gone a step further. I would have strangled Royan with my bare hands before I'd allow him to hurt Maeve or her babe." The other man simply stared at him and he added, "I just want you to know that."

At his continued silence, Ryan said, "I can understand how angry you'd have to be, hearing that story. My sister Claire—" *why did I bring her into this?* "—and I thought it was horrific. Beyond horrific, actually."

He could hear Dee sucking on the man's thumb. Christ Almighty.

"Why didn't you want the story told?"

"It's part of the fun of it, isn't it now?" He smirked. "Imagine. Generations of Kellys, their hearts broken, their lives destroyed, and not a one of them knowing why."

"So you also have records of the man who killed Rían Kelly's fiancée?"

"What does it matter?"

"How many times has this played out before?"

"It's all about family to you, isn't it?" he said suddenly.

"Aren't you close to your family? I'd like to know more about them."

He snorted.

"Truly I would. Do you have brothers? Sisters?"

"And are they like me?" he added.

"Like you or not like you, it doesn't matter. I'm sure they love you."

"Emotional blackmail won't work with me, Detective. You should know that."

He wanted to think and he knew he had to keep talking. If he could only think, he might be able to figure out a way to take his child out of Delport's arms. "Can I hold her?" he asked.

"Oh, sure," he answered amicably. "Let me just hand her over to her papa so there'll be no one standing in the way of your snipers."

His mouth felt dry. "Snipers?"

"I'm not stupid, Detective." He kicked the radio toward him. "Pick it up. Tell them to remove the snipers or the kid gets thrown over."

Ryan kept one eye on him as he bent to retrieve the radio. They were on a channel closed to regular police business but he had no idea how many officers might be listening, or where they were. "O'Clery here," he said, intentionally disregarding radio protocol. "Remove the snipers or the hostage will be thrown from the tower." He thought the use of the word *hostage* would help him distance his emotions from the helpless bundle he'd helped to bring into this world, but it didn't. And he was beginning to wonder how long this could go on before he was in danger of losing his composure.

"We are removing the snipers," the chief's voice crackled through the radio.

"Tell me something," he said. "Why did you come back?"

Delport dragged his finger across Dee's cheek, pausing when he reached one ear. Then with an eye on Ryan's face, he very slowly dragged it across her throat to the other ear.

"I mean," Ryan said, struggling to keep his emotions in check and the anger that threatened to overcome him tamped down, "everyone thought you were dead. You could have lived out the rest of your life anywhere in the world, and no one would have been looking for you."

"If you must know," Delport said, "I was enjoying my life when Skovgaard found me."

"She—she contacted you?"

His smirk turned into a grotesque sneer. "She had the audacity to tell me what she knew about Baldr."

"And that upset you."

"She'd pieced together his lineage and tracked me down halfway around the world."

"Why?"

"Precisely my question. Our family history is not one for the public. It is intensely private."

He half-waved his arm as if he was talking with his hands as he took a small step closer to Delport. "I suppose you told her that."

"Of course I did."

"And she didn't listen."

Delport adjusted Dee in his arms as she began to squirm and Ryan took another step closer. As he glanced back at him, Ryan added, "I guess she's listening now."

"The radio." His tone had changed; it was curt and low.

Ryan held the radio where Delport could see it.

"Demand number one," he said, nodding toward the radio, "I want both those laptops delivered to me."

Ryan held the radio with his finger just short of the button. "Where do you want them? At the base of the tower?"

"Tell them to get the laptops."

He continued watching Delport as he said into the radio, "O'Clery here. You're to deliver Mrs. Skovgaard's and Miss Janssen's laptop computers."

"Where do you want them?"

Ryan shrugged as he looked at Delport.

"Demand number two. Say it."

He pressed the button. "Demand number two."

"I want ten million dollars in small bills."

He held out the radio to him. "I think you might want to tell them that."

"Say it." He stepped closer to the edge of the tower so Dee was inches from the abyss beneath them.

"He wants ten million dollars in small bills."

There was a slight hesitation. "Can we talk directly to Delport?"

Ryan shifted his feet, stepping a bit closer to Delport, which also placed him closer to the edge than he wanted to be. He knew the officers were listening to every word on the second mike. Out of the corner of his eye, he noticed movement near the perimeter; an officer was climbing the fence as Delport's back was turned to him. "I'm telling you," Ryan said, trying to keep his voice casual, "I know exactly how they think."

"Demand number three. Say it."

He repeated his words into the radio.

"A helicopter."

"He wants a helicopter."

There was another pause. "Is that all?"

Delport half-nodded.

As Ryan spoke into the radio, he waved his arm and nudged a bit closer. "That's right. The two laptops, ten million dollars and a helicopter." He leaned a bit toward Delport. His bare foot nearly tripped on a bunched-up piece of tarp. "And I suppose safe passage to... somewhere?"

"The laptop and the helicopter we can get right away," the chief answered. "The money could take some time."

"You're out of time," Delport said.

Ryan's eyes locked on his. The man was taller than he was by about three inches and outweighed him by at least twenty pounds. He appeared to be all muscle. He'd fought him once and barely survived. And with his infant child in his arms, fighting was out of the question. And he knew it.

He hadn't brought his child to the top of this water tower as assurance that Ryan would not fight him. There was no doubt in his mind that he intended to take Dee on that helicopter with him. And there was no way he could allow that to happen. There was no way he could stand here and watch his child taken away from him, whisked into the sky and heading for parts unknown.

What would he do with her? His mind screamed that he shouldn't allow his thoughts to go in that direction, while another part of him could think of nothing else.

"What are you willing to give us in return?" the chief's voice broke the silence.

"Nothing," Delport responded.

Ryan did not repeat his answer. He hesitated only a moment before saying, "It's me you want, Delport. They'll expect you to give up something. Let it be the child. Take me as your hostage, and do with me what you will."

A bloodcurdling laugh turned Ryan's stomach. "It isn't *you* I want, Detective. It's never been the *men* we've wanted. It's been the women they loved." His fingers squeezed Dee's cheek and she began to cry.

He gritted his teeth. He wanted nothing more than to throw himself at Delport. If it was just the two of them, he'd have no regrets plummeting over the side of this damned monstrosity as long as he knew the man would be dead when he hit the pavement below. Even if every bone in his own body was broken upon impact, he'd use his last breath making sure this evil monster was torn apart.

Dee began to cry louder.

"Let me take her," Ryan said. His voice was thick with tension.

Delport moved so close to the edge that the toe of his shoe extended beyond the scaffolding. He shifted Dee's squirming body so she was nearly over the precipice. The officer below froze as he glanced upward, and Ryan moved suddenly to one side so the other man would be forced to look at him, cocking his head away from the movement below. Ryan was closer to Dee now and he stared at the small bundle held in the crook of the man's arm. His thumb had been removed and Delport seemed oblivious to the noise she made in protest.

"If you kill her," Ryan said, unable to keep the venom from his voice, "there will be no reason to meet your demands."

He laughed again but as Dee wriggled her entire body, he shifted his weight.

He heard the sound of the helicopter almost as soon as he saw it rise from the airport a short distance away. His mind flashed through the scene unfolding before him: the helicopter would arrive at the tower within two minutes, tops; officers had breached the fence and were somewhere below or climbing the ladder; and a killer still held his daughter securely in the crook of his arm.

Delport turned his head in the direction of the helicopter.

"Jesus," Ryan breathed.

Delport jerked his head back in his direction. One shoe was halfway off the scaffolding; the other slipped in a tangle of water and tarp folds. For the briefest of moments, Ryan caught a glimpse of his expression. His eyes widened in surprise and his mouth opened slightly.

An explosion rocked the ground beneath them and they both turned in complete astonishment as a ball of flames shot into the sky, followed by a much larger plume of black smoke. It rose over the airport, temporarily obscuring the helicopter.

Within that split second, Ryan jumped. He had no time to think about the poorly constructed supports or about the impact that four hundred pounds of abruptly shifting weight would do. His eyes were riveted on his daughter. As his hands reached her and he, too, began to slide, he knew if he had to tear her in two to get her out of Delport's arms, he was now beyond retreat.

She screamed, causing his hair to stand on end. Delport had an iron-clad grip on her. He was righting himself but Ryan was still falling.

His legs were sliding out from under him as he grabbed for Dee. Twisting his body unnaturally, he crashed into Delport as he swung around, tucking his daughter under both arms as he lunged for the far side of the scaffolding. As they fell atop the tarp, the material wrenched free from the supplies. He caught a glimpse of the larger man swaying as the tarp was pulled out from under him. Time seemed to stop as Delport teetered right on the edge. Ryan waited for the shots to ring out, but they didn't. There was nothing but the man above him, beginning to right himself, the unmistakable look of rage in his eye, his clenched jaw promising Ryan a fight for his life—and his daughter's.

He slid Dee among the supplies, his soul urging the angels to look over her but the words freezing on his lips. Then he felt as though fire had ripped through his shoulder. He cried out and struggled to rise as he realized Delport had wrenched one of the two by four's loose and was wielding it like a bat. As he raised it above his head, Ryan spotted his own blood on the wood and a piece of flesh dangling from a jagged nail. He fought the instinct to raise his arms to fend off a second attack. He sprung to his knees and jerked the tarp from under Delport's feet. He let out a guttural yell as he prepared to throw himself at the larger man, even if it meant that both of them would plummet through the gaping hole left by the wood Delport had yanked free.

The large albino righted himself once more, kicking the tarp over the side of the tower. His legs were planted far apart. One hand wielded the thick piece of wood while the other beckoned for Ryan to come to him. His face was contorted into an amused grin, his eyes gleaming with the pleasure of a fight, his exposed skin dripping with the weight of the storm's humidity.

There would be only one movement. Ryan knew that. And he knew it would most likely mean death to them both. He struggled to his feet and locked eyes with Delport. He started to take a deep breath but his body seemed out of sync with his mind as his legs sprang forward. With the air caught in his throat, he spread his arms wide to push them both over the edge.

When the shot rang out, his feet had already left the scaffolding. His mind registered an astonished look on Delport's face just as a second and then a third shot followed. As the man tumbled backward, Ryan struggled to catch himself but realized it was too late. Delport plummeted over the edge, spraying Ryan with blood as he skidded to a stop, his legs straddling a vertical post in the scaffolding.

Time seemed to stand still. Diallo Delport appeared like a grotesque doll, his arms and legs splayed apart, his eyes still locked on Ryan's as he fell. The ground seemed so far away that it felt as if he would never reach it. When he did, the sound of his body diving into the concrete below was thunderous, as if a tractor-trailer had run straight into a concrete barricade. As Ryan stared straight down into his face, the ground around Delport grew bright red with his blood.

Slowly, he tore his eyes away from the man. He looked out across the great expanse around the water tower. The helicopter was moving toward him. The fire and the smoke seen only seconds ago were gone. Sirens began in every direction and in an instant, police vehicles, fire trucks and ambulances were converging just beneath him.

It registered that Dee was screaming and he turned back, pulling his legs from where they'd hung over the abyss. He hadn't realized that he'd fallen and now he held the vertical post between his hands and delicately tilted it. It was hanging on by just one nail that was partially protruding.

He looked behind him, expecting to see the officers who had rushed across the ground below. Instead, he looked directly into Cait's face.

Her eyes were still riveted on the gaping hole where Delport had plummeted. She held her pistol in both hands as it remained pointed where the albino had once stood. All color had left her cheeks, leaving her pale, her expression immobile, her eyes wide and dazed. The wind caught her hair, sending the strands upward to swirl around her.

He rose to his feet and crossed the scaffolding. As he reached her, he wrapped one arm around her slender waist while his free hand sought the pistol. The barrel was still hot. He gently pulled it from her grasp as he buried his face against her hair.

~~~~~

Ryan held Dee in his arms as Cait stepped into the rescue basket. The wind, already strong, was whipped into a frenzy from the helicopter blades that churned directly overhead. Once she was settled, he placed his daughter into her waiting arms. He could have sworn that Dee smiled. He glanced into her eyes and then did a double-take as he realized the light blue eyes he'd become so accustomed to had turned into the same stormy gray-blue of her mother's. It seemed to reflect the tumultuous clouds overhead, the swirls of silver, sapphire and black with the tiniest sprinkling of gold.

He kissed Cait lightly before tugging on the cable. Then he stepped back to watch the helicopter whisk her off the water tower and to the ground below, where a team waited beside an ambulance with a stretcher. In his heart, he knew Dee was unscathed. And she was alive. The hospital would no doubt run every test possible to ensure his child had suffered no damage at the hands of a madman who still stared back at him with wide, unseeing eyes.

As the helicopter hovered below and Cait passed the child to a paramedic before stepping out of the basket, he looked across at the horizon. Delport had been right; he could see all the way to South Carolina from this height. He started around the water tower toward his discarded pants and shirt, marveling at the streets below, the interstate traffic, the people wandering across parking lots and down city streets. He supposed if he studied it long enough, he'd figure out which of those rooftops represented his home.

He slipped on his clothes and made his way to the ladder. He passed two officers who were beginning to process the scene. One reached out and touched him lightly on the arm. "The helicopter will be right back."

It was then that he noticed the blood saturating his shirt sleeve. The pain had ceased to register but now he felt it returning in full force. The nail had no doubt created a tear that reached from his shoulder to midway down his arm.

He stood at the top of the ladder and peered straight down 120 feet to the concrete below. "It's alright," he answered. "I won't need it." Then he swung around and placed his foot on the first rung and prepared to descend.

33

A shout went up as Ryan and Cait entered the detectives' office. Tables had been cleared of paperwork to make room for a punch bowl filled with ice, rows of soft drinks, and platters of food. A clamor of voices hit them at once.

"Good job, Cait," one said. "Ever thought of joining the force?"

"Congratulations, Ryan. You got him!"

"Saved the city the effort of trying the bastard."

He waved off their congratulations, pausing only when the women employed at the police department approached to coo over Dee or Darcy. It was true what they said, he thought; Darcy was the spitting image of him with her deep green eyes and black hair, and Dee was a miniature version of Cait with her gray-blue eyes and soft brunette locks.

Arlo approached, holding his hand as if he carried an ice pop. "We don't need this evidence anymore," he laughed as Dee reached out with both hands to grab her pacifier from him. She smiled broadly, the tiny teardrop birthmark engulfed by a deep dimple.

"Welcome back!" The chief's voice could be heard above the others as he made his way toward them. He stopped just short of Ryan and pointed at his bandaged arm. "How's the arm?"

"Twenty stitches," Ryan answered. "It was a helluva nail."

"I'd say. They give you a tetanus shot?"

"They did. And I'll be cleared to return to work by the end of the week."

"You sure you want to come back so soon?"

"It's in my blood."

Chief Johnston nodded before motioning for them to follow him. "You too, Arlo," he said before the evidence technician could duck away.

They gathered in the chief's office as the sound of the party behind them continued to grow.

"Just wanted to say," he said, leaning against his desk, "that you both did a great job."

Ryan turned toward Cait, who was settling into a chair with Darcy on her lap. "How did you—?"

"—manage to give the officers the slip?" she finished. She smiled shyly. "Zuker trusted me way too much."

"I'll say I did." They turned to watch him enter the room. "How she managed to climb out the bathroom window without being seen by the other officers, I'll never know."

"They were a bit preoccupied."

Ryan turned to the chief. "The snipers—?"

"They couldn't get a clear shot. I'm sorry, Ryan. I had four of them covering the tower from every angle. But with the tower being so high, it was difficult to get a shot upwards at that range."

"I suppose that's why you sent in the officers."

"Why I—" He stopped to look at Cait. "Actually, I sent two officers after Cait. Through my binoculars, I saw her climb the fence and scramble up that ladder."

"She has no fear of heights," Zuker interjected.

"I wanted the officers to stop her."

Ryan sat in the chair next to her. Clutching Dee with one hand, he squeezed Cait's hand with the other. "I'm glad they didn't."

"I'd hope to somehow get the gun to you," Cait said. "But things were happening so fast…"

"What was the explosion about?" Ryan turned back to the chief.

"Aviation fuel. I was hoping to create a diversion. I had officers partly fill a 50-gallon drum with aviation fuel. When they set it off, it created a bomb-like explosion."

"Singed the grass at the airport," Zuker chuckled.

"And the helicopter?"

"Eyes in the sky. I was hoping a sniper on board could get within range to fire."

He nodded. "And Diallo Delport…"

"His body will be sent back to South Africa." He turned to pick up a large envelope on his desk. "Which reminds me why I wanted to talk to you. I received this in the mail this morning." As he watched Ryan open it, he added, "It looks like a journal Delport kept. I thought you'd want to have it."

"You don't want it as evidence?"

"Don't need it. The murders of Annelise Skovgaard, Jacqueline Janssen and Albert Petrironcalli are solved. Plus a kidnapping and attempted murder. Besides, what's in there looks personal. I thought you should have it."

Ryan began to rifle through the journal when Arlo cleared his voice. "Chief?"

"Oh," Chief Johnston continued, "I thought you'd want to know. Those black hair samples we found at the crime scenes."

"I've no doubt they were mine," Ryan said, closing the book and looking up. "Once I realized Delport had gained access to my house, I knew it would be easy for him to pull hairs from my comb or brush… It was all part of his plan to frame me for the historians' murders."

"You might find it interesting that the DNA also matched Delport's," Arlo said.

"It—?" Ryan stopped himself. "Interesting." The room was silent except for the cooing of Darcy and Dee. He met Cait's eyes. "I suppose that's to be expected, though I never would have imagined him to be a relative of mine."

Chief Johnston slapped one leg. "The party's waiting," he said abruptly. "Go. Enjoy yourselves."

~~~~~~

Ryan settled into the recliner in the living room. In one hand, he gripped a whiskey glass and in the other, Diallo Delport's journal. The wall clock ticked toward midnight, the sound of the hands moving the only noise in the otherwise still house. The girls had been asleep in their bed for hours and after an evening of lovemaking that rivaled his first time with Cait, she'd drifted off to sleep in his arms. He'd watched her for a time, softly racing a finger down the bridge of her petite nose, following the line of her jaw, and feeling the pulse of her heart through the vein in her neck. He kissed her brow and each eye, listened to her murmur, and held her closer than he ever had before.

After nearly an hour, he'd gently rolled her away from him and had climbed out of bed. He'd made his way down the still hallway and into the living room, where tentacles of light from a full moon made their way through the uncovered window near the ceiling to stretch across the length of the room.

Now he took a deep swig of the whiskey before placing it on the end table at his side. He held the journal in both hands for a long moment. It was a hefty book with a leather binding. He didn't recognize the raised pattern on the front; it swirled much like a Celtic knot but seemed somehow different. Then he realized it was a Viking symbol. At the bottom of the front cover, someone had etched the words "GINFAXI - Victory in Combat" with a dark, thick pen.

He thumbed through the pages. The journal was only half-completed. The remaining pages were cream-colored, the edges uneven, as if the book had been hand-cut and sewn. As he flipped back through, he discovered the latter pages contained increasingly smaller text that often slanted unevenly over the page. As he made his way from back to front, the words increased in size and went from script to block letters, and then text printed neatly atop carefully drawn horizontal lines.

When he thumbed back to the first page, the writing was very large. At the top was printed the date: January 1, 1981. Delport would have been five years old at the time of his first entry, he realized. Five years old. Would he have started to school by then? He wondered. He considered what he might have looked like:

perhaps small or even scrawny, his pale skin, white hair and odd blue eyes so different from other children…

Then his eyes drifted to the first entry. Each character was formed with painstaking precision:

> My name is Gunnar Baldrsen. They call me Diallo but I do not know why. A strange woman says she is my mother, but she is not Maeve…

OTHER BOOKS BY p.m.terrell

THE TEMPEST MURDERS (2013)
Ryan O'Clery Suspense Book 1

THE PENDULUM FILES (2014)
Black Swamp Mysteries Book 5

DYLAN'S SONG (2013)
Black Swamp Mysteries Book 4

SECRETS OF A DANGEROUS WOMAN (2012)
Black Swamp Mysteries Book 3

VICKI'S KEY (2012)
Black Swamp Mysteries Book 2

EXIT 22 (2008)
Black Swamp Mysteries Book 1

THE BANKER'S GREED (2011)

RIVER PASSAGE (2009)

SONGBIRDS ARE FREE (2007)

RICOCHET (2006)

THE CHINA CONSPIRACY (2003)

KICKBACK (2002)

About the Author

p.m.terrell is the pen name for Patricia McClelland Terrell, the award-winning, internationally acclaimed author of more than eighteen books in four genres: contemporary suspense, historical suspense, computer how-to and non-fiction.

Prior to writing full-time, she founded two computer companies in the Washington, DC Metropolitan Area: McClelland Enterprises, Inc. and Continental Software Development Corporation. Among her clients were the Central Intelligence Agency, United States Secret Service, U.S. Information Agency, and Department of Defense. Her specialties were in white collar computer crimes and computer intelligence.

The first book in the Ryan O'Clery suspense series, *The Tempest Murders*, placed as a finalist in the 2013 USA Best Book Awards and is a 2014 International Book Awards nominee. *Vicki's Key* was a top five finalist in both the 2012 International Book Awards and 2012 USA Book Awards.

Her historical suspense, *River Passage*, was a 2010 Best Fiction and Drama Winner. It was determined to be so historically accurate that a copy of the book resides at the Nashville Government Metropolitan Archives in Nashville, Tennessee.

She is also the co-founder of The Book 'Em Foundation and the organizer of Book 'Em North Carolina, an annual event held in the real town of Lumberton, North Carolina. For more information on this event and the literacy campaigns funded by it, visit www.bookemnc.org.

She sits on the boards of the Friends of the Robeson County Public Library and the Robeson County Arts Council. She has also served on the boards of Crime Stoppers and Crime Solvers and became the first female president of the Chesterfield County-Colonial Heights Crime Solvers in Virginia.

For more information visit the author's website at www.pmterrell.com, follow her on Twitter at @pmterrell, her blog at www.pmterrell.blogspot.com, and on Facebook under author.p.m.terrell.